Maggie was alone

And more terrified than she'd ever been in her entire life.

Then, from far above her in the dark stairwell, she heard another door open.

"No," she whimpered. "Please, no."

She couldn't face another attacker, couldn't fight anymore. If someone else was coming to finish the job, she didn't know where she would find the resources to resist.

"Maggie? Are you down here?"

It was Travis! For an instant she considered holding her silence, allowing Travis to go away until she pulled herself together. She didn't want to be weak in front of him.

"I'm here," she whispered softly.

She needed his protection. She needed him.

Dear Reader,

Sultry isn't a word usually associated with my home state of Colorado. Winter in the Rocky Mountains is cold and white with snow, so it fascinated me to venture into New Orleans in January when the carnival celebrations leading up to Mardi Gras are in full swing.

While I was writing, I switched to jazz on the radio and ordered Cajun food at restaurants. I imagined myself in the French Quarter, enjoying the elegant, sexy decadence of this lush old city where the trees never really lose their leaves and the humidity hovers at 80 percent. I'm caught by New Orleans, and I hope you will be, too, as you read *A New Year's Conviction*.

The heroine, Maggie Deere, is a woman close to my heart. And the hero, Travis Shanahan, is everything a Southern gentleman should be.

Cassie Miles

A New Year's Conviction
Cassie Miles

Harlequin Books

TORONTO • NEW YORK • LONDON
AMSTERDAM • PARIS • SYDNEY • HAMBURG
STOCKHOLM • ATHENS • TOKYO • MILAN
MADRID • WARSAW • BUDAPEST • AUCKLAND

ISBN 0-373-22402-8

A NEW YEAR'S CONVICTION

Copyright © 1997 by Kay Bergstrom

This edition published by arrangement with Harlequin Books S.A.

Printed in U.S.A.

New Orleans

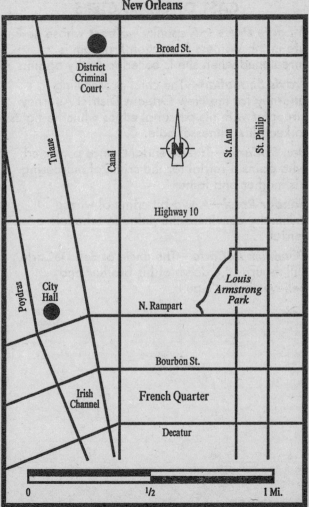

Broad St.

District Criminal Court

Tulane

Canal

St. Ann

St. Philip

N

Highway 10

Poydras

City Hall

Louis Armstrong Park

N. Rampart

Bourbon St.

Irish Channel

French Quarter

Decatur

0   1/2   1 Mi.

CAST OF CHARACTERS

Maggie Deere—A spunky waitress whose new life in the Witness Protection Program is threatened when she is called to testify again.

Travis Shanahan—The chief prosecuting attorney for the New Orleans District Attorney struggles with his personal ethics while he fights to keep his witnesses safe.

Ben DeCarlo—The defendant, once convicted, who gains a retrial for the crime of murdering his mother and father.

Sandor Rossi—A two-bit criminal whose testimony convinces the judge to schedule a retrial.

Dominick DeCarlo—The uncle of Ben DeCarlo still mourns the death of his brother and believes in Ben's guilt.

Prologue

December 15, 1993

Augustine's restaurant and bar in the heart of New Orleans was a dream come true for waitress Maggie Deere. The kitchen was pristine. The cooks in their high white hats and snowy aprons were honest-to-goodness chefs. And the tips? Well, the tips were unbelievable!

Maggie purely loved working the lunch crowd. The aroma of fresh bread from the stone ovens mingled with the spicy scent of boudin sausage and gumbo. The produce—red peppers, green okra, lush purple eggplant—was so fresh you could almost taste the dirt from the fields. Not like those sleazy diners where Maggie had to pinch off the wilted parts of salads and turn up the charm to make sure nobody noticed that the food was nothing but grease on grit. Augustine's had class. The atmosphere of dark wood and soft lights flattered the ladies and gave gentlemen the feeling that they were involved in a clandestine tryst.

Clandestine tryst, Maggie repeated to herself. Those were her two new words for the day, and she liked the way they fit together.

She swiveled between the tables in the long room with

practiced ease and delivered an order to a *clandestine* table in the back corner. The seafood salad with dressing on the side was for the elegant lady wearing a winter white suit that probably cost more than three months of Maggie's tips. And there was a huge muffuleta sandwich for her husband. "There you go, Mr. and Mrs. DeCarlo. Enjoy."

Mr. DeCarlo, a fine-looking older gent, stared straight into her cleavage. "Thanks, Maggie. And would you get me another bourbon Sazerac?"

"Can do, sugar." Maggie glanced at his wife. "How about you, ma'am? More wine?"

"One more glass." She was a handsome woman with a serene smile and weary eyes. "How have you been, Maggie? Still learning new vocabulary words?"

"Can't complain," Maggie said. "I mean, my life isn't one clandestine tryst after another, but—"

"What?"

"My words for the day," Maggie explained.

Mr. DeCarlo chuckled. There were people who claimed he was involved in crime, a big boss in the Dixie Mafia, but Maggie didn't believe it. As far as she was concerned, Mr. DeCarlo was a decent gentleman. He might take his time looking Maggie over, but he never touched. And his tips were more than generous. He and his wife were among her favorite regular customers.

"I just don't get it." His voice was gentle. "Why's a pretty little blonde like you working so hard?"

"Didn't know I had a choice."

"Heck, Maggie. I bet there's ten men in this room who'd volunteer to be your sugar daddy."

"Stop that," his wife chided.

"It's the God's truth. I want to know why our little Maggie doesn't settle down with a man who can support her."

"Support from a man?" Maggie had heard this line before, about one million times since her thirteenth birthday when she started developing bosoms and her foster daddy said he might find it in his cold black heart to buy her a new dress if she saw fit to pay him a visit in his bedroom while her foster ma was at work. Primly, Maggie said, "No, thank you, Mr. DeCarlo, sir. I support myself just fine. Besides, I'm taking college correspondence classes. I'm studying pre-law."

"Good for you," Mrs. DeCarlo encouraged. "You keep at it, honey. Maybe, someday, we can give you a job."

Her husband laughed indulgently. "That's right. I can't ever have too many lawyers in my line of business."

"Y'all enjoy your lunch." Grinning to herself, Maggie pivoted and headed toward the bar. Someday, she was going to make something of herself. She'd done real good on those first assignments from correspondence school.

She paused at another table and took another drink order. No, sir, she wasn't stupid. Bleached hair and big breasts didn't mean she was a dumb blonde. Besides, she liked looking pretty, like Dolly Parton or Marilyn Monroe.

On her way past the table where one woman sat alone, Maggie hinted again that the lady might want to order and give up on whatever man was apparently standing her up. But the lady in her Christmas red sweater ordered another wine and said she'd wait.

At the polished oak bar, Maggie went up on her tiptoes to lean across. "Hey, Kyle, I need two hurricanes, a bourbon Sazerac, a merlot and another glass of the chablis that Mrs. DeCarlo likes."

"The DeCarlos, huh?" Kyle Johnson, the bartender, wore a dopey Santa Claus hat. The white tassel flopped down between his shifty eyes as he juggled the bottles. "I'd like to have your tips from that table."

"You'll get your share, bud. Even if I am saving up for Christmas presents."

"What'cha gonna get for me, Maggie?"

"From what I hear, you haven't been a good boy. Santa's likely to put coal in your stocking."

Kyle nodded toward the front entryway where a tall gentleman in a dark brown overcoat had entered Augustine's. "Well, look at what just blew through the door."

"Ben DeCarlo," Maggie said, recognizing him immediately. Mrs. DeCarlo had introduced her son to Maggie once when he had joined his parents for lunch. His mama was obviously proud of her smooth, successful son. He was so handsome that it made Maggie's teeth ache. Rumor had it that he was preparing to run for the Senate, and she'd vote for him ten times if she could.

But something was wrong with Ben today. He looked angry enough to spit nails as he stormed through the restaurant with his overcoat flapping like a bat's wings. He made straight for his parents' table.

Maggie started back in that direction with her drinks balanced on a tray. If she hustled, she could talk to Ben and see what was making him look so harsh. Maybe she'd get lucky and he would notice her.

Ben's daddy rose up and welcomed him. His mama's proud eyes turned suddenly frightened. What was going on here? Ben was talking rudely to his parents.

Then she saw the gun. "Oh, my God, no!"

The tray of drinks fell from her hand and crashed on the hardwood floor as she charged toward the rear table, the clandestine table, the distant table that seemed miles away. "No, Ben! Don't—"

Two shots rang out.

Maggie didn't take her eyes off Ben. As he turned and

ran toward the exit, she stepped in front of him. "What have you done? My God, what have you done?"

Inches from his face, she stared into his ice-blue eyes and saw a flat emptiness. There was no light within. No emotion. No soul.

He shoved past her and ran from the restaurant. She didn't need to look back at the corner table to know her two favorite customers were dead. Killed by the hand of their own son.

Chapter One

Despite repeated warnings from Judge Leland Howell, the atmosphere in the courtroom lacked the solemnity typically associated with justice. The oak benches in the high-ceilinged, paneled room were filled by jaded members of the press, an artist making sketches, friends, family and associates. Some of the women were spectacularly beautiful. Some of the men looked like they'd be right at home in a police lineup. The air crackled and fizzed with the thrill-seeking excitement usually found at a carnival freak show, and the main exhibit was the defendant, Benjamin Wilson DeCarlo.

Travis Shanahan, chief prosecuting attorney for the New Orleans District Attorney's office, rose from his chair behind the prosecutor's table. His gaze fell on DeCarlo, and then he quickly looked away. He couldn't stand the sight of this man who sat so calm and smug in spite of his prison pallor. Never before had a defendant been so clearly guilty.

Over two years ago, Travis had prosecuted DeCarlo and had won a conviction. Two counts of murder in the second degree. Ben DeCarlo was sentenced to life in the Louisiana State Prison in Angola.

Now, due to new testimony, alleged impropriety in the New Orleans Police Department and possible jury tampering, it seemed likely that DeCarlo would have a second chance. A retrial? Such a procedure was almost unheard-of, especially in a murder conviction.

However, at this morning's hearing, it seemed likely that the dozens of appeals filed by DeCarlo's high-priced team of attorneys, led by the invincible Ezra Dean Slaughter, would bear results. After weeks of legal wrangling, the only thing standing in the way of a retrial were the final statements to the judge.

"Your Honor..." Travis paced, hoping to shake off his sense of futility. Though everyone had predicted the certainty of a retrial from the moment the judge agreed to these hearings, Travis wouldn't give up. This was his last chance to make his former conviction stand.

"It was just over three years ago," Travis said, "on December 15, 1993, at Augustine's restaurant, that Benjamin Wilson DeCarlo walked through the lunchtime crowd, raised his gun and fired point-blank.

"He killed his mother and his father."

Travis looked into the steel gray eyes of Judge Howell and saw impatience. The judge had already made up his mind. The retrial was a foregone conclusion.

Still, Travis continued, "Ben DeCarlo committed murder. He was convicted based on the testimony of five eyewitnesses. Five citizens came forward to do their duty. They gave up their normal lives and careers to enter the witness protection program.

"Another trial for this man is a mockery of their sacrifice, a perversion of our justice system. His entire defense is nothing more than a very expensive bag of legal tricks. It's a con job, Your Honor, based on the convenient memory of a two-bit criminal, Sandor Rossi."

Travis almost choked on the name. When this little slimeball came up with his ridiculous tale of a frame-up and an alibi, he should have been laughed out of the Criminal District Courthouse. Instead, his words had set the wheels to turning, and DeCarlo's elite defense team had stoked the engine until the system was on a runaway course toward retrial.

"Your Honor, we cannot, in good conscience, waste any more of the court's time or the taxpayers' dollars. Ben DeCarlo is guilty—no matter how much money he has to spend on his defense. He's guilty as Cain. If we allow the luxury of another trial, we send the devastating message to our community that it's okay to commit murder as long as you can afford the best lawyers. In the state of Louisiana, justice can be bought."

Judge Howell winced slightly, and Travis knew he'd struck a chord. Had the judge been paid off? Judge Howell, who had served for twenty-four years on the bench?

"Don't dishonor our courts with this high-priced mockery of truth," Travis concluded. "Don't reward the liars and the cheats and the murdering scum that would drag us through another heinous trial of this vicious and guilty man."

That was all Travis had to say. He returned to his place behind the prosecutor's table.

"Thank you, Mr. Shanahan." Judge Howell inclined his head toward the defense table. "Rebuttal, Mr. Slaughter?"

Travis gnashed his rear molars together. Asking Ezra Dean Slaughter if he wanted to rebut was like asking a bullet if it wanted to leave the chamber after the trigger had been pulled. The prominent defense attorney had built a reputation over the past seventeen years for brilliant rhetoric. When he addressed the judge, he actually removed his glasses and wiped crocodile tears from his eyes. Travis couldn't stand to listen to Ezra Dean's orator's voice when he talked about the tragic injustice perpetrated on his client.

"And then, there's the matter of Sandor Rossi," he said, turning to address Travis directly. "Shame on you, Mr. Shanahan, for denigrating this brave man. Disregarding great personal danger, Sandor Rossi brings forth new information on this case, information proving the innocence of my client. Sandor Rossi lays his words before us, like a guidepost leading the shining way to truth."

Travis exerted extreme willpower to keep from sneering. Not only was Sandor Rossi a shoddy crook, but this supposed "guidepost" was nothing more than a vague statement with names blanked out. The prosecutors had not received permission to take a deposition, allegedly because Rossi would be in peril as soon as the names were revealed.

Flamboyantly, Ezra Dean raged at the supposed unfairness of the first trial. He roared, then whispered, pleading and demanding simultaneously. The wrap-up was a gesture toward Ben DeCarlo's sister, Maria, a dark-eyed beauty who had steadfastly stood beside her brother. Maria had been Ben's alibi for the time of the murders. Of course, Travis knew she was lying like a dog, but even he had to admit that Maria radiated sincerity and sadness. Her presence in the courtroom was a strike against him.

"Be brave, Maria," said Ezra Dean. "Your parents can never be returned to your sweet and loving arms, but soon, dear lady, justice will be done. We trust in the wisdom of the court to grant a retrial. Maria, you will again have your brother."

A few nefarious characters in the courtroom actually applauded as Ezra Dean returned to his seat beside Ben DeCarlo.

"Order." Judge Howell rapped his gavel. "Thank you, Mr. Slaughter. I will retire to my chambers to deliberate, and we will reconvene here after lunch."

Travis and his two assistants turned to face the waiting press and the curious public that had hung on every word of the first trial. It had been a glamorous spectacle, widely viewed on court television, except for those closed portions when the parade of witnesses testified. The media loved taking photos of the handsome Ben DeCarlo, and his face had graced the covers of more than one national magazine.

Travis nodded to his assistants and said quietly, "We're going to have no comment right now. Understand?"

"Yes, sir."

Briskly, Travis strode through the courtroom into the marbled hallways of the courthouse. He was careful not to move so fast that he appeared to be fleeing, but he kept up a steady pace as he made his way through the media to the towering marble columns in the entryway.

Outside, the January drizzle suited his mood. The rain falling from the thick gray skies was wet and miserable without being cleansing. As always, the contrast between the magnificent old court building and the seedy streets of midcity New Orleans reminded him that high ideals were, too often, rooted in muck and mire. This retrial, he knew, was going to get dirty.

Halfway across Broad Street, the media gave up the chase. Instead of trailing Travis and his assistants, they focused on the fiery Ezra Dean, who could always be counted upon for a dramatic flourish. Only Farris Quinn of the *Times-Picayune* newspaper stuck beside Travis. Last month, the shaggy-haired Quinn had broken a story about police corruption. He loped around in front of Travis and walked backward. "What about your witnesses, Mr. Shanahan? Are there any left who are willing to testify?"

"The retrial hasn't been set. It's premature to speculate."

"Come on, Travis. We all know there's going to be another trial. You're the only person in New Orleans who won't admit it."

Not publicly, Travis thought as he dodged around Quinn and pushed open the door to the old stone building where the district attorney had his offices. "Sorry, Quinn. No comment."

Before the door closed, Quinn shouted, "Brently Gleason has been excused from testifying. What about the others?"

What about the witnesses? That question had plagued Travis from the moment the motions for retrial had started to be taken seriously. In the first trial, his case against DeCarlo had rested upon the testimony of five people who were then stashed away in the witness protection program. As Quinn pointed out, Brently Gleason, who had nearly been killed owing to corruption in the police department, would not be called. Another of the original five, Kyle Johnson, had been murdered. That left three—an accountant, an ex-model and a waitress.

Shaking the dampness from his shoulders, Travis punched the elevator button and turned to his assistants. "Soon as we get upstairs, our preparations for the trial go into high gear. First thing we've got to do is contact our witnesses."

"Maybe Judge Howell won't rule for a second trial," said Janine Carlson, a petite and shy attorney who'd been working in the district attorney's offices for a little over a year.

Travis stared into her hopeful face. Surely she wasn't naive enough to think they had a chance. "Do you think we won, Janine?"

"We're in the right," she said. Her small hand clenched into a fist. "DeCarlo is guilty as sin."

"Sometimes, being right doesn't matter." The disappointment in her eyes made Travis feel like he was deflowering a virgin. "It's all in how you play the game."

The elevator doors swished open. This area was restricted. There would be no reporters, photographers or curious onlookers. There should have been a quiet hum as the lawyers, legal assistants and researchers plied their trade. Instead, Travis heard an angry female tirade spilling through the open door of one of the offices.

"If you think you've caught the real killer, you're out of your mind! I'm not going to let this happen. No, ma'am, I am not."

"If you don't leave, I will have you forcibly ejected."

"Don't you threaten me, Miss Gold. Don't you dare. I'm trying to help you."

Travis stepped into the open doorway. "What's going on here?"

A slender, raven-haired woman whirled around so quickly that her curly hair flew in front of her face. Her intense blue eyes flared like laser flames.

When a sudden grin curved her lips, he thought she looked familiar.

"Hi, Travis. Long time, no see."

"Pardon me, but have we met?"

She braced her fists on her slim hips and tossed her head. "I'm insulted, sugar. Don't you remember all those long nights together? I'd say we had ourselves some fine clandestine trysts. 'Course, that's not exactly the way it was."

His memory cleared, like the sun coming out from behind a cloud. He knew her. "Maggie Deere."

"In the flesh."

There was much less flesh on the well-toned, tanned body of this former waitress who had witnessed the double murder in Augustine's. She'd lost weight. There were other changes as well. Her formerly platinum blond hair was black and cut in an easy-care, casual style that framed her gamine face. Subdued makeup enhanced her big blue eyes and highlighted those lips that always looked like she was on the verge of laughter. She wore an attractive, fashionable pantsuit instead of one of those too-tight sweaters that he remembered so well.

Travis growled, "What the hell are you doing here?"

"Well, I do enjoy southern California. That's where they sent me in the witness protection program. But I had to hightail it back here when I heard about the murder of Kyle Johnson. How could you arrest Pete Fontana?" Her full lips pulled into a frown. "Honestly! You people are handling this case wrong. All wrong."

Dryly, Travis said, "So, you came back here to tell us how to do our jobs."

He wasn't surprised. Maggie Deere was one stubborn woman. As a witness, she was impossible, totally incapable of answering a question with a simple yes or no. She'd balked at every suggestion he made. Her testimony gave new meaning to the word embellish. She was the most contrary, sassy, determined female he'd ever known.

And, strangely, he was glad to see her.

"Listen here, Travis. I was just telling Miss Gold that I might be able to assist you with this case."

"And why is that?"

She hesitated for a fraction of a second before replying, and Travis had the impression that Maggie was hiding something.

"I know I can help," she said. "On account of I knew Kyle and Pete. I can tell you, right now, that you've got the wrong man in jail. Pete Fontana is gentle, kind and really smart. Besides, he and Kyle were friends.''

"Friendships sour," Travis said.

"Sometimes," she said, "but a friendly argument doesn't usually end with something that looks like a gangland execution.''

Not unless the murderer is "really smart," Travis thought. "Does the phrase 'crime of passion' mean anything to you?"

"Passion?" She shook her head, and her hair bounced. "If you're implying that Kyle and Pete were lovers, you're wrong, sugar. And I can tell you why.''

"I'm sure you will. Let's step into my office and discuss your opinions.''

"I don't think so." Maggie tossed her head. "From what I understand, Miss Gold is handling the prosecution on the Kyle Johnson murder. I should be chatting with her. Not you.''

"Yes, of course. But right now, I need to—''

"Don't you trust her, Travis?" Maggie turned to Sharon Gold. "He's not giving you much credit here.''

Sharon Gold, a highly competent prosecutor who was on her way up, came around her desk to stand beside Maggie. The two women made an interesting contrast. Sharon was at least five inches taller. She seemed to be constructed of hard-edged angles from her helmet of blond hair to her square-toed shoes. Maggie, on the other hand, had an undeniable softness.

Crisply, Sharon said, "She's right, Travis. Maggie should talk to me. This is my case.''

"Fine. But right now, I need to get Maggie back into protection. I need to keep my witnesses safe. Even as we speak, Judge Howell has retired to chambers to deliberate on the motions for the retrial of Ben DeCarlo.''

"Oh, that!" Maggie said dismissively. "Ain't no way! Any judge worth his robes will not allow that man to be retried. With my own eyes, I saw Ben DeCarlo kill his poor, sweet mother and father."

"Gosh, I hate to undermine your faith in the system," Travis said. He seemed to be doing that a lot lately. "But everybody in New Orleans expects Judge Howell to rule in favor of DeCarlo."

"Dang!" Maggie's blue eyes widened. "I should run across Broad Street and give that judge a piece of my mind."

That was exactly what Travis was afraid of. The last thing he needed was Maggie Deere facing the press and letting loose with a string of unfounded testimony. He needed to build up the credibility of his witnesses. And he needed to protect them. "Maggie, what are you doing in New Orleans? Does your handler with the U.S. Marshals know you're here?"

"I do not need a handler, thank you. I am not a zebra on display in a zoo."

"When you entered the witness protection program, you made certain promises."

"Yes, I did. Believe me, I am most grateful for all the wonderful help I've gotten in this program."

Travis eyed her suspiciously. Was she being sarcastic? Most witnesses complained about being torn away from their friends and family and career, but Maggie seemed pleased.

Sharon Gold voiced his question, "Are you joking?"

"No, ma'am."

"You like being a protected witness? Being dumped in a strange town? Having no contact with your family?"

"I've got no family. Never knew my daddy, and my mother died when I was eight." There wasn't a hint of self-pity in her attitude. "I'll tell you, Miss Gold, this witness protection program is the first time in my life that I felt like anybody gave a damn about me and my safety."

Sharon's gaping amazement stretched into a smile. "You're really something, Maggie. Tell you what. Why don't you come back here tomorrow morning at nine o'clock and we'll go over the evidence in the Kyle Johnson murder."

"Thank you." Maggie took her hand and gave a strong pump. "You know, Miss Gold, since I'm here right now, maybe I could make a copy of your case file. That would save us some time in the morning."

"Don't push your luck," Sharon warned.

"Do you suppose it would be okay if I swing by the Parish Prison and pay a little visit to my old friend Pete?"

"Whoa," Travis said. "You're not taking off anywhere until I've arranged for someone to keep an eye on you. Let's go, Maggie. To my office."

"Right behind you, Travis."

But she had no intention of following him at a humble and subservient distance. Maggie fell into step, right at his side, and they proceeded down the hallway to the large corner office.

She was pleased that she'd won this small victory with Sharon Gold...and with Travis. Their prior contact when he was coaching her on how to give testimony in the DeCarlo trial was one confrontation after another. He'd had power and all the arrogance that went with it. This time, it was going to be different.

He closed the office door behind her and gestured toward the padded leather chair opposite his huge, cluttered desk. "Sit down, Maggie."

"I'd rather stand."

He flashed a smile. A killer grin, she thought. Most of

the time, Travis looked like a serious man whose mind was occupied by gloomy, complex problems. But when he smiled, his whole face lit up. His dark eyes twinkled with mischief.

"You haven't changed a bit, Maggie. Your appearance is different, but you're still as contrary as a weed in a tulip patch."

"Why would you say such a thing?"

"I ask you to sit." He pointed to the chair. "You say you'd rather stand. If I offered you coffee, you'd say you want soda pop. If I said the sky was blue, you'd insist that it was orange."

"You're being silly. I know the color of the sky."

"Blue as your eyes." He sat behind his desk, flipped through a Rolodex and picked up the telephone. "I'm calling the district office for the U.S. Marshals."

While Travis untangled the federal bureaucracy over the phone, Maggie wandered over to a tall, narrow window and looked down at the midcity traffic and clutter. A trash can had been overturned on the street, and a raggedy man pawed at the contents. A soggy newspaper was scattered on the sidewalk. Though it was only noon, the streets seemed dark and foreboding. This was the New Orleans that the tourists didn't see. An air of sultry deterioration, like the heartfelt sigh of a terminally ill patient, breathed on the chilly January winds.

Yet, when Maggie gazed on the marble columns of the Criminal District Court, she felt a surge of pride. The parish of New Orleans might be as rotten as a termite-infested mangrove tree, but that beautiful old building was the place where Jim Garrison pursued his conspiracy case on the assassination of JFK. Garrison, a former district attorney, had fought for what he thought was right. And Maggie admired that courage.

She turned around and looked at the man behind the desk, a man of New Orleans. Travis Shanahan was fine, handsome, tall and...*elegant*. That was a word she would always associate with him. Travis was smooth as satin, but there wasn't anything soft about him. He looked stubborn and strong, with features hewn from granite. His light brown hair was always neatly combed. He always dressed in beautifully tailored clothes. A soft white shirt with his monogram on the cuff. A perfectly fitted navy blue suit. Silk tie. Travis reminded her of a gentleman from the antebellum South, but his attitude was one hundred percent modern.

In spite of what Travis thought, she wasn't purposely trying to be difficult. She wanted to cooperate with him and with Miss Gold and everybody else in the D.A.'s office because something was way out of whack, and Maggie wanted it set right. That was what lawyers did, wasn't it? Get things straightened out?

Travis hung up the phone. "A marshal will be here within half an hour."

"You know, Travis, I didn't refuse to sit because I wanted to annoy you. It's just that I've been driving for three days to get here, and my butt is still asleep."

"What about your brain? It wasn't smart for you to come back to New Orleans. It's dangerous for you here." He raised his hand before she could object. "I know you never believed that Antonio DeCarlo was involved in racketeering, smuggling and all manner of organized crime. But those are facts. That's how I managed to get you and the other witnesses in the protection program."

"Well, duh! I know that, Travis."

"Why did you come back?"

"Because I think you might be right," she said.

Maggie would never forget the moment when she read

the newspaper article about Kyle Johnson's murder. He'd been shot twice in the head. His body was stuffed in the trunk of a rental car and left at the docks.

"What are you saying, Maggie?"

"I still don't believe that Mr. Antonio DeCarlo was a crime lord, but Kyle's murder sure as heck looked like a gangland execution to me."

"No way," Travis protested. "Don't even go there, Maggie. That dog don't hunt."

"I suppose that you considered the idea," she said archly. "I mean, it does seem powerfully obvious that somebody—maybe somebody who was working for Ben DeCarlo—lured Kyle back to New Orleans and killed him so it would scare off the other witnesses."

"That was our first supposition. Especially since the timing of Kyle's murder coincided with the motions for the Ben DeCarlo retrial. But we have a great deal of circumstantial evidence to the contrary. Murder weapon, fingerprints, blood spatters, the whole nine yards." He shrugged. "I'm sorry, Maggie, but your friend Pete killed Kyle Johnson."

"You're wrong."

"And you are the most stubborn woman on the face of the earth."

She stared in his face. There was something she needed to tell him, but it was hard. Maggie was happy in the witness protection program. She didn't want things to change, didn't want to give up the life she'd established in southern California. "I'm right, Travis. You've got to listen to me. I'm fixin' to save you a heap of embarrassment."

"Don't do me any favors." He pushed away from his desk and stood. "Let's talk about something else before the marshal comes to get you. Do you like California?"

"I like it as well as anyplace I've lived. I've got a job. I'm going to college, studying pre-law. But I'm not here to chat. I came back here to get my friend out of jail and to—"

"The change agrees with you," he said.

He was looking at her in a way that brought her up short. His gaze shone with appreciation as he studied her the way a man studies a woman. Maggie stammered, "What are you talking about?"

"The new hair color. New style. You look great. Did your handler suggest that you change your appearance?"

"Nope. I did this all on my own." She eyed him suspiciously. Was he tossing out compliments to confuse her?

"How did you decide on black hair?"

"At first, I was going back to my natural color. Except I couldn't recall exactly what that hue might be. I decided black would be kind of dramatic on account of everybody in southern California is blond."

"Looks good with your blue eyes."

High praise, indeed. Travis had spent most of their time together when she was a witness complaining about her clothes being too tight. He was virtually the only man who had ever disapproved when she displayed her breasts.

Now, Maggie thought, there weren't many curves to show off. "I started myself on an exercise program," she said. "In the first two months of the protection program, they gave me a real nice little apartment, rent-free, and a stipend. It was the first time since I was fifteen that I didn't need full-time employment, so I did all those things I'd been putting off. You know, working out, taking long baths, lying in the sun, pampering myself. I even went to a dentist and got my teeth fixed."

Travis nodded. "What about your new clothes? From what I recall, a beige linen pantsuit isn't your style."

"After I lost weight, none of my old clothes fit. One of my friends in the apartment building is a clerk in a department store, and she helped me pick out new stuff at a big, juicy discount." Shyly, she asked, "Do you like the way I'm dressed?"

"I do. If I can just get you to control your motor mouth, you'll make an excellent witness."

That was the only way he thought of her—as a pawn in his legal chess game. A witness for the prosecution. Two years ago, Maggie had been foolish enough to hope that there might be something more intimate between Travis Shanahan and herself. For a while, it seemed like there was a spark. But she knew better.

"Travis, you don't really think there's going to be a retrial, do you?"

"Afraid so."

"I cannot believe that." She came to his desk, pushed aside a manila folder and perched on the edge of his desk top. "I can't think of a single precedent for a new trial on a murder conviction with five eyewitnesses."

"Nor can I. I kept telling myself that it wouldn't happen, but I suppose the retrial was inevitable from the minute that Judge Howell scheduled a hearing."

"When was that? Around about December 10?"

"Earlier than that. Why?"

Maggie dug into her shoulder bag, in which she carried enough of life's basic essentials to survive anywhere. In the otherwise empty photo section of her wallet, she found what she was looking for. A scrap of newspaper with a photo of Kyle Johnson, looking very dapper in a tuxedo. The accompanying article identified him as Emmet Wyatt, which was Kyle's name in the witness protection program. The story told of his murder.

She dropped the article on his desk. "The date on this is December 10."

"I'm aware of when Kyle was murdered," he said. "I already told you, Maggie, we considered the connection with DeCarlo."

"Consider this," she said. "I received that article and photo in the mail. The letter was addressed to Maggie Deere, but everybody in California knows me as Margaret Compton."

"It came to your address?"

"Yes."

He circled his desk and came to her. He was moving fast, like he was shot from a cannon. His hands grasped her shoulders. His fingers tightened, and she thought he was going to shake her. "Dammit, Maggie. Why didn't you tell me this right away?"

"I was getting to it."

"Your cover was blown. That means the whole damn witness program is compromised. Again."

Her heart raced as she looked up at him. She hadn't known what to expect from Travis when she told him, but this wasn't it. His eyes were furious. His jaw tense. "You're scaring me."

"Good." He was wound tighter than a watch spring. "Did you tell your handler about the letter?"

"No. At first, I thought he might have been the one who sent the article to me. He knew that me and Kyle were friends."

"Did you—"

"You're the first person I've told, Travis."

"Thank God nothing has happened to you."

His touch gentled. She thought, for a moment, that he was going to pull her into an embrace, that he would hold her against his broad chest and shelter her from those who would harm her. Then he said, "I can't afford to lose another witness."

"Right." She wasn't anything more to him. Just a witness. Important only as a witness. "Well, you don't need to worry. I'm damn good at taking care of myself."

"Why did you come to New Orleans?"

"Because of Pete." Though she avoided looking up into his eyes, she couldn't help being super-aware of how near Travis was to her. His touch was light on her shoulders. She could feel the heat radiating from his body.

"So, you came back here, into certain danger, because of Pete. Why?"

"It was near Christmastime when I read about him being arrested, and I kept thinking about him in a cold jail cell. All alone. He didn't kill Kyle."

"What do you think happened?"

"I don't know." She dared to look into his face. "That's why I came back."

"When you were relocated, did you tell anyone where you were going or what your new identity would be?"

"No, sir."

Travis dropped his hands from her shoulders and stepped away from her. His forehead wrinkled as he concentrated. "Somebody knows your new identity, and that means there's a leak. The witness program isn't going to be any sort of protection at all. I can't turn you over to the custody of a U.S. marshal."

"You can't?"

"The traitor might be in the marshal's office. I've had my suspicions about those boys."

Though Maggie knew he was right, she found it difficult to accept that federal officers had been corrupted. "So, what happens? I go with the police?"

"You don't know everything that's been happening

around here, Maggie, but we've had problems in the police force. I wouldn't leave a bowl of goldfish in their care.''

"I still have some people I know here in town," she suggested. "I could stay with them."

He rolled his eyes. "You still don't get it, do you? This isn't hide-and-seek. These are dangerous people. I have to make sure nothing happens to you."

There was a tap on his office door, and Travis called out, "Come on in."

A tall, reedy-looking man with a weathered face sidled through the door. "I'm Marshal Babcock. I have an order to come over here and pick up one of your DeCarlo witnesses." He focused on Maggie. "Are you Maggie Deere?"

"I am."

"Then I guess you're coming with me."

"No, I'm not," she said defiantly.

"What's the problem, lady? I'm just doing my job."

"I understand, Marshal Babcock. I also know that under the terms of the contract I signed with your office, you can legally compel me to accompany you. However—" She took a deep breath, keeping her voice low and controlled the way they'd taught in the debate classes she'd been taking in college. "When I volunteered as a witness, I did not give up my right to free speech. If you force me to come with you, I guarantee I will turn your life into a living hell with the press. And I will immediately start legal procedures to un-volunteer my testimony. There's plenty of precedent for that. It's my right as a citizen and as a lady to change my mind. So, don't you think that you can order me to come and go."

"Hang on just one minute here. I'm not ordering you to—"

"It's all right," Travis said. "I apologize for your inconvenience, Marshal Babcock. I will need to spend more time with Miss Deere.''

''And what's that supposed to mean?'' Maggie demanded. She thought she'd handled this situation pretty well by herself. She didn't need for Travis to step in and undermine her words.

He flashed another of those killer grins. ''It means that I'll personally arrange for your housing, Maggie.''

She swallowed hard. Did he mean to take her home with him? A brand new terror crept into her heart. This was a fear she'd never felt before. What if she started to care about him? What if she started to believe that he thought of her as someone more important than just a witness?

As she watched the tall, elegant attorney who summarily escorted Marshal Babcock from his office, Maggie knew that Travis had it within his power to hurt her more than she'd ever been hurt before.

Chapter Two

Travis wasn't exactly sure what he was going to do with Maggie, but he had to find a way to protect her that wouldn't involve any of the usual law enforcement officials. She was vital to the case against Ben DeCarlo. If anything happened to her...

"What are you going to do with me?" she demanded.

"For now, you're staying right here."

"Well, then. Long as I'm here, there's no real good reason why I shouldn't start working on the Kyle Johnson murder."

"You're not an attorney, Maggie. You're a witness, and you've got to keep that in mind. We can't do anything that would compromise your testimony."

"What did you have in mind, sugar?" She flashed a seductive little grin. "In terms of compromising?"

"This is no joke, Maggie. You can't be involved, in any way, in our strategy planning for the DeCarlo case. On the witness stand, Ezra Dean can question you on anything you might have overheard."

"I know that, Travis. Didn't I tell you I was studying pre-law?"

"We'll use that as our cover," he said. "If anyone questions your presence here, we'll tell them that you're here as a student, observing.''

She nodded with satisfaction. "That's a fine idea. I might even learn something."

He announced their cover story during a box lunch that was served in the third-floor conference room, a dismal old space with dark paneling. Travis marched to the head of the table.

"I'd like to introduce Maggie Deere," he said, glancing around the long rectangular table at the eleven attorneys and legal aides who made up the core staff handling criminal prosecution. "Some of you might remember her as a witness on the DeCarlo murder trial."

"No way," said Dave Dermott, a husky young man with red hair and freckles who—like Travis—was from one of the best old families in New Orleans. "I remember Maggie. A blonde. And she had—" Dave's hands rose in the shape of torpedo-sized breasts before he remembered he was in the presence of several female attorneys. "Maggie Deere was kind of, um, round. Not that there's anything wrong with that. What I mean is—"

"I understand." Maggie winked at him. "And I appreciate your attention to detail, Dave."

"Over the next few weeks, Maggie will be in our offices frequently," Travis said. "She's taking a little break from studying pre-law in college, and we're her homework assignment."

"There's more bologna in that sentence than in this sandwich," said Sharon Gold as she pushed aside her lunch.

Though Travis appreciated Sharon's assertiveness in the courtroom, everything about her was annoyingly argumentative. "What's the problem, Sharon?"

"You aren't leveling with us," she said. "Why isn't

Maggie with the U.S. Marshals? You still need her as a witness. We all know that Judge Howell is going to rule for a retrial.''

"Let's talk about the retrial," Travis said, grabbing a new topic and hanging on tight. He didn't want to explain to his staff that he didn't trust the federal marshals or the NOPD to provide adequate protection for any of his witnesses. It had also occurred to him that the leak concerning Maggie's address might have come from within these offices. One of his own trusted staff might be feeding information to the men who worked for DeCarlo.

"Sharon is correct," he said. "In half an hour, I fully expect that we once again will be prosecuting Ben DeCarlo."

There were groans all around the table.

"We need to get started," Travis said. "I already have the files on my desk. As far as I'm concerned, our approach to the case will not change substantially. We have eyewitnesses to the crime."

"But not Brently Gleason," said Dave, picking up a giant-sized hero sandwich. "Damn, she was good. An eyewitness with a photographic memory. We're going to miss her testimony."

"We can't call her. After that story that Farris Quinn ran in the *Times-Picayune*, Miss Gleason is up to her neck in alligators with regard to police corruption. That's a line of inquiry we wish to avoid whenever possible."

"Police corruption is one of the reasons for the retrial," Sharon Gold reminded him. "The defense claims that our cops were paid off to frame DeCarlo."

"There goes all our forensic evidence," moaned the gloomy-faced legal aide named Roy Hackman. "The fibers on his shoes. The blood spatters on his coat. Worthless!''

"Not that we ever had the murder weapon," Sharon reminded him.

"We don't need the gun," Travis said firmly. "We've got eyewitnesses. We've got Maggie."

"Why, thank you." She smiled like a homecoming queen and waved. "I'll do my best."

Travis addressed the other attorneys. "Also, I need to remind all of you that anything you say to Maggie might be repeated on the witness stand. Be careful around her. She is a witness and will be compelled to tell the whole truth."

"What's next?" Dave Dermott asked.

"We need to juggle some scheduling and shuffle around the caseloads. The DeCarlo retrial is going to be full-time work for me and at least two other attorneys."

While they discussed agendas, he watched Maggie as she poured herself a cup of coffee from a thermal carafe. She looked so calm, he thought. With her new hairdo and makeup, she seemed less like a tough blond waitress and more like a sophisticated, intelligent law student. She smiled pleasantly aᵗ the man seated to her left. "Would you like some coffee?"

"Yes, please."

"Cream and sugar?"

Even her voice was different, Travis thought. She was softer in every way, gentler, more complaisant. With a little coaching, he might transform her into a stellar witness.

The guy sitting next to her was obviously captivated by her new presence. He was oozing charm as he accepted her offer of cream and sugar.

"Don't expect me to take up all of the slack," Sharon Gold complained. "I've already got two murder trials coming up. Not to mention that I'm plea-bargaining ten to twenty cases a day."

Maggie was on her feet, refilling the coffee carafe from a large urn. "Anybody else want coffee while I'm up?"

"I do," said Dave through a mouthful of sandwich.

Maggie poured for him and glanced over at Janine Carlson, who nodded as she said, "I think we need to talk about police corruption on the DeCarlo case. Do you think Ezra Dean will use the Mark Fuhrman defense?"

"Of course he will," Sharon Gold said. "Cops all over the country are being charged with brutality and entrapment."

"That's purely a shame," Maggie put in as she refilled another attorney's coffee cup. "I mean, if people can't trust their law enforcement officials, who can they turn to?"

"The police evidence doesn't matter," Travis said. "NOPD could be run by gerbils and it wouldn't matter to our case. We have eyewitnesses. Ultimately, that's where the defense is going to attack. They'll try to cast doubt on our witnesses."

"What's our position with the press?" Dave asked.

"I think some outrage about the injustice of retrial would be in order. Sharon, I would appreciate if you would accompany me in the courtroom this afternoon. You do outrage very well."

"Thank you, Travis."

"Otherwise, with regard to the press," Travis said, "we want to repeat, over and over, that a whole dining room full of people watched Ben DeCarlo shoot his loving parents."

"I don't know," Dave cautioned. "We might not want to hit too hard on the loving parents angle. Everybody knows that Antonio DeCarlo was a big man in organized crime.''

"But never convicted," Travis reminded. "And his wife, Bethany, was blameless."

"A lovely woman," Maggie put in. "The DeCarlos were my favorite customers at Augustine's. Anybody else want cream and sugar?"

"No coffee for me," said Roy with a heavy sigh. He had to be the most pessimistic individual this side of Job. "But I sure would like an orange soda pop from the fridge down the hall."

"Okay." Maggie picked up a legal pad from in front of him. "That's one orange soda. Anybody else?"

"Maggie, what are you doing?" Sharon demanded.

"As long as I was up, I thought I would—"

"Don't." Sharon snatched the legal pad from her hand. "If you behave like a waitress, nobody is going to take you seriously as a law student, a witness or anything else."

Maggie's backbone stiffened at this snotty criticism of her profession, and Travis braced himself for a scathing Maggie counterattack. To tell the truth, he was looking forward to hearing Maggie put Sharon in her place. Instead, Maggie nodded. "I believe you're right, Miss Gold."

"I usually am."

Maggie plunked down in her chair. "You're a big boy, Roy. You can fetch your own soda."

"Thanks, Sharon." Roy sneered at her. "Now I have to go all the way down the hall."

"The exercise will do you good," Sharon taunted. "That's some little potbelly you're growing there."

"Listen up," Travis said. "We need to work out our schedules. Dave will sit second chair for the DeCarlo trial."

"I'm your man."

"And, Janine, I want you there, too. I need a sweet-talking woman to counterbalance the silver-tongued Ezra Dean."

Janine chirped, "Okeydoke."

"Oh, please," Sharon said. "No offense, Janine, but you're no match for Ezra Dean Slaughter. That's like pitting a baby lamb against a king cobra."

"Bah, bah, bah," Janine bleated. "You just might be surprised."

Silently, Travis agreed with Sharon. Janine was a young, unseasoned prosecutor while Ezra Dean Slaughter was a formidable, brilliant, highly paid defender who managed to fight aggressively for his clients without ever abandoning an aura of fellowship. His demeanor caused jurors to think of him as a favorite uncle or a football coach or—when he launched into his orations—a kind-hearted preacher. In his prestigious career, Ezra Dean Slaughter had lost only two cases. One was long ago. The other was the first Ben DeCarlo trial.

After the verdict, he'd confronted Travis with fangs bared and dripping with venom. There was no jury present, so Ezra Dean hadn't bothered with a pretense of friendship. Like a deadly reptile, he'd spewed his lies, accusing Travis of railroading DeCarlo, of working out a sleazy political agenda, of being in the pay of organized crime. Snarling, Ezra Dean had promised that the case wasn't over.

And he'd been right. His confounded ability to manipulate the system infuriated Travis.

"Travis?" Janine said quietly. "Do you really want me on the DeCarlo trial? Sharon's much more experienced and—"

"Of course I do. I want you to cross-examine their alleged star witness, Sandor Rossi. I want the jury to see the contrast between your dewy-eyed innocence and that sack of slime."

"Fair enough. I won't disappoint you."

"Besides," Travis admitted, "if I were to question Rossi myself, I'd be hard-pressed not to jump into the witness box and strangle him with my bare hands."

Before they ended their lunch conference, Travis meted out tasks and recruited one more person. "Roy, I want you to keep an eye on Maggie this afternoon."

"Don't I have enough to do?" he whined. "Why do I have to take care of everything around here?"

As the other attorneys filed out of the room, Travis clarified, "Don't let her leave this floor, Roy. If anybody says they're here to pick her up, you refuse. If she tries to sneak out of here, you have my permission to hog-tie her to a bench."

"Why would I sneak away?" Maggie batted her eyelashes with overplayed innocence. "I wouldn't dream of causing trouble."

"Just like you wouldn't dream of taking off from southern California without notifying your handler?"

"I'll be fine." She patted his arm. "Good luck, sugar."

As soon as Travis, Sharon and Dave boarded the elevator and departed for Judge Howell's courtroom, Maggie changed her mind. She wanted to be there to hear with her own ears when Judge Howell proclaimed a retrial.

She sank down on the worn leatherette sofa in the office that Roy shared with three other legal aides. Thoughtfully, Maggie studied her long fingernails. Though she preferred bright red, or even magenta, her new friends in California convinced her that the plain French manicure was stylish. Probably they were right. Probably all this transforming was worth it.

Her new look certainly made a difference to Travis. More than once, she'd caught him looking at her as if she were a human being instead of a witness.

The best thing was to do as he said. Sit here quietly and do as she was told.

Maggie watched the legal process at work. Two of the aides were diligently engaged in computer searches. Another, who was on the phone, scribbled furiously on a legal pad.

Roy was at the desk nearest to her, and she smiled at him sweetly. "Tell me, Roy, did you do any of the research for the Kyle Johnson murder?"

"Of course I did. I always end up doing everything around here."

What a grouch! "I understand that they found the gun in Pete Fontana's apartment."

"That's right. The investigation was a no-brainer once we got the tip that Kyle was staying with Pete Fontana. Initially, the police had found the key to a mighty nice room at the Lafayette Hotel in Kyle's rental car, so we had assumed he was staying there."

Maggie nodded encouragingly. From the article, she knew that Kyle's body was found in a rental car, but she hadn't realized that the car was one that Kyle had rented for himself. "The Lafayette? Ooh-la-la. I guess Kyle had come into some money to be able to afford a room there and not even use it."

"He had a credit card from his new girlfriend." Roy lowered his voice, obviously enjoying this chance to gossip. "Not that she was much of a girlfriend. Seems that those two boys—Pete and Kyle—were the real item, if you know what I mean."

Maggie whispered back, "I don't know what you mean."

"Well, Kyle rented the room so his girlfriend wouldn't get suspicious. In fact, she was supposed to join him. But he was staying with Pete. In his one-bedroom apartment. We think Pete and Kyle were lovers, and they had an argument."

"Crime of passion," Maggie said. Except she knew for a fact that Pete wasn't gay.

"I probably shouldn't be talking to you about all this." Roy picked up the telephone on his desk. "I've got a lot of work to do."

"Come on, Roy. I think your job is fascinating. Please talk to me." She cajoled, "I'll get you that orange soda."

"Maybe later," he conceded. "Right now, I have to contact the Marshals office about the other two witnesses. This is going to be hard. They won't want to tell me anything."

"Why not?"

"They just won't." He pouted.

"Well, I'd love to talk to Monique if you get ahold of her."

Maggie thought of the beautiful, coppery-haired woman who had given up a high-profile career as a model to testify against Ben DeCarlo. Losing her glamorous livelihood was a huge sacrifice, and Maggie admired her for doing the right thing.

But it was all for nothing, Maggie thought, if Ben DeCarlo won a retrial. Damn, she wished she could be down there, in the courtroom, watching.

And why not? Travis had been concerned about two things: that she might talk to the press. And that she was somehow in danger.

Worrying about the press was irrelevant, she decided, if she simply didn't talk to anybody. What about the danger? Nobody knew she was here, so who could be after her?

Besides, she looked different. Travis hadn't even recognized her when he first saw her. With her new appearance, nobody would pay her the least bit of attention.

Having fully rationalized the issue in her own mind, she rose to her feet, stretched and yawned.

Roy looked up from his phone call. He spoke into the receiver, "Could you please hold?" To Maggie, he said, "What are you doing?"

"Just shaking off the afternoon drowsies." She whispered, "I'm fixin' to go to the bathroom, if you don't mind."

"I should go with you. Travis said to watch you."

"Oh, sugar, you're so busy. Don't fuss with me."

"You're not going to pull anything, are you? Travis will have my head on a platter if—"

"Tell you what, Roy. I'll leave the office door open." Grabbing her huge purse, she stepped into the doorway. "The ladies' room is down this hall to the left. The elevators are to the right. You'll see me if I sneak to the right."

"Okay," he said hesitantly.

"Don't you worry, sugar. I wouldn't dare do anything to make Travis mad."

She strode down the marble-floored corridor. In her personal history of untruths and half truths, the part about not upsetting Travis was a whopper of a lie. In a teasing, perverse way, she enjoyed watching Travis get riled up...maybe because it gave her the illusion that he actually cared about her.

Passing the ladies' room, Maggie headed toward the last door in the third-floor corridor. When she was first a witness two years ago, she'd discovered all of the catacombs in this old building across the street from the courthouse.

She knew there was a narrow stairway at the end of the hall. From there, she could escape to the street.

Maggie slipped into the stairway and started down. The doors locked as soon as they were closed, so she had to play with the catch on the first-floor door so she'd be able to get back through it when she returned to this building.

Maggie peeked into the first-floor corridor. There were only a few people and nobody seemed to notice her.

As she exited the building, Maggie smiled at the policeman who sat at the front desk beside a metal detector. She dashed across Broad Street. If she was going to get back before Roy got suspicious, she needed to hurry.

Inside the courthouse, she checked the dockets and proceeded to Judge Howell's courtroom, slipping inside just as he took the bench. Maggie sat on the far end of the last row nearest the door.

A sense of excitement welled up inside her. She loved the drama of the law. Both sides stated their cases as best they could, and then…a decision. Lives were changed by the edicts spoken in these courtrooms. *Edicts.* That was a good vocabulary word.

She liked being here, being in this beautiful, spacious room with the tall desk where the judge sat. Here was where all those intangible ideals, like justice and truth, came first. *Intangible,* she repeated to herself. It seemed like she got smarter just by being in a courtroom.

The problem here, in Judge Howell's crowded courtroom, was that a wretched miscarriage of justice was about to occur. If Ben DeCarlo won a retrial, the whole system was shaky. DeCarlo was guilty beyond a reasonable doubt. She'd seen with her own eyes when he fired that pistol.

Maggie shuddered, remembering that horrible moment. When she'd finally summoned the courage to look, she saw the ugly scarlet bloodstain on Mrs. DeCarlo's winter white suit. Her husband hadn't quite been dead, and his hand had reached toward his wife before it went limp. There was blood everywhere. On the white tablecloth. On the paneled walls. On the flagstone floor.

In her mind, Maggie heard the echoing screams of the other people in the restaurant. Chaos ran rampant. *Rampant.*

Most of all, Maggie recalled her own helplessness.

Her memories were full of recrimination. If only she'd run up to Ben when he entered and started talking, he might have come to his senses. If only she'd been faster getting to the DeCarlos' table, she could have grabbed Ben's arm and held on real tight until somebody came to help her and they disarmed him. Could have... Might have...

But she hadn't. She'd been as stunned as anyone in Augustine's. And the DeCarlos were dead.

The droning voice of Judge Howell reviewed the appeals filed by the defense. New evidence. Jury tampering. Tainted forensic procedure. Couldn't he just get to it? She glanced at her wristwatch. What about the eyewitnesses? What about the truth? Maggie wanted to believe in the law, to make the practice of law her life. There had to be someplace for people to turn for a fair decision. There had to be some way that people who were wronged could be helped.

"In conclusion," Judge Howell said, "I will honor the appeals of the defense. I call for a new trial for Benjamin Wilson DeCarlo."

There was a murmur from the watchers in the courtroom, and Maggie recognized two of the reporters who slipped past the bailiffs and out the doors. A lovely woman, seated right behind the defense table, buried her head in her hands and began to weep softly. She was Maria, Ben's sister, who had always believed in his innocence. When Ben himself turned to comfort his sister, Maggie saw a cruel smile on his handsome face. He'd won. His expensive attorneys had manipulated the system and overturned the truth. She imagined, for a second, that his gaze rested coldly upon her, sinking to the depth of her soul, threatening her.

He was a dangerous man, a murderer. And what about the people who worked for him? They must be equally dangerous. They might have killed Kyle Johnson and framed Pete Fontana. They might be coming after her.

"Jury selection will begin tomorrow," the judge declared.

Travis was on his feet. "Your Honor, the prosecution requests a few weeks, at least, to prepare."

"Sorry, Mr. Shanahan. I've taken to heart your closing statement that we should not waste the court's time and the taxpayers' money with a prolonged trial. We will get underway immediately. I want this wrapped up by the end of the month."

"But Your Honor—" This time it was Ezra Dean Slaughter who objected.

"I will not entertain any objection on this point, Mr. Slaughter. Your client is entitled to a speedy trial, and that is what I intend to give him. This court is adjourned."

Just like that! Maggie blinked. One snap of the gavel, and justice crumbled. It was up to Travis and his team of prosecutors to rebuild the evidence.

Maggie hadn't expected to be so disturbed by the judge's decision. Not only was this a miscarriage of justice, but the decision for a retrial put her in deep jeopardy. If Ben DeCarlo would kill his own mother and father, the people who worked for him would not hesitate to ax down a nobody like Maggie Deere.

As unobtrusively as possible, she joined the throng exiting the courtroom and hurried onto Broad Street. She needed to get back upstairs in the building across the street. Travis had been right when he warned her. The minute she'd looked into Ben DeCarlo's eyes, she understood that her life could be in peril now that her witness protection cover had been blown.

Instinctively, Maggie could feel danger closing around her. The dank January weather rolled over her, consuming all light. The hairs on the nape of her neck prickled. Goose bumps chased up her forearm.

She was at the door to the building that housed the D.A. and his staff when she felt a hand on her arm. "I know you."

She pivoted. Surely, no one would attack her here! Not in broad daylight! Not when she was within shouting distance of the guard at the doorway! She faced Farris Quinn.

"You're Maggie Deere," he said.

A voice inside her head told her to deny her own identity. But how could she? Farris Quinn knew her pretty well. After the last trial, she'd granted him an interview—an interview that had made Travis furious. With a shrug, she said, "Hi, Mr. Quinn."

"What are you doing here? You're supposed to be in the witness protection program."

"I'm back here for the trial," she said, "and I really mustn't be talking to you."

"Have you changed your mind about Ben DeCarlo?"

"Are you plumb crazy? I know what I saw. Ben DeCarlo pulled that trigger. He did it, Mr. Quinn."

He pressed a card into her hand. "Call me when you can talk."

She darted inside the building and allowed the guard to run her purse through his metal detector. Then she hurried to the stairway where she'd kept the door unlocked with a piece of tape from her giant-sized purse. Maggie whisked inside and peeled off the tape, allowing the door to latch.

As soon as it closed, she knew she'd made a mistake. The light above the door was out. Though she could see a faint glow from far above, other lights were out, too.

She twisted the knob in her hand. Too late. Someone had set the lock to fasten tight when she returned. She was trapped in the semidarkness.

Squinting, she could barely discern the edge of the metal banister in front of her. She groped toward it. Her foot had touched the first stair when she felt the presence of another person. Intangible but near.

Carefully, she crept forward. Up one step, then another. So far, so good. Was she safe? Had she imagined the danger? She moved more surefootedly. She was halfway to the first landing.

Then…Maggie gasped. All her terror was expressed in that single, swift intake of breath.

She was caught. Someone had grasped her ankle.

Wrenching frantically to get free, she went down hard on the metal-edged stairs. Though her arms rose to protect her face, her forehead cracked against the banister. Pain exploded behind her eyes. A scream rose in the back of her throat, but no sound escaped her lips.

The world was spinning. She was dizzy, fainting. No! She couldn't pass out now! She had to escape!

But how? Her arms wouldn't move. Her knees weren't strong enough to support her. She was being dragged down the stairs. Her huge purse spilled cosmetics and notes and wallet and wadded tissues that shone in the dim light like camellia petals.

Gathering every last shred of her strength, she managed to stand up. He grabbed her from behind. One arm caught her by the throat, the other gripped her waist. *Oh, my dear Lord, I don't want to die.*

His forearm pressured her windpipe. *Help me! Somebody help me!* She needed to scream, but all she could manage was a strangled cry.

"Shut up," he snarled in her ear.

"No!" She wouldn't give up. She hadn't spent her whole life fighting to concede so easily. She pushed away the ragged edges of unconsciousness. Nobody was going to drag her down. Nobody was going to make her say uncle.

Maggie struggled with all her strength. Her elbows were flying. Her feet kicked backward at her unseen attacker.

The man yelped when she connected with his shin. Then he tightened his grip on her throat. *I can't breathe.*

Her lungs throbbed. Her mouth tasted dry and hot.

"I'm not going to hurt you," the man said. "Not yet, anyway."

She didn't believe him. With her last breath, she was going to fight.

"This is a warning, Maggie Deere. Pack up and get out of town. Don't testify. You can't win. Ben DeCarlo is going to walk."

Abruptly, he flung her away from him. She spun around. Flailing with her arms, her hand connected with his head. She grasped at his head and clawed, fighting to regain her strength. Her fingertips slid through his greasy, long hair. She felt his loop earring. Viciously, she raked the skin of his face with her long fingernails.

"You little—"

He slapped her, and she fell to the hard concrete floor at the base of the stairwell. On her hands and knees, she gulped down air in precious gasps.

Then she heard the click of a safety catch being released from a pistol. He was going to kill her.

"Leave town," he said. "Or you're a dead woman."

She was panting, gathering strength to fight back. "Did you kill Kyle? Did you murder Kyle Johnson?"

A muffled gunshot echoed in the stairwell. A thud. He was using a silencer.

Behind her, the doorway to the first-floor corridor flew open. Briefly, a slash of light illuminated the stairwell. Then the door closed again.

Maggie was alone. And more terrified than she'd ever been in her life.

From far above, she heard another door open.

"No," she whimpered. "Please, no."

She couldn't face another attacker, couldn't fight anymore. If someone else was coming to finish the job, she didn't know where she would find the resources to resist.

"Maggie? Are you down here?"

It was Travis!

For an instant, she considered holding her silence, allowing him to go away until she pulled herself together. She didn't want to be weak in front of him.

"I'm here," she whispered softly.

She needed protection. She needed him.

Chapter Three

Travis heard her voice, a tiny whimper, from the bottom of the stairs. "Maggie?"

"I'm down here," she said weakly. "I'm okay. Just give me a minute."

That was brash, bold, demanding Maggie? And she was whispering? My God, she must be at death's door! He flung wide the third-floor door to the stairwell and snapped at Roy, "Hold this so it won't lock."

"This isn't my fault," Roy whined. "Really! She said she was going to the bathroom."

Travis charged down the stairs. At the second floor, he encountered darkness. The red exit light was broken as well as the bulb above the landing. Someone had darkened the stairwell for an ambush. That much was obvious to him. But how the hell had they known Maggie was going to be here? They must have been following her, must have picked up her trail as soon as she hit town.

Dammit! Travis rounded the twist in the stairwell. Why had she returned to New Orleans in the first place? If she was right about Kyle Johnson's murder being a hit, she had put herself in severe danger. How many damned times did he have to tell her?

All thoughts of recrimination washed from his mind

when he saw Maggie in the dim light. She sat at the base of the stairs with her back leaning against the iron banister and her feet tucked beneath her. Her head was tilted up, eyes closed. Her face was a perfect oval—pale in spite of her California tan.

And she was beautiful.

The realization occurred to him at the same time he experienced a jolt of fear that hit his heart with the force of a lightning bolt. He cared about what happened to Maggie Deere. He cared about her beyond the normal concern for a witness.

"Maggie." His voice was husky.

Her eyelids blinked open. Her blue eyes shone like glass, and her features were bleak. In slow motion, she held out her arm toward him. "Give me a hand, Travis."

Standing at the bottom of the stairwell, he pulled her to her feet. Her grip was weak. She seemed wobbly on her feet, barely able to stand. Travis dragged her against his chest and held her, lightly stroking her back and shoulders, assuring himself that she was all in one piece. Her body was delicate, as fragile as a wounded dove, and his hands felt big and clumsy.

"My God, Maggie, you scared me."

"Did I?"

He buried his face in her soft curls, and he smelled the clean fragrance of her shampoo. "I'll get you a doctor."

"I'm all right."

But when she tried to move away from him, she stumbled. Seeking balance, she clung to him. Her small, round breasts crushed against his chest. The pressure of her body was tentative, uncertain and exquisite. More than anything, he longed to protect this woman, to make the world safe for her.

"Hey!" came Roy's shout from the third-floor landing. "What's going on down there?"

"I'm all right," Maggie yelled back. She had regained volume, but her voice trembled.

"The hell you are," Travis muttered. He shouted, "Roy, call 911. Get an ambulance."

"Don't you dare!" Maggie countered. "Don't call 911."

They heard Roy's plaintive whine. "Make up your minds. What am I supposed to do?"

In a firmer tone, she said, "Really, Travis. I'm fine. Shaken up like a vanilla malted, but fine."

He squinted through the shadows at her face. Her eyes. Her lips. "All right, Maggie. Let's get you upstairs to my office, then we'll decide."

"Travis?" Roy wailed. "What should I do?"

"Just hold the door," he yelled back.

They started up the stairs, then Maggie remembered. "My purse. It's spilled all over."

She wriggled out of his arms and knelt down, fumbling around on the stairs, picking up an odd assortment of articles, ranging from a flat-head screwdriver to a silvery tube of lipstick.

"Let me get it," Travis said.

"It's okay. I'm perfectly capable of—"

"Capable of driving me crazy." He lifted her by the shoulders and stood her against the wall of the staircase. "I'll pick up your stuff. Doggone it, woman, do you have to object to every word I say?"

"Isn't that what lawyers do? Objections?"

"You're overruled, lady. Just stand there."

He picked up the clutter that had spread over several stairs, then slung the strap of her bag over his own shoulder. "This thing is heavy. What's in here?"

"Everything I need for a quick escape."

He linked his arm through hers. Slowly, they mounted the stairs. "Escape, huh? Well, you're overruled again. You're not going anywhere."

"That's not going to please the man who attacked me."

Travis swallowed the anger that rose in his throat. "What did he say?"

"He told me to get out of town. And that if I testify, I'm a dead woman."

"NO DOCTORS," MAGGIE repeated. She leaned back in the padded leather chair in Travis's office. "How many times do I have to tell you? I'm fine."

"Nothing hurts?" he asked.

"I'm not some kind of fancy little porcelain figurine. Nothing's busted. I'll be okay."

But it did hurt. Her right temple, where her head had smacked the banister, ached. Even though she didn't bruise easily, she was going to have an ugly lump on her forehead. Her right knee throbbed. Her throat was so sore that it seemed like she could still feel that man's forearm gripping, strangling the breath from her lungs. *Stop it! Don't think about it!* She couldn't give in to a paralyzing fear. The attack was over. She'd survived. There were various other pains from her tumble down the stairs, but she'd been beat up worse, much worse.

She glanced over at Travis, who sat in the leather chair beside her. With an air of finality, she reassured him, "I'm fine. Don't call the paramedics."

"You're scared of doctors," he said.

"Well, who isn't? Have you ever been in a doctor's office when it didn't hurt? All that poking and probing with an ice-cold metal implement! Then they push on a bruise and ask if it hurts." She shuddered. "Thank you, no. I'd rather heal myself, settle back and let nature take its course.''

"I understand your fear of doctors. I've seen this reaction before from people who have been abused.''

"Excuse me?'' Maggie hadn't shared her past with him, not with anyone. Immediately, she threw up a steel wall of defense. Some things did not bear thinking about. "I don't know what you're talking about.''

"Come on, Maggie. I've seen your juvenile records. We went over the details during the first trial. You were arrested as a runaway. You bounced from foster home to foster home. It's my guess that some of those places weren't Sunnybrook Farm. One of your foster fathers was convicted of child abuse and served time.''

"That's none of your business.''

"It's why you're afraid of doctors,'' he continued. "The pattern is set in childhood. You're afraid to go to the doctor because if the doctor finds out what's really wrong with you, the abuser will get into trouble. Then you'll be beaten again.''

"Thought you were a lawyer,'' she muttered. "Not a doggoned social worker.''

"In the D.A.'s office, we're a little bit of both.''

Maggie stretched out her legs, scooted her chair a bit closer to his desk and propped her feet up on the cluttered surface. She laced her fingers together and looked down at her hands. "Well, shoot!''

"What's wrong?''

"I broke a nail.''

"How? Is there anything else you remember about the attack?''

Unbidden, her mind replayed the terrifying scene in the stairwell. Her breath jumped up in her throat in a stifled scream and she gulped it back down, forcing her fears to be still. "I scratched the guy on the face. I could feel his hair. Kind of greasy. And he had a loop earring in one ear."

"That's helpful," Travis encouraged. "From the earring, we can assume he wasn't a cop on duty or a marshal. Can you remember anything else about him?"

"It was too dark to see. I know he was taller than me from the way he grabbed me, but that's not saying much." She studied Travis carefully. There was something he wasn't telling her. "Why would a cop attack me?"

"I don't know." Travis shrugged. "Was there anything unusual about this guy's voice? An accent?"

"He was Southern, not Cajun," she said. "But why would you even think it was a cop?"

"The guy had a gun. Roy tells me that he shot the lock at the bottom of the stairs. How would he get a gun into this building unless he was licensed to carry one?"

"Oh, puh-leeze." She rolled her eyes. "It wouldn't be all that hard to smuggle a gun in here."

"There are metal detectors at all the doors."

"But there are ways in and out that don't require walking through the front doorway. The last time I was here as a witness, I didn't find it all that difficult to sneak out and grab myself a hamburger."

"Okay," Travis allowed. "Our security measures aren't perfect. That's why we need to find someplace safe to stash you, and you need to go there, immediately."

"No," she said.

"Excuse me?"

Maggie lifted her feet off his desk and stood. "I'm fixin' to pay a visit at Parish Prison this afternoon."

"Oh no, you're not." He was on his feet, glaring.

"I am," she said simply. "It's real convenient, since

Parish Prison is right next to the courthouse. In fact, I left my car in the prison parking lot.''

"And you just strolled past the prison?"

"Of course I did. And I mean to tell you that it was not a pleasant walk in the park. Those criminals are hanging out the windows and whooping and hollering all kinds of filthy comments." She frowned at him. "But why would you be surprised by where I parked? Practically everybody who gets called for jury duty parks there."

"Did it occur to you that there are snitches in the prison who might have recognized you?"

"How could they? You hardly knew me when you saw me. That's why I didn't think it made any difference if I ran across the street and sat in Judge Howell's courtroom. And I must say that he was—"

Travis threw his hands in the air. "You are the most exasperating woman it has ever been my misfortune to come into contact with."

"I'm not trying to be."

"That's what makes it worse! This talent of yours is inborn, unchangeable, impossible—"

"Settle down, Travis. I'm sure that once you understand what I'm doing, you'll agree with me."

"Not likely."

"The way I reckon," she said, "this guy who attacked me knows something about Kyle's murder, and that's a defense for Pete Fontana. So, I need to get over to the prison and talk to Pete. Poor Pete."

"Poor Pete?"

"He hasn't got any family. I'll bet he's sitting in his jail cell, feeling miserable and abandoned." She lightly touched the sore spot on her forehead, hoping the aspirin would alleviate her aching head. "Pete needs a friend."

"Does it have to be you?"

"I don't see why not."

He spoke slowly, dropping every word like a thud on her brain. "Because people are after you. You're an important witness."

"I'm also a human being, Travis. I've got to go forward with my life."

"With no regard for your own safety?"

"I'll be careful." She stuck out her chin. "But I'm still going to see Pete."

Why couldn't she make him understand? She couldn't sit quiet and let anybody—not even a man with a gun—push her around. She had to keep moving. It was harder to hit a moving target.

"Fine," he said, turning away from her. He rested both hands on the desk top and leaned forward heavily. Beneath his soft white cotton shirt, she could see the play of muscles across his broad shoulders as he inhaled and exhaled.

Though she hadn't meant to push his buttons, she obviously had ticked him off. Once again, they were confronting each other. And that wasn't what she wanted. Maggie would have liked nothing more than to cuddle up close and be agreeable. When he'd held her in his arms at the foot of the stairwell, she'd felt—possibly, for the first time in her whole life—that someone was there for her, to protect her, to care about her.

"I'm sorry, Travis." She couldn't help who she was.

"Ever play with a yo-yo, Maggie?"

"Sure, when I was a kid."

"Well, I'm feeling like a yo-yo with the string wound tight. One more twist and I'm about to go flying."

"Maybe I should just leave now." That would be best. She could slip out the door and keep her distance from this overstressed attorney who obviously had enough problems without worrying about her.

"We will leave now. *We.* That means both of us." He snatched his suit jacket from the back of his office chair and shrugged his arms into the sleeves. "Is that clear, Maggie? We will be going together. You and me. Together."

A bright ray of sunshine cut through her anger and her fear. He was coming with her! Travis cared enough to put up with her demands and still want to be with her. She was so completely relieved that she didn't object. "Thank you, sir. I would be most pleased to have you as my escort."

Though a visit to Parish Prison couldn't really be considered a first date, Maggie experienced the same kind of pleasant giddiness when Travis took her arm and led her to the elevators. On the first floor, he guided her to a rear exit that was also guarded by a uniformed policeman with a metal detector. They went into the private parking lot, and Travis took her to his car, which was a sedate BMW sedan with a couple of discarded fast-food bags in the back seat. He opened the passenger side door for her and tucked her inside. *Just like she was somebody!*

"It's only two blocks," she said. "We could walk."

"This is easier."

He was right. At the prison, the D.A.'s office had reserved parking near the entrance. With practiced ease, Travis handled all the details of visitation, bypassing the embarrassment of having cops paw through her purse and the inconvenience of filling out endless forms detailing why she needed to see the prisoner.

Quicker than the flick of an alligator's tail, they were seated in a small, windowless room. Maggie sat at one of the three chairs that had been placed around a plain wood table. "Very nice," she commented. "Other times I had to come to a jail, it wasn't nearly so simple."

"Other times?" Travis questioned as he sat. "Please don't tell me that you make a habit of consorting with known criminals."

"Friends," she explained, "not criminals. Sometimes, I've had to arrange bail for somebody who got picked up for being drunk and disorderly. Or for possessing an illegal substance. Sometimes, I came for a visit, but that was mostly when I lived in Texas. Actually, I've never been here in the Parish Prison, but the inside of one of these places looks a lot like another." She winked at him. "Do you suppose they all use the same decorator?"

He raised an eyebrow. "Interior design by Incarceration, Unlimited?"

"Featuring designer cells with decorative but practical iron bar grillwork."

When he flashed his devastating grin, Maggie blushed from the inside out. This sure as heck felt like a date. She enjoyed being in his company, and he seemed more contented and relaxed than ever.

Then the door to the room opened. A uniformed prison guard directed Pete Fontana through the door. His skinny wrists were in cuffs. The trousers of his baggy prison clothes were pinched by leg irons. The sight of him, so unjustly shackled, broke Maggie's heart. With a little cry, she leapt from her chair.

"Sorry, ma'am." The guard stepped in front of Pete. "No physical contact. Those are the rules."

Maggie remained standing. Her gaze still focused on Pete's face. "How are you doing, sugar?"

"Not bad, I guess. I can't believe this is you, Maggie. You look so different."

"Do you like my new style?"

"You're still the prettiest gal I've ever seen."

"Didn't I write and tell you that I'd be here? I'm not somebody who goes back on her word, Pete."

She glanced at Travis. "Can't we get those cuffs removed?"

He nodded to the guard. "You can release him and then leave. I'll take full responsibility."

"Sure thing, Mr. Shanahan. I got better things to do."

When Pete had been freed and the guard departed from the room, Maggie did the natural thing. She pulled her friend into a warm hug. "Oh, Pete, honey, I'm so sorry this happened to you."

"I didn't kill Kyle," he murmured as he held her close.

"I know you didn't. And I'm fixin' to get that all straightened out. You can count on me."

"I always could."

With as much warmth as she could muster, Maggie hugged his scrawny body. Pete had always been thin, but now he was positively skeletal. "Don't you see who I brought with me? Travis Shanahan, himself. He's the chief prosecuting attorney in the D.A.'s office."

"Hi, Mr. Shanahan," Pete said without ending the embrace. "Thanks for coming."

"Sure."

Travis couldn't see Maggie's expression because she was facing away from him, but he had a clear view of Pete Fontana. From the blissful look in the prisoner's eyes, Travis could see that this young man adored Maggie in a way that went far deeper than the bond of friendship. Had they been lovers?

In some ways, Travis found the idea of Pete and Maggie together hard to believe. She was a tiny ball of energy and grit. Pete had a soulful look, like a poet, and he seemed to be knee-deep in self-pity. How could Maggie fall for a guy like that?

Yet, the pairing of Pete and Maggie made logical sense. They had worked in the same restaurant. If Pete were her lover, that would explain Maggie's intense desire to see him cleared of the murder charges. It would explain why she'd risked her life to return to New Orleans.

A sick feeling churned in the pit of Travis's stomach. Her personal life—beyond that which pertained to her credibility as a witness—was none of his business. Hadn't she just informed him of that? Still, he didn't like the idea that she was in love with Pete Fontana. He didn't care for the idea that she had any lover at all.

She separated herself from Pete. "You'd better sit down. We have a lot to cover and not too much time."

"Hell, Maggie, I've got all the time in the world." He offered a sad smile. "I've got nothing but time."

"Your trial is getting under way in a week. I understand that you're represented by a public defender."

He slumped in the chair behind the table. "Yep, I've talked to this guy, who looks to be about fourteen and still has acne behind his ears. He tried to tell me I should plead guilty to manslaughter for a reduced sentence. But I won't. I didn't kill Kyle."

"I know you didn't, sugar." Maggie dug into her suitcase-sized purse and produced a small tape recorder, a pen and a spiral notebook. Thus prepared, she turned the recorder on and picked up her pen. "Tell me what happened."

With a slight show of energy, Pete gestured toward Travis. "Should I be talking in front of Mr. Shanahan? Isn't he going to be prosecuting me?"

"Good point." She turned to Travis and cocked her head. "Maybe you should leave."

"Can't. There's no way the police are going to leave you and Pete alone together."

She opened her mouth to object, then closed it. "I think it's okay for Travis to be here, Pete. We're all looking for the truth, aren't we?"

"Okay," he said, sullenly.

"So?" Maggie probed. "Tell me about it. You and Kyle."

"Me and Kyle stayed in touch."

"Hold it," Travis said. "You corresponded? In spite of the witness protection program?"

"That's correct."

It was also illegal, but Travis supposed that to a man who was facing a murder charge, the idea of a reprimand for breaching the protection program was small potatoes. "Why'd you stay in touch?"

"You see," Pete drawled, "I'm studying investments and going to night school so's I can become an accountant. Anyhow, I've been dabbling around and handling money for some of my friends."

"Not me," Maggie told Travis. "I never did have much of a nest egg."

"But Kyle did," Pete said. "I was managing his money in the amount of about five thousand dollars, and I couldn't withdraw the cash until recently. That's why Kyle came back to New Orleans. I gave him his money, in cash."

"How'd the investment turn out?" Travis asked.

"I almost doubled his nut in two years' time," he said proudly. "Less my commission, Kyle got eight thousand, nine hundred and forty bucks."

An excellent return, Travis thought. He wondered if Pete's investment source was altogether legal. That was an issue he would need to bring to Sharon Gold's attention in her preparation for this case.

While Pete rambled on about how he was doing really well with all his financial dealings and how he wished they would let him have his computer in the jail, Travis considered the case against this young man. Their forensic evidence indicated that the murder took place in Pete's apartment. Also, Pete had left fingerprints in the rental car used to dispose of the body. The murder weapon was registered to Pete Fontana. Motive was a problem. Travis knew that Sharon Gold had intended to use "crime of passion," assuming that Pete and Kyle were lovers. However, after seeing Pete with Maggie, Travis doubted that the prisoner was in love with another man.

Maggie asked, "After you gave the money to Kyle, what happened?"

"He was real cool about it, and hinted that he was coming into a whole heap more cash."

"From what source?"

"He didn't say, and I didn't ask."

Maggie turned to Travis. "I'll bet you it was a payoff from somebody connected with the DeCarlo case. Somebody was fixin' to pay Kyle for not testifying. Or maybe for changing his testimony."

"Why would you assume that?" Travis asked. "I thought Kyle was your friend."

"An acquaintance, not a friend." She frowned. "Kyle wasn't always on the up and up. He tended to get himself into trouble by taking risks."

"Always testing himself," Pete added. "Driving too fast. Staying up for two days running."

"Obsessive," Maggie said with that little smile she always used when she'd spoken one of her vocabulary words. "He was an alcoholic, you know."

Travis asked Pete, "Did he mention the DeCarlo case?"

"Nope. I kind of had the idea he was getting this huge sum of money from his rich new girlfriend, Francine. She was the one who rented that fancy car for him. And he used her credit card to get his hotel room.''

"But he stayed with you," Maggie said. "Is that right?"

Pete chuckled. "I don't think Kyle was all that fond of Ms. Francine Bentley. She was at least fifteen years older than him, and he told me that she was skinny as a whippet."

"That's cruel," Maggie said. "Most guys don't refer to their girlfriends as dogs if they're intending to give a compliment."

"Anyhow," Pete continued, "Kyle asked if he could stay with me, and I said he could. No big deal. He slept on the sofa bed in the front room."

"On the night of the murder," Maggie asked, "where were you?" Then, she chuckled and glanced at Travis. "I just always wanted to say that. 'Where were you on the night of the murder?' Sounds so official." She looked at Pete. "Well? Don't make me repeat it."

"Working the night shift at Augustine's. I didn't get home until one in the morning, and Kyle wasn't there." He shrugged his narrow shoulders. "I didn't think nothing of it. Figured that old Kyle probably changed his mind and went to the hotel. Or maybe he found a new girlfriend."

"What did you do next?"

"Went to bed. Got up the next morning. Did some errands. Then worked another night shift."

"And then?"

"Nothing. I read about Kyle getting murdered in the newspaper, and I was real upset about it. But there wasn't nothing I could do. It wasn't until a week after they found him that the cops came busting into my apartment, looked around, found my gun in the bedside table and took me in for questioning." He breathed a ragged sigh. "Guess I didn't answer their questions right, because they arrested me for murder. I don't know why. It wasn't fair.''

Maggie bristled. "You listen to me, Pete Fontana. Stop feeling sorry for yourself. You stop that right now. We're going to beat this.''

"Oh, come off it, Maggie. We both know I'm going to jail. For something I didn't do. The cops quit looking as soon as they picked me up.''

"But I'm here. I'll do my own investigation. How do I get into your apartment?''

"The manager's got a key and he knows you.'' He sighed again. "My stupid attorney says they got a lot of evidence against me.''

"But you didn't have the opportunity to kill Kyle. You were at work.''

"My apartment is only ten minutes away from Augustine's. Nobody can swear I was there continuously.''

"No motive,'' Maggie said. "You didn't have any reason in the world to murder Kyle, did you?''

Pete frowned for a minute, thinking. Then he shook his head. "Nope.''

"There you go, sugar.'' She reached across the wooden table and patted his hand. "You're practically free already.''

He caught her fingers between his hands. "Means a lot to me, Maggie, that you care enough to come here and help me. I can't tell you how much.''

"Heck, I'd do the same for anybody else who was wrongly accused.'' She smiled gently. "Remember, Pete. We talked about this a lot. I'm going to be a lawyer. This is what I want to do. If I could, I'd fix all the injustice in the world. There's so much wrongdoing. If I can take one little piece and make it right, my life is worth something.''

Despite his cynicism, Travis believed her. Though she

didn't have a law degree and possibly didn't have the patience to build an effective case, she had the fire and passion of a great attorney. If anybody could slap the world into shape, it was Maggie Deere.

She proved her determination a few minutes later when they were leaving Parish Prison and came face-to-face with Clayton Bascombe, the district supervisor for the U.S. Marshals. The usually easygoing Bascombe seemed to be at the end of his tether. Instead of pausing to chat with Travis, he merely nodded and growled, "Where y'at, Travis?"

"Hey, Clayton." Travis nodded back. "What's going on?"

"I heard about what happened today." Bascombe riveted Maggie with a glare. "I'm taking this woman into protective custody. Ms. Deere, you may come with me quietly or I will have you incarcerated."

"What for?" Maggie protested.

"Let me count the ways," Bascombe said through clenched teeth. "Leaving California without informing your handler of your whereabouts. Coming to New Orleans, a city where your presence is specifically forbidden in the terms of our contract with you. Refusing to come quietly with the marshal sent to pick you up this afternoon."

"You'd put me in jail?"

"You bet I would, missy. The protection program is not a joke. You have blatantly disregarded the terms of a contract you signed with the federal government."

"I have to do what's right, Marshal Bascombe. That's why I agreed to testify in the first place."

Reaching behind his back, the marshal unclipped a set of handcuffs from his belt under his suit coat. Travis had never seen Clayton Bascombe in this mood. Generally, the big man with thinning gray hair and lazy grin was congenial and kind. Right now, he had the appearance of a highly intimidating authority figure.

Maggie didn't back up one inch. Tilting her head up to look into Bascombe's face, she let loose. "Technically, sir, you are obeying the law. You *can* force me into protective custody."

"Don't make me use these cuffs, Ms. Deere."

"If you do, I guarantee that my memory is going to start fading real fast. I might be so upset that I won't recall the name of the restaurant where I worked. And I surely won't be certain about seeing Ben DeCarlo."

It was Bascombe who took a backward step. "You'd lie under oath? That's contempt. That's perjury."

"Memory is a funny thing. You can ask Travis about that. If I screw up on the witness stand, it's worse for him than if I didn't testify at all. Isn't that right, Travis?"

"Unfortunately, yes."

"Not to mention, Marshal Bascombe, that I will be most certain to speak with the press. Probably with Farris Quinn. And I would be certain to tell them how the federal Marshals treat United States citizens who come forward to do their duty."

Bascombe sputtered.

"On the other hand," Maggie offered sweetly. "I'm sure we can work out a compromise that will be agreeable to everyone. I know! Why don't you join us for dinner?"

"Dinner?"

"Please say you will," Maggie cajoled. "It's time for an evening meal, isn't it? And I'm so hungry I could eat a rattlesnake. How about you, Travis?"

Her lightning-swift change of strategy amused Travis. She'd transformed from vengeful attacker to pleasant hostess, throwing Bascombe completely off kilter. The poor guy didn't know whether she was going to rip his face off or force-feed him pralines.

He turned toward Travis. "Is she always like this?"

"Always," he promised.

Chapter Four

Maggie prevailed.

Half an hour later—whether they liked it or not—Travis and Marshal Bascombe were seated in a red leatherette booth at a truck-stop café off Interstate 10 toward Biloxi. Outside the trailer-shaped diner, a huge black-lettered sign read simply, Eats. Not only had Maggie picked the place but she had also overruled Bascombe's objection to taking two cars. She insisted on driving here alone with Travis while Bascombe followed.

On their route away from New Orleans, Travis discovered that no matter how decisive Maggie appeared to be, she had no sense of route or street signs. Her navigation was solely by landmark. "Past the bowling alley, then down to the corner, where we go that way. I think."

Following her directions, with Bascombe in the car behind, they'd gone down the second dead-end road when Travis inquired, "Are you trying to elude anyone who might be following us or are we lost?"

"I think we go east," she said, pointing into the sunset.

"West," he corrected her. "The sun sets in the west."

"Then it must be the other way. Just off the highway going east, because I found this place when I was coming from Alabama."

But they'd finally located the diner. As soon as they entered, Maggie excused herself and greeted the cook and one of the waitresses, a tired-looking redhead.

Travis watched her flit around the clean but tacky dining area where leftover Christmas tinsel hung limply from the green plastic wreath above the door.

Bascombe groaned. "What are we going to do with her? I don't think there's a leash long enough to allow her the freedom she wants and still keep some kind of control."

"She's a problem," Travis readily agreed. "We can't take any chances. Dammit, Clayton, I can't afford to lose another witness."

Maggie rejoined them and slid into the booth beside Travis. "Don't look at the menu," she said. "I know what you'll like."

When the gum-chewing, redheaded waitress sidled up to their table, Maggie said, "We're all going to have the étouffée." She explained to Travis and Clayton. "That's a Cajun crayfish stew over rice."

"I know what it is," Travis said. "I was born and raised here. For your information, we say crawfish, not crayfish."

"Then you know how to eat them, too."

"Boiled crawfish?" Travis put on a thick New Orleans accent. "Suck da heads and pinch da tails."

Maggie completed their order. "We'll also have blackberry pie and chicory coffee. Thanks, Becky. I would introduce you to these two fine gentlemen, but they are undercover."

Becky pursed her lips in a teasing kiss directed at Travis and purred, "Honey-lamb, you can crawl under my covers, any day."

"You stop that," Maggie chastised. "What would Tony say if he caught you carrying on that way?"

"He'd hose me down, like one of those tomatoes he

keeps trying to grow in the patch out back of the house.''
She pointed a sharp, pink fingernail at Travis. "You? He'd
kill.''

"No need," Travis said coolly. "I'd never poach in
another man's field.''

"Aren't you the gentleman?" Becky swung back toward the counter where she bellowed the food order to a
cook who waved a spatula in their direction.

Maggie leaned across the table to speak to Clayton Bascombe. "I told you that I knew a place where nobody
would find us.''

"Congratulations," he said dryly.

"Don't you like it?''

"Actually, I do.'' Bascombe leaned back in the leatherette booth. "I'm a man of simple tastes. A family man.
I take care of my little twin daughters and work on old
cars. I just finished reconditioning an Edsel so it runs like
a champ.''

Travis wasn't sure where the marshal was going with
this down-home discussion, but he respected Bascombe
enough to sit back and listen.

"A simple man," Bascombe repeated. "I like simple
solutions, Maggie. Now, it's my job to make sure you
survive long enough to give your testimony against
DeSharko—"

"Who?" Travis asked.

"DeCarlo. We call him DeSharko around the office for
obvious reasons. Anyway, Maggie, I can't do my job when
you're running all over town. We have a safe house. The
simple solution is that we keep you there. You'd be able
to go just about anywhere, accompanied by a bodyguard.''

"A bodyguard?" She wrinkled her nose. "Well, why
don't we just paint a sign with letters three feet tall, saying,
Protected Witness Here. Forgive me, sugar, but a body-

guard is way too obvious. And how safe is your safe house? Really?''

Travis cleared his throat. ''Actually, she does have an argument.''

''What?''

''I respect you, Clayton.'' There was a need to be diplomatic in his dealings with the marshal. Travis didn't want to alienate Bascombe, but he couldn't ignore the leak. ''You've got a hard job and a heavy caseload.''

Clayton picked up the plain fork in his table setting and turned it end over end. ''What are you getting at, Travis?''

''The fact that Maggie was assaulted in our building indicates that someone is feeding information to DeCarlo's men. Plus her witness protection identity has been compromised.''

''How do you know that?''

''She received an anonymous letter, addressed to her real identity, while she was at the supposedly safe address in southern California.''

''Damn.'' Clayton stabbed the fork tines into his paper napkin. ''I guess this ain't so simple.''

''There's a leak,'' Travis concluded. ''The only people who knew Maggie was in town are from your office and mine. Frankly, I'm worried about my other two witnesses, Monique LaRoquette and Gord Hoskins.''

''We're more secure with them,'' Clayton said. ''I handled the placement of those two witnesses personally. I've spoken with both of them. They have indicated no problems. I will, however, make their protection high priority. I don't much like Hoskins. There's something going on with him.''

Great, Travis thought. Another problem. ''Like what?''

''Can't put my finger on it. But you watch him.''

"Gord Hoskins, the accountant?" Maggie questioned. "But he was always so friendly to Pete Fontana."

"Fontana, the guy under arrest for murder?" Clayton raised his eyebrows. "I rest my case."

"As for Maggie," Travis said, getting back to the topic at hand, "she's going to be my own personal project for as long as she's in town."

"You'll protect her?"

"She'll stay at my house," Travis continued. "I will drive her back and forth to the courthouse and keep steady surveillance on her, wherever she needs to go. Is that satisfactory?"

"It's irregular. You're not trained in protection."

"I don't know what else to do," Travis said. There didn't seem to be anyone he could trust.

"Well, all right. Give me a memo to that effect and she's yours," Clayton said. "And welcome to her."

Travis pulled a Cross pen from his inner jacket pocket and scribbled a legally phrased note on the dinner napkin, which he pushed across the table to the marshal. Then he looked toward the black-haired woman with the laughing blue eyes. Under the table, her thigh was inches from his.

The mere fact that he was aware of their nearness warned him to be careful. Having Maggie stay with him might be a terrible mistake. She was a witness. He needed to be clear about that in his own mind. Anything that happened between them could be questioned when she was on the stand, and it wouldn't look good if she testified that she was involved in an affair with the chief prosecuting attorney on the case.

However, Travis knew he wouldn't feel safe unless he was personally monitoring her twenty-four hours a day. Maggie's penchant for taking off on her own was a problem for anyone who wouldn't stand up to her.

Her expression was almost demure as she smiled at him. "I'm grateful to both of you for allowing me the freedom to pursue my investigation on the Kyle Johnson murder."

Inwardly, Travis groaned. Chasing all over New Orleans on some kind of half-baked investigation with Maggie wasn't what he had in mind. He just wanted her to be safe. He never wanted to relive that moment when he saw her, bruised and battered, at the foot of the stairs. "Freedom has limits, Maggie."

"Well, excuse me, Mr. Abraham Lincoln, I would think that an attorney-at-law would—"

"You're not to go anywhere without notifying me. If you disobey this one simple rule, you will not be staying in a safe house, you will be locked in a very private, very solitary jail cell. Is that clear?"

"Crystal clear."

Their food arrived and Maggie suggested that they eat it while it was hot. She could barely taste the deliciously spicy crawfish stew. Her senses were already on overload when she thought of going home with Travis, staying at his house, saying her final good-night to him before she shut off the lights and went to sleep.

After they left the restaurant, with both men raving about the étouffée, Maggie wanted to return to the prison parking lot to pick up her own car, but Travis refused.

"It's late. We're going directly to my house."

"Only eight o'clock. We have plenty of time."

"If we go back to the courthouse, we might pick up a tail. And we don't want anyone to know that you're staying with me," he explained. "One of the reasons this plan might work is that nobody will suspect that I would take you home."

"Of course not." She forced a laugh. "Nobody would

suspect that a well-bred gentleman like yourself would have anything to do with the likes of me.''

"That's not it, Maggie."

"No?"

"Nobody would suspect that an intelligent attorney like me would be dumb enough to put himself in a potentially compromising position with an important witness."

Potentially compromising? Maggie pondered that phrase with delight while they drove through uptown New Orleans in an area where she'd never been before. Did Travis feel drawn to her? Did he think that if they stayed in the same house, he might want to become intimate?

She wasn't altogether sure how she felt about that possibility. Of course, she liked Travis a lot. When he flashed that killer grin, he was the most handsome man she'd ever seen. But they could never have a relationship, not a permanent kind of commitment. For one thing, she was going to be leaving town and going into the witness protection program right after the trial.

The BMW pulled up in front of an ornate wrought-iron gate and Travis clicked a remote-control button. In response, the gate creaked open. The sedan circled a short drive around a heavy oak tree draped in Spanish moss. The grounds were thickly landscaped. Old growth, Maggie realized. This gracious stucco house had been standing for a long time.

When he escorted her into the foyer of his beautiful old home, Maggie stifled a gasp of amazement. Everything was lovely, delicate. She didn't have the vocabulary to describe how perfect his home seemed to her. A sweeping staircase, fit for Scarlett O'Hara, descended from an open balcony. There were fresh flowers in crystal vases. A chandelier illuminated the marble floors and the gleaming antique furniture.

What a dope she'd been to take him to the diner where she used to work! He must have been disgusted. How could she have plied him with crawfish stew?

"This is so…elegant."

"This house has been in the family for as long as I can remember. I always liked it, and I bought it—complete with furnishings—from my mother two years ago." He grinned, "Surprised?"

"It's so clean. I've seen your office, Travis, and it's not a place where Martha Stewart would feel at home."

"I have a cleaning lady," he said. "Twice a week."

It must be wonderful, she thought, to be able to afford someone to clean for you.

"Come on upstairs," he said, "I'll show you your bedroom."

At the top of the stairs and down a hall, he opened a door into a spacious area with a desk, two chairs, a little table, a dresser and a huge four-poster bed with a lacy white comforter and dust ruffle. "Will this be okay?"

"Add a refrigerator and a hot plate and I could live here." She went to the bed and hesitantly stroked the soft lace. "It's real pretty, Travis."

"So are you."

Had she heard right? Maggie whirled around to confront him, but he was already on his way out the door. "What?"

"If you need anything—"

"Actually, I do. I had to leave my suitcase in my car. Though I do carry a change of underwear in my purse, I don't have anything else."

"There's a terry-cloth robe in the bathroom," he said, opening the door to that room. "But I don't have a ladies' nightgown."

"I could make do with one of your shirts," she said.

"Of course. I'll be right back."

After he left the room, she sat primly in one of the brocade claw-foot chairs beside the skirted table. As she gazed around the lovely room toward the bower of draped windows, reality sank in. She had been purely deluded to think there might ever be any sort of relationship between herself and Travis. They were from different backgrounds. Heck, she told herself, they were from different planets. She came from a dirt-poor place. He hailed from a world where everything was soft, clean and perfect.

There was a tap on the bedroom door.

"Come in, Travis."

He held out one of his monogrammed white cotton shirts. "Will this do? It's laundered without starch."

She'd been expecting an old T-shirt, but she rose to accept his offering. "It's fine."

Their fingers touched beneath the fabric, and she felt a dangerous thrill chase up her arm and spread through her body. It would have been smart to say thank you and goodnight, but Maggie had never been one to play it safe. She needed to know if he felt the same kind of spark between them that she felt, but she couldn't ask that sort of intimate question. What to say?

She gazed up into his dark eyes. "Why'd you become a prosecutor?"

"Why not?"

"All this." She gestured to the room. "I understand enough about the law to know that prosecutors spend most of their time dealing with the dregs of the legal system. If you were a defense attorney, like Ezra Dean, you could be in a high-tone, walnut-paneled office with three secretaries."

"I didn't become an attorney for the money," he said. "I wanted to make a difference."

"That's what I want, too." She brightened. Maybe they did have something in common, after all.

"When I first joined the D.A.'s staff, I thought my efforts would change things. I wanted to make sure that the guilty would be punished and the innocent would go free."

"Yes," she said.

"But that's not how it works. Look at DeCarlo. The man is guilty, but he has enough money to afford Ezra Dean Slaughter as an attorney, so he wins a retrial."

"At least the judge didn't overturn the verdict and set him free."

"The first conviction should have stood. DeCarlo should be in jail with no hope of pardon." His smile faded. "Have you got everything you need, Maggie?"

"I think so."

"I'd like to get out of here early in the morning. To be at the office by eight, we need to leave here at twenty past seven in the morning."

"Good night, Travis."

She shut the door behind him.

After a long soak in the tub, she enumerated the bruises from when she was attacked and decided that she was, in fact, just fine except for a particularly painful bump on the knee and the knot on her forehead. Toweled dry, Maggie slipped into Travis's shirt. The shirttail fell almost to her knees. Soft cotton caressed her skin. And it smelled like Travis.

She glided between the bedsheets and tried to read from the novel she had in her purse, but the aroma haunted her. When she turned out the bedside lamp, she could almost imagine him in the bedroom, lying beside her.

With a smile on her lips, she slept like a baby, a dreamless rest. In her subconscious, she was aware that many hours had passed. The night had deepened, and the darkness was breaking into day.

"Maggie."

She heard a voice calling from far away.

"Maggie, are you up?"

She wakened in fear, vulnerable to the terrors of her childhood when she'd often heard a man's deep voice calling to her, demanding horrible acts from her, things she would never give.

She sat bolt upright on the unfamiliar bed. In the light from the door, she saw the dark outline of a man's broad shoulders. Where was she? She blinked hard, but the man didn't vanish. He wasn't one of her nightmares. He was real. Fully dressed. It looked like he was holding a belt strap in his hand.

Who was he? What did he want from her?

Instinctively, she reacted. Her legs curled up, ready to flee. She yanked the covers up to her chin. Frantic, she fumbled in the half-light, searching for a weapon. "You keep away from me! You hear? Get back!"

"Maggie, it's me. Travis."

Her heart hammered so loudly that she barely heard his words. All she knew was that he was coming at her, closer and closer.

"Don't touch me," she warned fiercely. "Don't you ever touch me."

"It's okay, Maggie. I'm not going to hurt you."

The realization struck her. She recognized him. "Oh, my God, Travis. It's you."

"I didn't mean to frighten you."

She drew a ragged breath, willing the demons to be silent and safely buried in her dark and wounded past. "Sorry."

"I'm the one who should apologize."

Travis stood very still, not approaching, not sure of how to handle this moment. What a jerk he was! Travis couldn't imagine how he could have been more insensitive. What made him think he could barge into her bedroom...as if he had the right. "Are you okay?"

"Fine. I guess I should be up and out of bed, huh?"

He lifted the necktie he held in his hand and slipped it under his collar. "We should leave in about an hour."

"Give me a minute," she said, turning on the bedside lamp.

She looked adorable in the morning light with her black hair disheveled and her tanned skin making a contrast to the white of the comforter and whiteness of his shirt. Even though she'd rolled up the sleeves, the shirt was huge on her.

Her blue eyes, clear as the day that was breaking outside the windows, gazed lazily at him. She was so damned cute! He wanted to pull her into his arms and soothe away all the fears.

"I made coffee," he said, feeling like he was trying to patch a gaping wound with a Band-Aid. "It's downstairs."

"I'll get dressed and find the kitchen."

Cursing himself, he closed the bedroom door. From her reaction, he assumed that his suspicions about her childhood must have been right on target. She had been abused. Her suffering infuriated him. As a prosecutor, he'd seen all manner of atrocity, but it still made him angry. How could anyone harm a child?

How could anyone harm Maggie?

He turned out the hall light, allowing the glow from the windows to illuminate the second-floor hall that led to the balcony. Shadows seemed appropriate. Half-hidden facts were beginning to become a way of life.

AT THE OFFICE, their first item of business this morning was one that Travis dreaded: a briefing with the District Attorney, Wiley Henderson. There was something about Wiley that Travis instinctively mistrusted. Though Wiley was cordial, intelligent and full of good advice, he was far too political for Travis's taste. He and Maggie took their seats in Wiley's huge office on the first floor. Generally, the D.A. liked to get the agenda for his day over with early so he'd have the afternoon free for golf. Though it was only fifteen minutes past eight o'clock, his desk top was clear.

He glanced at Maggie and arranged his features in an expression of concern. "I heard about yesterday, and I do apologize."

"No real harm done," she said.

"We're going to keep you safe, little lady." He turned his head toward Travis. His full lips, beneath his ginger mustache, pulled into a frown. "Where is she staying?"

"I've made arrangements," Travis said. A natural caution warned him against telling Wiley that Maggie was staying with him. "Jury selection for the DeCarlo trial starts today. I'm planning to have Dave handle it."

"Dave Dermott. He's a good kid. Be sure his jurors are not opposed to the death penalty. I'd like to see a murder-one conviction this time around." Wiley dragged his hand through his bristly curling hair. "You didn't answer my question, Travis. Where is Maggie staying?"

"She's safe. You can check with Clayton Bascombe."

"Ah, the U.S. Marshals are taking care of her. Good."

"I need to talk to you about the DeCarlo case," Travis said, deftly changing the subject. He turned toward Maggie. "Would you excuse us, please? Wait for me in the outer office."

"Sure thing." She smiled and slipped through the door.

As soon as she left, Wiley commented, "Pretty little thing, isn't she? You be careful, Travis, that she doesn't overhear anything that could be used in court."

"Yes, sir. That's why I asked her to leave."

Wiley went to the windows and gazed out. "Beautiful day. Good weather for the tourists."

"Yes, sir."

"There's always a mob of them here for Carnival."

While Travis waited for the small talk to abate, he had the distinct impression that Wiley would like to distance himself from the DeCarlo case. Politically, this trial was a hot potato. Ben DeCarlo had money, influence and power in New Orleans. His uncle Dominick, who had taken over Antonio DeCarlo's nefarious business, was a force to be reckoned with. A District Attorney needed to pick his fights, and Wiley might have already decided that his office would be unable to win this one.

"Sir, we need to discuss strategy for the retrial."

"Hell, I suppose so." Wiley sank back into his chair behind the polished desk top. "What about it, Travis?"

OUTSIDE THE D.A.'S OFFICE, Maggie had requested a cup of coffee from the secretary in the outer area. As soon as the woman left the room, Maggie crept down the short hallway that led to Wiley's office. She leaned close to eavesdrop.

Travis said, "We are severely hampered without access to the complete testimony of the main defense witness, Sandor Rossi. All we have is a transcript alleging a frame with all the pertinent names blanked out."

"I know."

"We're being rushed into a trial without a chance to investigate. I need to take a deposition from Rossi."

"Ezra Dean is a hell of a good attorney, no matter what else I think of him. I'll work on that end, Travis. Is there anything else you need to prepare for this case?"

"I have a sense, nothing more than a gut feeling, that Judge Howell might be prejudiced in DeCarlo's favor. He seemed uncomfortable during my closing statement when I mentioned the practice of buying justice."

"Howell? Leland Howell? You're mistaken, Travis. I've played poker with the man. Even if he was dirty, he wouldn't betray a single trick."

"Nevertheless, I'd be pleased if we could have a different judge sitting on the bench for this trial."

"I'll see what I can do, but don't count on it."

"What are you saying, sir?"

"It's your problem, Travis. This is your case."

From outside the door, Maggie heard chairs being pushed back and she scurried back to the outer office in time to meet the secretary at the door.

As Wiley and Travis emerged from the inner office, the District Attorney said, "I'm off. I have to do breakfast with the mayor and the police chief. You get one guess as to the topic of our meeting this morning."

"Police corruption," Travis said.

"Bingo. Chief Royce Monk has a lot of explaining to do." Wiley opened the door to his office, ushering them out. "Keep me posted on developments."

"Yes, sir."

Coffee in hand, Maggie followed Travis to the elevator. When Wiley was out of sight, she said, "So that's what a D.A. does, huh? Passes the buck and makes sure he stays in office."

"What are you talking about?"

"Seems to me, Travis, that you're getting the DeCarlo

mess dumped totally on your shoulders while Wiley plays golf and shakes hands.''

He glared down at her. "Were you listening to our private conversation?''

"Well, I couldn't help overhearing some of it. The door wasn't quite shut. And I don't mind telling you that I'm downright disgusted with Mr. Wiley Coyote.''

"Maggie, this isn't a joke. I don't want you overhearing anything that might be used against us in court.''

"Don't you worry about me, sugar.'' She shrugged her shoulders. "You go ahead with your work. I'll be in Sharon Gold's office, getting information about Pete Fontana.''

She'd lugged her suitcase to the third-floor bathroom and had changed from yesterday's businesslike pantsuit to more casual red slacks and a matching rayon tunic with polka dot collar and sleeves. Travis thought she looked cute as a ladybug. "No disappearing acts,'' he said firmly.

"You have my word.''

Maggie didn't need to knock on the door to Sharon's office because it was standing open. She looked up when Maggie entered. "You're early. That's good. I've got a busy schedule today.''

Maggie plunked down in a straight-back chair on the opposite side of Sharon's desk. "You're not from around here, are you?''

"How did you guess?''

"No accent. So, where's home?''

"Southern California, not far from where you're staying in the witness protection program. I came to Louisiana to attend Tulane University, liked it and stayed.''

"Tulane has a fine law program.'' Maggie took note of Sharon's blunt haircut and her no-nonsense style. This lady attorney embodied many of the attributes that Maggie herself hoped someday to achieve. "You planning to stay in the District Attorney's Office?"

"For a while. I need seasoning and practice." She cocked her head to one side. "So, Maggie, what do you want to know about the Kyle Johnson murder?"

"What directed the police toward Pete Fontana?"

"An anonymous tip. Our informant sent a note on a scrap of paper that was hand-delivered to Chief Royce Monk. Amazingly, the police chief took quick action."

"Why amazing?"

"I have no respect for the NOPD," she said. "After learning last month that at least four officers were in the pay of organized crime, I'm shocked when they do anything right."

"But they did all right in investigating Pete Fontana?"

"I'm sorry, Maggie, but it was pretty much open and shut. The homicide cops got a search warrant and went to Pete's apartment, where they found the murder weapon, a .357 Magnum, in the drawer of the bedside table. A search revealed blood spatters, mostly cleaned up, in the kitchen."

"Blood spatters?"

"When someone is shot, especially at close range like Kyle was, there is a pattern. From forensic reconstruction of the crime, the police determined that Kyle was kneeling when the murderer drilled one bullet through his forehead. The second bullet in his head came after he slumped to the floor."

"So, it's certain that he was killed in Pete's apartment." Sharon nodded.

"But that's still circumstantial," Maggie said. "What makes you so sure that Pete did it?"

"We identified his fingerprints on the rental car. Even on the trunk where Kyle's body was stashed."

"What about motive?" Maggie asked.

"Crime of passion. Assuming the two men were lovers and had an argument. But it could also have been greed. Earlier that evening, Kyle had been flashing a wad of hundred dollar bills. When the body was found, he had no money."

"But Pete gave him that money," Maggie said.

"And maybe he wanted it back." Sharon steepled her fingertips and leaned back in her chair. "There was also an indication that Kyle might have been coming into more money. A great deal more money."

"A payoff from DeCarlo?"

"For your sake, I hope not." Sharon shook her head. "It might have been coming from his girlfriend. I've spoken to Francine Bentley, and the woman is a bit of a ditz."

Maggie recalled Pete's comment that he didn't think Kyle really cared for Ms. Bentley. "What kind of relationship do you think she and Kyle had?"

"According to Ms. Bentley, they were the greatest lovers since Romeo and Juliet. It was a May-December kind of thing. I would guess that Kyle was quite a bit younger than she."

"Hard to believe," Maggie said. "I knew Kyle pretty well, and he wasn't a man to see beyond the purely physical. More likely, Kyle would be dating in the opposite age direction."

"Maybe he matured in the witness protection program."

"Did you investigate any connection with DeCarlo?"

"That was our first line of inquiry. We were pretty much certain that Kyle had been murdered to keep him from testifying in the event of a retrial. However, we rounded up the usual suspects, checked their alibis and whereabouts. Nothing. We came up totally empty-handed."

"Could have been a hit man from out of town."

"Of course," Sharon said patronizingly. "And it could have been aliens, but it wasn't. Nobody associated with DeCarlo knew Kyle was here. He checked in at the hotel, using Ms. Bentley's credit card, and he stayed with Pete Fontana. Though he was out on the town for one night, it's too huge a coincidence to believe that someone who was gunning for him just happened to run into him."

"What if he came here to meet with them, then they double-crossed him?"

"If you can find reasonable evidence to that conclusion, I'd love to see it, Maggie. Otherwise, I'll be trying Pete Fontana on murder in the first degree."

That meant Pete could get the death penalty. Maggie felt the blood in her veins run cold. There was damning evidence against Pete. Circumstantial, but heavily weighted against him. It was just possible that Pete would be convicted and condemned.

Sharon Gold regarded her through determined eyes. "And, Maggie, if I try this case…I'll win."

Chapter Five

Obediently, like a good little protected witness, Maggie sat with her feet up in Travis's office, paging through the novel she carried in her purse. Though there were dozens of things she'd rather be doing, she had promised to be no trouble—even if the idleness drove her crazy.

And she wasn't the only one. Travis seemed to be a little bonkers himself. He hunched over his desk, appearing preoccupied with his work. As she watched him out of the corner of her eye, he glanced down at a document, then looked up, then shoved the closely printed paper aside. He scribbled a note on a legal pad, crumpled the yellow paper into a ball and pitched it toward the circular wastebasket. His shot missed, and he left the paper there, on the floor, with several others.

"Travis?"

He turned toward her. His elegant features pulled into a tense frown. "What?"

"I know what your problem is," she said.

"And I'll bet you're going to tell me."

"You're worried about the jury selection process that's going on right now in Judge Howell's courtroom, and I don't blame you, sugar. Why don't you go down there and give Dave a hand?"

"Worried? I didn't say I was worried. I have complete faith in my staff. If I hang around in the courtroom, it might make Dave feel that I don't trust his ability."

"Honestly, Travis, you're more nervous than a mother robin pushing her chicks out of the nest for the first time."

"Dave will do fine, just fine." He raised his eyebrows and looked at her. "Won't he?"

"I've never seen Dave work."

"Of course you haven't." He rose from behind his desk and began to pace. "I have. He's good. He'll pick a good jury."

"In the meantime," Maggie suggested, "why don't we get out of the office?"

His gaze narrowed. "What did you have in mind?"

"Oh, this and that. A couple of little errands."

"Like what?" he demanded.

Her first impulse was to gently misguide him until they got out the door, then she could point him in the direction she really wanted to go. But Maggie thought better of that manipulative tactic. If there was one thing she was learning about Travis Shanahan, it was that he didn't appreciate subterfuge.

Maggie took a deep breath and spoke the truth. "I want to do my own investigating on the Kyle Johnson case. It might help to take a look around Pete's apartment."

"I don't like the idea," Travis said.

"Also, it has come to my attention that Kyle's girlfriend, Ms. Francine Bentley, happens to be in town, staying at the Lafayette Hotel. If it's okay with you, I might make an appointment with her."

He wadded up another piece of yellow legal-sized paper and slam-dunked it into the circular wastebasket. "Okay, Maggie. Make your call to Francine Bentley."

She could hardly believe her ears. He was actually assenting to her investigation! Maggie wasted no time in punching out the number for the Lafayette Hotel. Luckily, Ms. Bentley was in and could see them at once.

Travis held the door for her, and they were on their way. She leaned back in the soft leather bucket seat of his BMW. This was nice, real nice. She hadn't expected his cooperation.

"I want you to know, Maggie, that this isn't a game or an exercise in one of your pre-law classes."

"No, sir, it is not. Pete Fontana's life and freedom depend on finding the truth."

"You might not like what you discover," he warned. "Do you mind if I give you a few tips?"

"I would appreciate your help," she said sincerely. "Think of me as a sponge, soaking up all the knowledge that I can."

"Okay, Sponge Girl. When you talk to Ms. Bentley, what will be the focus of your investigation?"

"I thought I'd ask some questions about what she was doing on the night of the murder. Stuff like that."

"But she isn't a suspect for murder. Her alibi is perfect. She didn't arrive in New Orleans until several days after the murder was committed."

"Right," Maggie said. She could feel the wheels in her head beginning to turn. "In pursuing an investigation, I'm trying to discover reasonable basis for suspicion. Then, evidence."

"And why would you suspect Francine Bentley?"

"She was close to Kyle. Maybe he was going to break up with her, and it was a crime of passion."

"But she was in Atlanta."

Maggie guessed, "She could have hired to have it done."

"How would you put that in the form of a question?"

The ideas formed more clearly in her mind. "According to Sharon Gold, Ms. Bentley claims that she and Kyle were passionately in love. But Pete didn't have that impression. So, I should ask her about their relationship, if they were planning to get married, stuff like that. Was she angry with him?"

"Good," Travis said. "Now you're thinking."

"I also want to know why she gave him her credit card. Was she fixin' to give him more money?"

"Don't forget the airplane tickets to Paris," Travis said.

"What airplane tickets?"

"Kyle had two one-way tickets, for Mr. and Mrs. Emmet Wyatt. He bought them with cash at a travel agent here in town. We never did find a satisfactory answer to why he booked that flight."

"Oh, Travis. I think I know. What if Kyle took a payoff from whoever was working for DeCarlo," she said. "They'd give him money not to testify, and he'd leave the country for good."

"Then, why would they kill him?" Travis asked.

Maggie was still pondering that contradiction when Francine Bentley welcomed them into her luxury suite at the Lafayette and poured them each a cup of coffee from a silver pot.

This well-groomed lady was in her late forties or early fifties, and she certainly wasn't Maggie's idea of a bowwow. Slender and long-limbed, she had a smooth, clear complexion beneath ash blond hair that was pulled back in a chignon at the nape of her long neck. She wore a pearl necklace and earrings. A high-class lady. So why had she been hanging out with Kyle Johnson, former bartender at Augustine's?

"This is a beautiful place," Maggie said.

"Thank you. I always stay here when I come back home to New Orleans."

Maggie tried to organize her thinking. "I wonder why Kyle didn't stay here after he checked in."

"I haven't the slightest notion," said Francine. "Cream and sugar?"

"No, thanks," Maggie said. "You were planning to join him when he came to town, weren't you?"

"Of course," she said. "But business matters kept me in Atlanta. I will always blame myself for his death. If I had been here, he wouldn't have put himself into the clutches of that terrible man who murdered him."

Francine Bentley dabbed at the corner of her eye with a delicate lace hankie, being careful not to smudge her makeup.

Maggie said, "I'm so sorry for your tragedy."

"We planned to be married. Emmet and I."

Francine used Kyle's witness protection name—Emmet Wyatt. How close were they, really? "Did Kyle tell you that he was a protected witness?"

Nervously, Francine glanced at Travis.

"Go ahead and tell the truth," he said. "You won't get into trouble."

"He told me," Francine said, and there was a hint of triumph in her voice. "Even though it might be dangerous, he wanted me to know everything. Even though it went against the rules, he didn't want to hold anything back. We were that close."

Maggie found the woman's declarations of devotion to be unbelievable. If you really cared about somebody, it didn't seem necessary to tell other people again and again. "How'd you and Kyle meet?"

"Oh, it's the most romantic story. It was a lovely April in Atlanta. Emmet was the bartender at a dinner dance that

I was obliged to attend as a board member of a charity for the care of orphans. My date had canceled at the last minute, but I really couldn't stay home. I was expected."

Maggie nodded.

"I ordered my favorite white wine from Emmet. Château Louis Noir. And he told me that I was not only beautiful but had excellent taste."

That sounded like Kyle, Maggie thought. He was great at pumping up his tips with compliments to the women.

"I thought nothing of his comment," Francine said. "But then he asked me to dance. Oh, my dear! He was masterful on the dance floor, and I confess that I was swept away. We strolled in the moonlight. He'd brought a bottle of Château Louis Noir, and we chatted the night away."

Francine exhaled a longing sigh. "It was the most beautiful night of my life."

"Like Cinderella at the ball," Maggie said encouragingly though she would never have cast Kyle Johnson in the role of Prince Charming.

"Exactly."

"So, you and Kyle were dating through the summer, and then you decided to head to New Orleans in December. Why was that?"

"For Christmas and Mardi Gras," she said. "I'm originally from New Orleans, and I always come back for Carnival."

"To visit with family?"

"I have no family. My parents are both deceased. And I'm divorced from two husbands. I never had children."

"So, you came back here for the Carnival balls? Even though Kyle would be in danger?"

Again, her eyes welled with tears. "I didn't believe it. Everything was so perfect. We were planning to be married. I simply couldn't believe there was really danger."

Maggie had heard enough lies in her life to know when someone was dancing at the edge of falsehood, and that was the sense she had with the classy Ms. Bentley. But what was the deception? Was it simply that this lady had deluded herself into believing she had a fiancé? Or was there something more ominous?

She asked, "Had Kyle already popped the question?"

"Oh, yes. We hadn't set a date, but he'd asked."

"Was that why he bought those tickets for Paris? For a honeymoon?"

"I'd like to think so," said Francine. "It's so like Kyle to whisk me off on a romantic vacation."

A one-way vacation? Now Maggie was sure that Francine was deluded.

"I had heard that Kyle was about to come into some money. Did he mention that to you?"

"Yes. The dear boy felt so dreadfully bad that he wasn't in my league, financially. I had offered to pay for the engagement ring, but he said no. He had his pride. That was why it was so important to him to return here to check on his investments."

"The money he placed with Pete Fontana?"

"The murderer." She stiffened. "I never knew his name until after he was arrested, and now I curse him daily."

"You didn't know of Pete Fontana?"

"Certainly not."

"That's odd," Maggie said.

Francine's chin came up and she looked down her nose. "What are you implying, young lady?"

"Just wondering." Maggie shrugged. "Seems like Kyle would want to introduce you to his old friends."

"Well, he didn't," she said huffily.

"How come?"

"I don't know," Francine said. She shielded her eyes

with her hand, and Maggie noticed that there was no lack of costly jewelry on this lady's fingers.

"Maybe," Maggie suggested, "he was ashamed of his old friends. Maybe he didn't want you to know his background."

"I'm overcome," she said. "I simply can't talk about this any longer."

"But I'm trying to help," Maggie said. "Don't you want to make sure the right man is in jail for Kyle's murder?"

"What does it matter now?" She rose to her feet. "Mr. Shanahan, I will have to ask you and your associate to leave."

Maggie started, "But I—"

"Thank you for your time," Travis said, interrupting Maggie. Gently, but forcefully, he took her arm and hoisted her to her feet. "It was a pleasure to meet you, Ms. Bentley."

"And you, Mr. Shanahan." She scowled at Maggie as the door to the suite closed.

Maggie frowned. In the hallway of the deluxe hotel, she looked down at her feet and traced the pattern of the carpet with the tip of her toe. She hadn't done a terrific job of interrogating Ms. Bentley and had wound up getting them thrown out of her room. Still... "I think she's lying."

"Agreed," Travis said.

Her gaze flew to his face. "Really? You don't think I screwed up too bad?"

"I didn't say that," he cautioned. "You started out well, getting her to open up about their first date. Then you pressured her, and she wouldn't tell us anything."

"But you thought she was lying."

"I don't think she and Kyle Johnson had the love affair of the century. From my brief acquaintance with Kyle, when he was a protected witness, I can practically guarantee you that if he proposed matrimony he wasn't sincere."

"Do you think that's her only lie? The Cinderella fantasy about getting married?"

He shrugged. "It's been my experience that a person who will lie about one thing will lie about another."

"Is that so?" Maggie chuckled as she sauntered down the posh hallway toward the elevators. "You don't understand women very well, do you?"

"Enlighten me."

"Well, there are some things that just don't count as lies. For example, lots of women lie about their age. And there's not a female alive who won't knock at least five pounds off her weight on her driver's license. But those are fibs."

"If Francine is lying about her relationship with Kyle, is that a fib?"

"Might be." Maggie frowned. "What's even sadder is that she might have talked herself into believing it."

As they drove to Pete Fontana's apartment, Maggie pondered Francine's words. Lies or fibs? Usually, Maggie was pretty sharp at telling the difference. She'd learned to read people in her childhood when she was shipped from foster home to foster home and survival was a matter of knowing who to trust. With Francine, a very sophisticated lady, it was tough to tell.

It took only fifteen minutes to go from the valet-parking luxury of the Lafayette Hotel to the rather shabby apartment building where Pete lived. Kind of an urban irony. *Irony.* That was a good vocabulary word.

"Travis, do you think I could make it as a lawyer? Do you think I've got the smarts?"

"Better than that, you've got desire. You want to make

it. You're willing to fight for your goal. You've got courage, Maggie, and that's half the battle."

He parked on the street, and they walked half a block. It was a temperate day in New Orleans, but the skies overhead were a steely blue, shrouded by heavy clouds. The air dripped with humidity and seemed heavy with portents.

On the sidewalk, a man and woman argued loudly about broken promises, and Maggie shivered.

"Are you nervous about going inside?" Travis asked.

"Why would I be?"

"It's a murder scene, Maggie. Your friend Kyle was killed in that apartment. His blood has soaked into the woodwork. He took his last breath in that room."

She scowled at him. "Why, thank you for pointing all that out, Travis. If I wasn't tense before, I surely am now."

"Murder is a grave offense against man and nature. Always think of the victim. Always."

After obtaining a key from the landlord, Maggie hesitated at the door to Pete's apartment. She'd been here so many times before, sharing a beer and a couple of laughs. Would it be different? Would it be stained by violence?

She fitted the key in the lock, and they walked inside. Immediately, she hit the light switch, banishing the darkness. Pete Fontana's one-bedroom apartment gave every appearance of being a typical bachelor's pad. In the kitchenette, which was visible from the middle of the living room, there were moldering, foul-smelling dishes in the sink. The coffee table in front of the large screen television was cluttered. The lumpy sofa was a hideous shade of puke green.

The only relatively tidy area was the large desk by the window and the computer that sat upon it.

"Lovely," she murmured. "Why would Kyle stay here instead of in that fancy hotel room?"

"Some guys prefer living like this."

Maggie stuck her head into the kitchenette and made a face. "This is downright awful. Seems to me that the police could have tidied up a bit when they left."

"They're not supposed to touch anything," Travis said. "And neither are we, Maggie. We can look around, but we're not allowed to remove anything from the murder scene."

"I really wasn't thinking of souvenirs." She turned to him. "You know what it looks like to me? I think Kyle came here to hide out."

"From what?"

"Maybe from Francine. She'd never think to look in a place like this for her Prince Charming, now, would she?"

"But why?"

"Think about it, Travis. Kyle wouldn't even introduce her to his buddy, Pete. He was hiding something from her."

"Okay, that makes sense," Travis said. "And that was the conclusion that Sharon Gold had reached in her investigating. Sharon, however, took it a step further. She figured that Kyle wanted to stay with Pete because the two men were lovers, and Kyle was hiding his homosexuality from Francine. Ergo, his murder was a crime of passion."

"But that's wrong," Maggie said. "They weren't lovers."

"And you're sure about that?"

"I'm dead certain." She meandered over to the computer and flicked it on. "Before I went into the witness protection program, I could only dream about having a machine like this. Now I know how to work one."

"Do you have a computer?" Travis asked.

"I have twenty-four-hour-a-day access to the computers in the student lab at school. That's just as good." She punched a couple of buttons on the keyboard. "Actually, I was saving up for one with my Christmas tips from Augustine's before the murders."

"What happened?"

"I had to use my savings to live on during the trial."

"I'm sorry," Travis said. "It's not supposed to work that way."

"I'm not complaining." She hit another button and the screen flashed a menu. "Pete and I used to talk about computers all the time. He had a billion brochures, and he explained the programs to me until I thought I would die of boredom."

Though she was aching inside, her lips twitched with a smile. She was glad that Pete had achieved this much of his dream of being a C.P.A. specializing in investment counseling. He had his computer and his programs. It seemed doubly tragic that he wouldn't be able to continue.

Remembering the lessons Pete had gone over with her, Maggie accessed his files. "Do you think it would be a breach of ethics, Travis, if I made a printout of this information?"

"Probably," he said. "But I'm sure we have the information in our files, anyway. Go ahead."

She turned on the printer and started it running, then turned to Travis. "So, where did the police find their evidence of Kyle's murder?"

"In the bathroom."

Resolutely, Maggie headed in the direction. At the last moment, she veered into the bedroom, where the covers were askew on the bed and the striped sheets looked like they were growing fungus. There was a definite stench in the closed apartment. "Purely nauseating," she pronounced.

"Not entirely," Travis said. He reached toward the

dresser and picked up a framed photograph. "Here's one beautiful thing."

"Let me see."

He held up a five-by-seven picture of Maggie with platinum blond hair and a tight purple sweater outlining her breasts. In her hand she held a can of soda pop, and she was laughing.

"Well, look at me!" She studied the woman in the photograph, the woman she used to be. "Where did Pete get that?"

"It looks like a snapshot he had enlarged."

"I like the way I looked," she mused. "Kind of flashy and carefree. When I was a little girl, I wanted to grow up and be Dolly Parton. But I couldn't sing."

"I like the way you look now," Travis said.

When she shot him a sharp glance, he quickly backtracked. "Not that I didn't like your former appearance, but—"

"It's okay, sugar. I like the new me, too."

Her black hair was much less trouble to maintain because she didn't have to keep touching up the roots. Since she had a California tan, she'd pretty much given up wearing foundation and powder. With all her exercising and eating healthy, she'd gone from a C-cup bra to an A. Her body was now firm, slim, different.

She felt complimented that Pete had missed her enough to keep her photograph in a nice silver frame. "Don't you think it's sweet that he kept this? I never even knew he had a picture of me."

"Come on, Maggie. You don't have to play coy with me. You don't need to tell one of your little white lies. Pete kept your picture in his bedroom because he loved you."

"Pete? Naw, we were just friends."

"Only friends?" His voice had a hard edge to it. "You came back to New Orleans in spite of great personal danger. You're pursuing this investigation, even though you'd be safer in a different state with a different identity. That's too much effort for someone who's just a friend."

"What are you saying, Travis?"

"It's not a big deal. You and Pete Fontana were lovers."

"The heck we were," she snapped.

"Isn't that the reason you're so dead certain that Pete wasn't gay? Because you were his lover?"

"No. I wasn't in love with him."

"Then, why? Why are you putting yourself in peril to clear his name?"

"It's more than his good name," she reminded. "Pete could be condemned to death."

"You can tell me, Maggie. Tell me the truth about you and Pete Fontana."

"We were friends. I haven't had many real friends in my life, so I take that kind of relationship seriously." She was angry at his arrogant hints. How dare he assume that she and Pete were lovers! "You don't know anything about me."

"I can make a reasonable assumption."

"Let me save you the trouble by telling you the flat-out, one hundred percent honest truth. There's nothing I wouldn't do for a friend. And I've never had a lover."

Maggie regretted those words the moment they flew from her lips. She had, in effect, confessed to Travis Shanahan, the chief prosecuting attorney for the city of New Orleans, that she was still a virgin. It wasn't anything she was particularly proud of, nothing she had planned to happen. But there hadn't ever been the right man, the man she could trust, the man who could vanquish the frightening ghosts of her past.

She couldn't believe she'd said something so desperately personal. Hoping to cover her admission, she stormed from the bedroom. "Let's take a look at this murder scene."

At first, it only looked like a bathroom that was in the same sorry state of filthiness as the rest of the apartment. Then Maggie noticed the rust-colored dots that formed a pattern against the wall. More faintly, she saw a splotch on the tile floor and against the side of the bathtub. Bloodstains, she realized. Kyle's blood. The thought of his death suddenly became real and sickening to her. "How could the blood still be here? Why didn't Pete clean it up? He had a week."

"He probably thought it was clean. These spatters have been chemically treated to stand out."

She swallowed hard, reminding herself that she had chosen to be here. She'd insisted upon investigating this herself. "How do they know... I mean, are they sure this is Kyle's blood?"

"There have been tests," Travis said. "DNA and such. It's amazing how little is needed for conclusive proof. They probably dug a tiny bit from the cracks where the floor meets the wall."

This was it, Maggie thought. This was the place where Kyle had died. She shuddered. Could Pete have killed him? Here was the blood, a mute witness to murder.

Trying to remain in control, Maggie recalled the explanation that Sharon Gold had read to her from the file. "Kyle was there." She pointed to the blood. "Against the wall."

"That's right."

"From the angle of the first bullet, Sharon said that the killer was standing over him when he pulled the trigger."

She cocked her fingers like a gun and aimed, slowly lowering her pointing finger. "That means Kyle was on his knees, begging for his life."

"His hands had been tied behind his back," Travis said.

In her mind, she saw his face, but it wasn't the face she remembered from Augustine's when they exchanged banter across the oaken bar. His features were distorted in fear, deadly fear.

Her mental picture was too vivid. Quickly, Maggie closed her hand into a fist and held it against her throat. Her heart was pumping in double time. If she hadn't been so angry at Travis and so embarrassed, she might have sought comfort from him, the same warm solace that he'd offered after she'd been attacked. She would have taken refuge in his arms from the stark reality of murder.

Maggie rubbed at her own arms, soothing herself, reassuring herself that everything was going to be all right. But it wasn't working. She was shaken to the core.

"I'd like to leave now," she said stiffly.

"Whatever you say."

On her way out, she paused to take the computer printout and to turn off the machine. This was the last time she would ever be in this apartment that had been the site of so many good times. She paused in the doorway without looking back. In her mind, she heard the echo of past laughter, the hopeful plans she and Pete had shared. Then there was only silence.

Chapter Six

"My car!" Maggie shouted. "Where's my car!"

Travis glanced at the space in the courthouse parking lot where he had told her to move her car this morning. Instead of Maggie's ancient Toyota, a silver Lumina occupied slot number twelve, which was designated for visitors. He'd meant to inform the police department not to ticket or tow, but he'd had a couple of dozen other things on his mind.

"Oh, my lord," she wailed. "What happened to my car? What happened to Junior?"

"Junior?" he said. "You named your car Junior?"

She unfastened her seat belt and dashed to the spot where her Toyota was last seen. Working herself into a frenzy, Maggie paced in a short path, back and forth, flapping her arms, mad as a wet hornet who'd lost the hive.

"Must have been towed," Travis said.

"No kidding!" She glared at him. "I thought maybe a fairy godmother had come, waved her magic wand, said 'bippity-boppity-boo' and turned my sweet little rattletrap into this fancy coach with the vanity plates that read *Ezra*."

"Ezra Dean Slaughter," Travis grumbled. The Lumina belonged to the defense attorney. Travis was struck with a sudden childish urge—unworthy of a prosecuting attorney—to scratch his keys along the perfect silver finish.

Maggie jabbed a fingernail at his chest. "You said you were going to take care of this. You said I shouldn't worry. You promised that you'd let the police know it was okay for my car to stay here."

"I forgot. So what?" He grinned. "So, shoot me."

"You think this is funny? Believe me, Travis, if I had a BB gun, you'd be hightailing it out of here with a spray of pellets embedded in your rump. I'm going to find out what happened to my car."

When she stormed up the stairs to the courthouse, he had no choice but to follow. Why was she getting so hysterical about an old Toyota? The problem would be easily solved. Her car had, undoubtedly, been towed. All he needed to do was contact the police impounding lot.

Maggie didn't stop marching until the uniformed guard at the door caught hold of her purse. "I'm sorry, Miss, but I've got to run that thing through the X-ray machine."

"What do you think I'm carrying?" she snapped.

"That handbag is big enough to tote a bazooka."

Travis stepped up beside her and informed the guard, "The lady is with me."

"Okay, Mr. Shanahan."

As the officer stepped aside, Maggie plunked her purse on the conveyor belt that funneled objects through the machine. "Go ahead and take a gander. I don't want any special favors."

"Contrary," Travis said. "You are so contrary."

When she grabbed her purse, he hooked his arm through hers. No matter how angry she was, he couldn't have her running amok in the courthouse. Too many people here might know her.

As he guided her toward Judge Howell's courtroom, he

said, "I'm going to have to insist, Maggie. Don't you talk to anyone while we're here. Don't say a word."

"I've got to find out about my car."

"In case you have forgotten, there are people here who might want to grab you so you won't testify."

"What do you suggest I do, Travis? Shake in my boots? Cower in my bed with my covers pulled up over my head?"

"Of course not, but—"

"In case you might have forgotten, the people who are after me already know I'm in town and they know what I look like."

She was right. There was no point in sneaking around and trying to hide her. The bad guys had identified her within a few hours after her arrival in New Orleans. In fact, Travis thought, it might be valuable for Maggie to meet with some of the major players in this drama. Their reactions to her might offer telling clues.

"Where are we going?" she demanded.

"I need to see how Dave and Janine are doing."

"I would prefer that you rectify the situation concerning Junior before we become involved in anything else."

He stopped outside the courtroom door, turned and faced her. "I thought you didn't want any special favors."

"This is not a favor. It's a payback. You made a mistake."

He gestured toward the closed courtroom door. "Do you mind if I check into the jury selection process for the DeCarlo trial first?"

"We're talking about my car!"

"Well, I'm glad you have your priorities straight. An old Toyota is certainly more important than convicting a man who murdered his parents in cold blood."

Her blue eyes blazed. "Do what you have to do."

They slipped quietly past the bailiff posted at the courtroom door. Travis left her seated near the rear. "Don't go anywhere."

He made his way down the center aisle to the prosecutor's table. Dave was posing questions to prospective jurors, and Travis leaned across to talk with Janine. "How's it going?"

"We're almost done. Maybe another half hour."

"Fine. Come back over to the offices, and we'll talk over the selection."

He returned to Maggie. "Let's go."

When they were in the marbled corridor, she said in a relatively civil tone, "Sorry I hollered at you."

"Apology accepted." They left the courthouse and headed toward the offices across Broad Street. "Tell me why this car is so all-fired important to you."

"Junior is the first thing I bought with my own money. It took me a year and a half of saving tips to buy him from a used-car lot, and he wasn't handsome like he is now. I worked on his engine, made the repairs myself and got him a fine new paint job in that midnight blue." She sighed. "I've had a better relationship with Junior than with any man I've ever known."

Because the car can't talk back, Travis thought, but he was wise enough not to provoke her again. "Didn't the Marshals make you give up the car when you went into the witness protection program?"

"They tried. On account of Junior could be traced, they said they'd replace him with a car of similar value. But I flat out refused. So, they agreed to change his registration number and let me keep him."

Travis held the door as she entered the office building. "At least you're consistent, Maggie. You're a pain in the rear for everybody."

"Junior is my freedom," she said. "That's why he's so important to me. That car and I traveled all over the south, from one job to another. If things got too bad in one place, I could move on. As long as I had Junior, I had my escape. Once, in Florida, I was dead broke, and I lived in Junior for a week before I could afford a room. We've been through a lot together, me and that little car."

Though Travis had barely begun to comprehend the complexities of this feisty and infuriating woman, he was beginning to have an inkling. For one thing, she was fiercely loyal—whether it was to her car or to her friends. "I'll get Junior back for you, Maggie. I promise."

In his office, he went directly to the telephone and called the impounding lot. After a few questions and explanations, he had the answers he needed. "Junior is safe," he said to Maggie. "He's been impounded."

She held out her hand for the telephone and spoke into the receiver. "That's my little car. Y'all take good care of him. If there is one tiny scratch on that body, I'll be all over you like spandex on an aerobics instructor. Understand?"

Travis took the phone back. "Thank you, officer. Please hold the car until someone from the D.A.'s office picks it up."

When he replaced the receiver in the cradle, Maggie was grinning sheepishly. "I guess maybe I overreacted."

"It was a sloppy mistake on my part," Travis admitted. "But impounding isn't an altogether bad situation. It might be best if we leave Junior right there. He'll be safe and—"

"And you won't have to worry about me taking off somewhere without the proper protection," she concluded.

"You're reading my mind."

"I'm really trapped here, aren't I."

Travis didn't answer. No matter how much he wished

she were safe, there was an undeniable danger, as real as the man who attacked her in the stairwell.

"For once in my life," she said, "I can't turn tail and run when things get tough."

"Not until after the trial," he said.

He wanted to hold her, to smooth the worry lines that had appeared between her fine eyebrows. He longed to tell her that everything was all right. But that was a lie.

"Travis? Do you believe in voodoo?"

"What?" Where had that question come from?

"Well, I was thinking that since you're from New Orleans and all, you probably know something about voodoo."

"A few years ago, I tried an assault case where the victim claimed to be under a voodoo curse by an old woman who danced around with chicken feet and poked needles in a doll. He wanted to charge the old woman instead of the perpetrator who actually beat him up. Of course, the old crone hadn't done anything. She couldn't be tried."

"What happened?"

"He won the assault case. The very next week, he was bitten by a dog, then run down by a city bus. He called me from the hospital and asked me to pay off the voodoo lady."

"Did you?"

Travis nodded. "I only saw that withered old woman once when I delivered the two hundred dollars that this unfortunate, beleaguered devil owed to her. I got to tell you, Maggie, this old dame was remarkable. Her face was a road map of wrinkles, but she had the eyes of a maiden, a young girl."

"Did she say anything to you?"

"Apparently, she liked me because she gave me a *mojo*, a good luck charm."

He felt silly, talking about voodoo and charms. Travis lived in a world of evidentiary fact and logic. There wasn't room for magic. "Why are we talking about this?"

"I need some good luck," Maggie said. "Losing my car reminded me of that. I thought, maybe, if you knew someplace, we could go and buy me a heap of luck. I went to a voodoo lady once before and got a charm. It was right before I got the job at Augustine's, which was the best waitress job I ever had."

"It was also the place where you witnessed a murder," he reminded her.

"That must have been part of my destiny." She exhaled a gentle sigh. "I always carry my charm with me in my purse."

Travis always took his *mojo* into court, but that wasn't something he intended to tell Maggie or anyone else. This slight bow to superstition embarrassed him.

Janine poked her head into his office. "We're back."

"In the conference room," he said, rising from behind his desk. "Maggie, you wait here."

"While y'all discuss the jury selection? Aw, Travis, let me listen in. It'd be like a full-fledged seminar on trial law."

"You're a witness on this case, Maggie. It's not appropriate for you to participate in jury selection."

"What if I sit real quiet?"

"No." He remembered this morning, when she had probably eavesdropped on his conversation with the district attorney. "And I mean no. This is information you shouldn't hear."

Travis strode into the conference room where the other attorneys had gathered. Dave Dermott was already complaining about Judge Leland Howell. "The guy hardly lets me ask two questions before he tells me to move along. You'd think, with the defense allegations of possible jury tampering on the last DeCarlo trial, that he'd be glad that I'm taking my time."

"How many have you already excused?" Travis asked.

Sharon Gold answered for Dave. "Five. He's only got five exceptions left."

"He had to bump them," Janine said. "They were all opposed to the death penalty."

"You did the right thing," Travis said. This was the first big, high-profile court trial for Dave, and he wanted to encourage him. "Any definite picks?"

"I'm pretty happy with these seven," Dave said, sliding a yellow legal pad across the table toward Travis.

Janine piped up, "But there are at least three of them that the defense is going to excuse."

"Why?"

"Two of the women sound like they've already decided Ben DeCarlo is guilty. And there's a guy who dated Maria DeCarlo and got dumped by her."

"If you ask me," said Sharon Gold, "we're going to have to compromise on the death penalty issue. Even if it means we can't get a murder-one conviction."

"Nobody's asking you," Dave snapped.

"Fine." She rose to her feet. "I have my own cases to work. I was only here to offer my expert opinion."

"I'm sorry, Sharon."

Dave was too quick to apologize, Travis thought, but the young redheaded man would toughen up quickly. The experience of the high-profile DeCarlo trial would age him considerably.

Travis didn't expect Dave or Janine to be in the D.A.'s office for long. Some high-class legal firm, offering big bucks, would woo them away within a few years, maybe less for Dave because his family was so well-connected in the legal community.

Sharon Gold was still sniping. "If you don't want my help, Dave, just say so."

"Hell, I'd accept assistance from the devil himself." Dave grinned. "But Ezra Dean hasn't offered."

For the next hour, they debated over the potential jurors, finally deciding that they'd have to give a little on accepting jurors who were opposed to the death penalty. The issue of police corruption was a huge problem, and they needed to be sure that none of the jurors had a personal grudge against the cops.

By six o'clock, they had nailed down the seven that Dave liked and come up with a possible six more.

"Are we done?" Dave asked. "Because I'm feeling the need for some liquid refreshment."

"We all are," Travis said.

There was a rustling outside the conference room door, and a knock. Maggie poked her head inside. "Are y'all about finished?"

Had she been listening again? Or was this a coincidence? Travis guessed the former was true.

"We're done!" Dave announced. "Looking for something to drown our sorrows."

"I'll get it."

"Down the hall to the lunchroom," Dave instructed, "there's wine in the fridge."

"Really, Maggie," Sharon commented, "I thought I told you about this waitress attitude."

"Just being polite."

Avoiding Travis's cool scrutiny, she hastened down the corridor to the lunchroom. He probably had every right to be angry, but she couldn't let this opportunity slip past.

After they'd closed themselves up in the conference room, she eased into a coat closet that opened in the hall and in the room. Listening really hard through the crack in the closed door, she had overheard almost everything.

Her head was spinning with all the bits and pieces of legal strategy she'd learned by sitting in the closet and listening like a fly on the wall. These attorneys were so smart! They considered more aspects of personality than a psychologist, trying to figure who was the best person to believe their case.

Someday, Maggie thought, she'd be one of them. She'd be perceptive, too. A lot of what they said was plain old common sense, fancied up with high-class words.

In the lunchroom, she went to the big old avocado green refrigerator that looked like it had been sitting here since the 1960s and opened the door. Inside, there was an assortment of soda pop, uneaten sack lunches, a six-pack of beer and two bottles of wine. Maggie turned the labels to read them, already deciding that she'd bring the better brand. She knew enough about wines to pick, and these hardworking lawyers deserved a treat. One was a cheap chablis. The other was a dark, handsome burgundy red. The label read Château Louis Noir. It was the same wine that Francine Bentley said she'd chosen to drink with Kyle.

A shiver went down Maggie's back. This burgundy was an unusual brand. It would have to be ordered special, and Dave Dermott had told her that it was right here. Was he somehow connected with Francine?

Though it seemed like a long shot, she mentioned Dave's burgundy to Travis that evening before she went upstairs to her bedroom in his elegant home. "You think it's a coincidence?" she asked.

"I sure as hell hope so." He scowled. "I don't like to

find connections between these two cases. If Kyle was murdered by one of DeCarlo's men..."

"It's probably nothing." Though she didn't want Pete to be convicted, Maggie wasn't comfortable with the supposition that somebody was killing off witnesses. "Maybe this Château Louis Noir is just the trendy flavor of the month."

Travis sank into the brocaded wing chair in his front parlor. "Did I make a mistake?" he murmured. His voice was so low that it seemed like he was talking to himself. "Should I have assigned someone other than Dave to this trial?"

"He's working hard," Maggie said. She perched on the matching chair beside him and dropped her huge purse with a clunk beside the antique rosewood table between them. "And I think the jury will like him. He looks like Huck Finn."

"I was counting on that," Travis said. "If Ezra Dean attacks either Dave or Janine, the jury will feel sympathetic toward them."

"What about you?"

"It's my job to be as hard and nasty as Ezra Dean himself. I'm the one who's going toe-to-toe with that sly old fox."

"He's a nasty one," Maggie said. "I remember my first testimony with him doing cross-examination."

"I remember it, too. Maggie, you are the master of embellishment."

"I did all right, didn't I?"

"When Ezra Dean asked you exactly how long you had been working at Augustine's and what kind of jobs you had before, you told him that it wasn't any of his business if you were a college professor or a mud wrestler in a girlie bar. There was nothing wrong with your eyes, and you knew what you had seen.''

Maggie cringed. After taking some law classes, she knew how difficult she'd been as a witness.

Travis continued, ''It took the judge two full minutes to quiet the giggles in the courtroom. And it wasn't just what you said, it was the way you said it. Tossing your platinum hair, planting your fists on your hips and sticking out your breasts at Ezra Dean like a couple of cannons.''

''Thank you so much for reminding me of that purely humiliating experience.''

''It was great. He was attacking your credibility as a witness, and you showed him—and the jury—that your personal background had nothing to do with what you had seen.''

''Well, a person's history shouldn't have anything to do with something they witnessed,'' she said.

''Not unless the attorney can prove that the witness is a pathological liar and a cheat by dragging in a string of character witnesses. Which is exactly what we intend to do with Ezra Dean's primary witness, Sandor Rossi.'' He pushed himself from the chair. ''I need to call the D.A. and find out if he made any progress in arranging for a deposition with Rossi.''

He was moving as slowly as one of the sloths she'd watched at the San Diego Zoo. *Lethargic,* Maggie thought. Another good vocabulary word that sounded the way Travis looked as he hauled himself toward the formal library that was next to the parlor.

Her impression of him during the last trial was all wrong. She'd thought he was a rich man who had everything fed to him by a silver spoon. But Travis worked hard. His devotion to his job was single-minded.

''Can I do anything to help with the case?'' she asked.

"Take care of yourself, and don't get into trouble."

"I feel like I'm not pulling my load. I mean, here you are, putting in full days with your trial preparations, and then you have to baby-sit me at night."

"You're the easy part. Today, when I was running around with you, it took my mind off jury selection. Otherwise, I would have been hanging around the office, snapping at everybody."

"Well, then, I'll be sure to figure out a field trip for tomorrow," she promised.

"I know where we'll be going," he said. "We're going to be looking into that wine. Château whatever."

"And how are we going to do that?"

"We'll have to go to the most exclusive wine shop in town," he said. "The Crescent Wine Cellar."

Maggie heard a click of fear inside her head. The Crescent Wine Cellar had, until his arrest three years ago, been owned and operated by Ben DeCarlo, and his manager still ran it for him. Waltzing in there seemed dangerous.

She followed Travis into the library. "Are you sure we want to go there? I mean, what if they recognize me?"

"They're not going to shoot you right there," he said. "Not in daylight. Not with me standing next to you."

"I suppose not."

"Like you said earlier, the people who are after you already know what you look like. If we get some kind of reaction from them, it might give us a direction."

That logic made sense to her. "Whatever you say, Travis."

The next morning, after some paperwork and plea bargaining at the D.A.'s offices, she and Travis aimed for the Crescent Wine Cellar. By going there, Maggie felt like she was pitching chum off the side of a rowboat, trying to attract a great white shark. *DeSharko.* That was what Clayton Bascombe called Ben DeCarlo. Maggie would make darned sure before she left this place that she still had all her fingers and toes attached.

The Crescent Wine Cellar was in the French Quarter, and she was delighted to return to that romantic part of town where the streets were cobblestone and the old buildings with their balconied facades were decorated with lacy grillwork. The old oaks were draped with moss, and there was a lazy air at noontime. The Quarter didn't really come alive until after dark.

Since it was Carnival season, there were banners of purple, green and gold, the Mardi Gras colors. Travis parked on Toulouse Street, in front of a charming building with an arched doorway. The Crescent Wine Cellar.

Before they got out of the car, he took her hand and gave a little squeeze. "Scared?"

"Naw. Taking action beats sitting around waiting for the next hit." She tightened her grasp on his fingers. "Travis, what if I see the guy who attacked me?"

"Would you be able to recognize him? I thought you said it was too dark."

"He'll have a scratch on his face," she said, touching her own cheek. "And a hoop earring. I might know him."

"We don't have to go in if you don't want to."

"I'm game."

Inside, the atmosphere was sophisticated, with dark woods and antique glass. Maggie had expected that. Before Ben DeCarlo became a murderer, he'd been a man of taste and standing in the community. A long bar stretched along one wall. Behind it, there were racks and racks of wines. The actual space for seating was small and most of the tables were for two. She and Travis sat near the door. At this hour of the day, there were only a handful of other patrons.

As soon as they sat, a large, barrel-chested man came through the front door and stepped up to the table beside them. His head was shaven clean. In the corner of his mouth, he clenched an unlit cigar. "Mr. Shanahan," he said. "To what does the Crescent owe this honor?"

"I wanted my lady friend to taste the finest wine in New Orleans." He leaned toward her. "My dear, this is Dominick DeCarlo. He's Ben's uncle."

The big man gave her a quick glance. Apparently, she was of little interest to him because he continued to watch Travis. "I understand that the retrial will start as soon as next week."

"Most likely."

"I'm disappointed in you, Mr. Shanahan. I had not expected to be put through this agony again. It is painful for me to relive the deaths of my brother and his wife."

"And Ben?"

He removed the cigar from his mouth. His lip curled as if he were ready to spit. "I have no nephew."

In his voice, Maggie heard an echo of his brother, Antonio DeCarlo, but there was none of the gentleness. It wasn't hard for her to believe that this man, Dominick DeCarlo, was involved in organized crime.

"I'll try not to disappoint you," Travis said. "I want to see Ben behind bars as much as you do."

"See that you succeed." Dominick strode away, moving quickly for a man of his size, and exiting back to the street. Had he been following them? Why?

A waiter came up to the table and placed a thick wine list in Travis's hand. When he turned to leave, Travis said, "On second thought, I don't believe we'll order anything for here. However, I would like a bottle for later. I've heard that Château Louis Noir is good."

"An excellent choice."

"Is that a popular wine?"

"Among our customers? Yes. For the general public? No."

"Why's that?" Maggie demanded. She didn't like the snooty waiter's implication that the general public didn't have the sophisticated taste buds to discern the difference between a fine wine and the stuff with a screw top.

"Château Louis Noir is pricy and relatively unknown. The vineyard is small."

"I'll take three bottles," Travis said. "Have them delivered to my home."

When he recited the address, the waiter looked upon him with new respect. Like the snob that he was, he drooled over Travis, asking if there was anything else—anything!—he could do.

"I'm curious," Travis said. "Do you have a preferred customer list, so I can place orders by phone?"

"We have a mailing list to notify special customers of special shipments and arrivals."

A mailing list! Maggie figured that they would be able to access such a list easily. Then they would know whether Dave Dermott and Francine Bentley were regular customers. In and of itself, taste in wine was no proof whatsoever. But the connection might bear further investigation.

When they left the Crescent Wine Cellar, the first thing Maggie saw on the street was a silver Lumina, illegally parked in a Loading Only zone. Ezra Dean Slaughter emerged from the driver's side, tugged at the front of his pin-striped vest, straightened his silk necktie and came toward them.

"Out of the frying pan and into the flames," Maggie whispered to Travis.

Chapter Seven

Maggie took a step closer to Travis as he offered an ice-cold smile to the famed defense attorney and said, "Well, Ezra Dean, what a coincidence!"

"Not really. I would assume that both you and I can afford to shop at the finest wine store in New Orleans." He scowled behind his wire-rimmed glasses. "But I see you're coming out empty-handed. What a shame!"

"I didn't find much to my taste in there," Travis said.

Maggie admired their exchange of double-meaning comments. These two men were equally matched as adversaries. The difference, she thought, was that Travis was decent and had a sense of ethics. Ezra Dean was a defense attorney who could be bought and paid for. In spite of his amazing success in winning verdicts, he often represented the very dregs of society. His only requirement for taking on a client appeared to be ready cash in hand.

It didn't matter, she thought, how slickly he dressed or how melodious his orator's voice was. Ezra Dean Slaughter was lower than a scorpion under a rock and twice as dangerous.

When he fixed his steady gaze upon her face, Maggie took care not to flinch. It wouldn't be smart to show fear to the enemy.

"My dear Miss Maggie Deere," Ezra Dean intoned, "allow me to compliment you on the changes in your appearance. The dark hair is very becoming. You no longer look like a cheap hooker."

A cheap hooker? She bristled. "Well, aren't you sweeter than praline pie?"

"I knew Travis was keeping you on a short leash, and now I can see why. You're very beautiful."

She'd had plenty of men look at her with that nasty smirk on their faces—like she was maple sugar and they had a painful ache in the sweet tooth. But she'd never been as wary as she was of Ezra Dean. It was as if he had the power to stare straight into the darkest depths of her soul, find her weaknesses and drag them out into the light of day.

"I'm pleased to have run into you," Travis said, no less insincere than Ezra Dean himself. "We need to talk about the Rossi deposition."

"Wiley has been pestering me about that, too." He frowned. "There's nothing to talk about. Rossi will make his testimony on the stand. Otherwise, he puts himself into too much danger."

"Then prepare yourself for a flurry of motions to stay the trial," Travis warned. "By not allowing us to review his testimony in full, you're impeding the prosecution's right to discovery. Come on, Ezra Dean, if there's really that much danger for Rossi, he can go into the witness protection program."

"And turn up dead? Like Kyle Johnson?"

Maggie's ears pricked up. "What do you know about the murder of Kyle Johnson?"

"Tsk-tsk, Ms. Deere. Curiosity killed the cat."

"I'll be filing my motions tomorrow morning," Travis said. "As you know, there's precedent and procedure in my favor. You cannot deny me access to discovery regarding your witness."

"I gave you the deposition."

"With all the pertinent information expunged. No names of alibi witnesses. All it said was that Ben DeCarlo was framed by certain persons. There was no explanation of how my five eyewitnesses—"

"Three eyewitnesses," Ezra Dean corrected him.

"Of how *any* witnesses could have seen Ben walk into that restaurant and pull a gun. That deposition you gave me was so marked over that it looked like you spilled ink on it."

"Your point?"

"I want access to Rossi. If I don't get it, I'm prepared to tie this process up for months and months."

"Wasting the taxpayers' money?" Ezra Dean said with a sneer.

"There's a principle of procedure and fairness involved. Sometimes, justice is expensive. I swear, Ezra Dean, I'll drag this all the way to the Supreme Court. How would your client like that?"

"Of course, he's anxious to get under way."

Travis took a step away from him. "Good afternoon, Ezra Dean. See you in court."

"Tell you what, Travis. I'm willing to work out a deal." Grandly, he added, "In the interest of fairness."

"When can I see Rossi?"

"You? Never." Ezra Dean took the time to adjust the precise one inch of cuff that showed beneath his suit jacket sleeves. "However, I would be willing to allow one member of your team, without a tape recorder or a court transcriber taking notes, to have informal access to a meeting with Rossi."

"What?"

"Let's say...Dave Dermott. He can meet with Rossi for one hour. Tomorrow after the jury selection concludes. I'll arrange it for him. Of course, I will be present."

"Why are you afraid for me to meet with him?"

"Fear has nothing to do with it," Ezra Dean said. "I just plain don't like you, Travis. Do we have a deal?"

"Two members of my team," Travis said. "Dave and Sharon Gold."

"No recorders and no transcription?"

"Agreed."

When the two men shook hands, Maggie half expected to see a flaming combustion. They disliked each other so much that there were sparks firing between them.

While Ezra Dean strolled into the Crescent Wine Cellar, they went down the street to Travis's car. It wasn't until they were on their way that Maggie ventured a comment. "You handled that real well. Got him to have two of your people instead of one."

"Then, why do I have this nagging feeling that I just took a wild swing at a low-and-away pitch? He's suckered me into something here. That was too smooth."

Travis had the sense that Ezra Dean had somehow managed to anticipate his every statement—from the demand for access to Rossi to the demand for Sharon Gold to accompany Dave Dermott.

And what about freckle-faced Dave, the resident Huck Finn of the District Attorney's Office? Had he bought that unusual wine from the business that was owned by Ben DeCarlo? Why had Ezra Dean specifically requested Dave?

Travis didn't like the direction his mind was taking. If Dave Dermott was playing footsie with the defense, he could sabotage the prosecution case.

"Travis?"

Maggie's voice startled him back to reality. He stopped for a light and turned toward her. Her shining black curls framed a worried face. Tense and confused, she was looking toward him for answers. If only he knew what to say...

"Travis, do you think we could somehow get access to the mailing list for the Crescent Wine Cellar?"

"Not a problem," he said. "If that information isn't readily available, we happen to have a computer hacker whiz in the D.A.'s office."

"Roy?" she guessed.

"Right the first time. How'd you know?"

"I figured he must be good at something. Why else would everybody put up with all his bellyaching?"

"I'm putting you in charge of that project, Maggie. Get Roy to tap into their list and run off a copy. Then you check the list and see if Francine Bentley is on it." Travis sighed heavily. He probably should discourage Maggie from investigating anything that might pertain to the DeCarlo trial, but who else could he trust? "I guess you should also see if Dave Dermott is listed, but don't let Roy know what you're looking for."

"And what will you be doing this afternoon?"

"I need to have a conference with Sharon Gold so we can go over the pertinent questions for Rossi."

Though Travis firmly believed otherwise, he would treat Sandor Rossi as if he were telling the truth. Fairness applied equally to honest citizens and slimeballs. Like Ezra Dean. Like Rossi. Like Ben DeCarlo.

MAGGIE SETTLED DOWN with Roy in his three-person office, and they first explored the strictly legal means for obtaining the customer mailing list for the Crescent Wine Cellar.

"Sorry," Roy said with a groan. "It's going to take a court order to open their files."

She seemed to remember a lot of clandestine evidence during the first trial, evidence that was never public record but was shared with the judge in his chambers. "Didn't you have a court order to investigate all the DeCarlo businesses during the last trial?"

"Not from this office." Roy lowered his voice. "There were court orders and wiretaps from the federal marshals that weren't strictly according to the rule book, if you know what I mean. Oh, I could tell you things about the DeCarlo family that would curl your hair."

"I really don't need to know." *Curiosity killed the cat.* "But I surely would appreciate it if you could find your way into those federal Marshals' lists."

"I'll try."

Roy perked up as he played with the computer, referencing forward and back. As he slid into a file marked Strictly Confidential, he made a noise in the back of his throat that sounded like amusement, though his face was smile-free.

"You're a downright whiz at this computer stuff," Maggie complimented him. "Looks like you can go anywhere."

"Not really. Not without passwords."

"How hard would it be," she wondered, "to access the federal witness protection records?"

"Almost impossible," he said. "Not only would you have to break the codes and figure out the passwords, but there's an alarm—like a burglar alarm—that tells the feds when somebody's broken in."

Then how had someone obtained her address in the protection program? The computerized records were pretty much closed to hackers, even sophisticated hackers.

Maggie leaned back in her chair and vaguely watched the ever-changing lists and flashes on Roy's high-resolution screen. This whole computerization thing fascinated her. These were the crimes of the future, she thought. High-tech crimes. Hackers could steal, cheat and falsify records without leaving the comfort of their own homes.

"Okay," Roy said, "I'm at the doorway of the Marshals' files on DeCarlo, but I need a password to get in."

"How do these files get passwords?"

"Somebody picks a word or phrase at random. Some places have a whole system, but I happen to know that the New Orleans branch of the federal Marshals stick with one word."

"You think Clayton Bascombe would pick the password?"

"Possibly," he said. "Clayton's been involved with the DeCarlo investigations from the start."

Maybe if they telephoned Clayton and told him what they were doing, he'd relent and allow them access, but Maggie kind of doubted that he'd be willing to cooperate with her. "Let me check in with Travis and see if he'll get us through the door."

She scuttled down the hall to Travis's office and tapped on the door. There was no answer. When she peeked inside, Sharon Gold was seated behind his desk. What was she doing here?

"Have you heard?" Her face was flushed with excitement. "I get to do the deposition on Rossi."

"With Dave Dermott."

"Oh, him. My little shadow. I'm so enthusiastic about this. If I ask the right questions, I can break this case wide open."

"And what does that mean?"

"For one thing, it means I'll be in the courtroom during the trial, maybe even as a witness. More exposure on Court TV. That can't be bad for my career."

"Where's Travis?"

"Who knows? I think he went over to the courthouse to watch Dave and make sure he doesn't screw up on jury selection." She moved away from Travis's desk. "I was just leaving."

Maggie returned to the office where Roy was poking at the computer keys. He looked up when she entered and said, "Okay, I went through the obvious passwords, like DeCarlo and Ben DeCarlo and other names of the family."

Maggie thought of the dinner she and Travis had shared with Clayton Bascombe. Had he mentioned anything that might be a password? His hobby was restoring old cars, and he was extra proud of one of his projects. "Try Edsel," she said.

Roy typed it in. "Nope."

What else had Clayton said? Where was the piece that might be a password. "Shark," Maggie said, remembering that Clayton referred to Ben DeCarlo as a shark.

"Not shark," Roy reported.

Maggie had it! This was her very best guess without running down to the courtroom and disturbing Travis. "DeSharko."

Roy typed the strange word in. "Well, I'll be darned. Here it is."

After a search, he located the customer mailing list for the Crescent Wine Cellar. Unfortunately, the list was a year old. Nonetheless, when Maggie scanned the runoff, she discovered a familiar name. Francine Bentley.

So Francine Bentley bought her fancy wine from Ben DeCarlo's shop. Although there was no mention of Dave

Dermott on the list, Maggie thought it was mighty suspicious that he'd shown up with a bottle of the same brand.

"Okay, Roy, close up that file, and we'll pretend we never did this."

"You're right about that. If the feds thought we were messing in their business, they'd chop off my nose."

After he'd exited the program, he looked up at her wistfully. "Isn't there anything else we can do on the computer?"

Maggie dug into her purse where she'd stashed the runoffs she had taken from Pete's apartment. She held them out toward Roy. "Can we access any of these records? They're off a private person's computer."

"Maybe," he said. "But why would you want to? Looks like you've got the whole runoff."

"You're right. I just need to sit down and go over this stuff the old-fashioned way."

Roy tapped the keyboard and returned to his regular work. "If you need anything else, Maggie, just let me know."

"Count on it. And thank you."

She took the pages into Travis's office and sat behind his desk to study the lists of names and investments that Pete had kept for himself. They seemed to be referenced two ways. First, there were project names for investments with a list of people underneath and a dollar amount. Second, she found special files for about fifteen clients whom Pete had developed complete portfolios for. Kyle was among these.

Maggie was fairly sharp with numbers. At least, she wasn't afraid of math. And it didn't take her too long to recognize how Pete had broken down Kyle's five thousand dollars into seven different chunks that had yielded varying returns. Only one investment was a loss.

The best return—the one where Pete had placed three thousand dollars of Kyle's cash—had recently paid out twice that amount. The name of the investment was TotalCom.

When she looked up TotalCom, Maggie found that Pete had placed every one of his portfolio customers in this investment, but there were no other names listed.

Back in Roy's office, she asked, "Can you find me the investor list for this TotalCom?"

"Normally, I couldn't," he said. "But your printout gives access instructions right up here at the top."

"Would you mind, sugar?"

In a flash, Roy had obtained the information she wanted. It was a listing of names and amount, similar to Pete's, but at least a couple of pages long. "Let's print it," Maggie said.

She returned to Travis's office with her new printout and started scanning the list, not sure of what she was looking for. A clue, a hint, some kind of reason why Kyle's investment had paid off at just this moment, drawing him back to New Orleans.

She stopped short when she read the name of a certain investor. *Ezra Dean Slaughter.*

The amount of his investment was one million, six hundred thousand dollars. He was the major single investor in TotalCom. By a long shot.

Maggie sat back in the padded chair behind Travis's desk and frowned. This wasn't the connection she'd hoped to find. She didn't want a link between Ezra Dean and Pete. Where Ezra Dean was concerned, Ben DeCarlo was not far away.

Too easily, Maggie imagined a plot where Pete would lure Kyle back to New Orleans for his payoff. Then DeCarlo's men would take the opportunity to kill off one of the witnesses. As soon as she thought of that scheme, it seemed so obvious. Pete hadn't killed Kyle, but he was involved, aiding and abetting the people who had performed the gangland execution with Pete's own gun.

There was only one way she could find the truth: talk to Pete himself. If she confronted him directly, Maggie didn't think he'd lie to her. Or, if he did, she could tell. She would see the deceit in his eyes and his manner.

Unfortunately, this wasn't a bit of information she was ready to share with Travis. Not just yet.

She returned to Roy's office. "I need to ask you a favor," she said. "Can you give me a lift over to Parish Prison?"

His eyebrows pinched with worry. "You're not supposed to leave this floor. Remember what happened the last time?"

"This if different," she said. "I'm going to the prison. It's full of guards. What could happen to me at the prison?"

"I don't like it. Why do you need to go?"

She didn't even have to think twice about this little fib. "My car," she said. "Travis screwed up, didn't tell the cops it was okay for me to park in the Parish Prison lot. If I don't pick up the car, the police will impound my vehicle."

A sneaky gleam lit Roy's eyes. "Travis screwed up."

"Yes, he did. And I'm plenty mad about it." She smiled sweetly. "Please, Roy. Give me a ride over there, walk me inside, and I'll take care of things from there."

"Okay."

At Parish Prison, it was easier said than done for Maggie to arrange for her own private interview with Pete, but the official in charge recognized her from when she'd been there with Travis. Maggie pushed until she got her way.

When Pete shuffled into the room, she was shocked by his appearance. He had a huge shiner on his left eye. There were bruises on his left forearm.

"What happened? Oh, Pete, who did this to you?"

Sullenly, he glanced toward the guard. "I slipped and fell down."

"Don't you even start to tell me those lies," she warned. "I know a beating when I see one. Was it the police?"

"I don't know what you're talking about, Maggie."

"Why? Who beat you?"

He painfully lowered his skinny body into the chair opposite her at the plain wooden table. He didn't even ask to have his cuffs removed, just sat there. His weary eyes were dull.

Outrage fired through Maggie's soul. How could this happen? As soon as she asked herself, she knew the answer. People were hurt all the time in jail. It was a violent place, filled with violent criminals.

"Did you go by my apartment?" he asked.

"Yes, I did. And I have never laid eyes upon such a pigsty in my entire life."

When Pete grinned, he winced. A groan escaped his lips.

Maggie couldn't stand to be here, seeing his bruises, wishing desperately that she could help him. "Pete, I want for you to tell me about TotalCom."

"You broke into my computer," he said.

"Well, of course I did. I'm investigating. And I remembered all that stuff you told me about it so I could access your files." She snapped her fingers. "Just like that."

"You shouldn't be messing in my private papers."

Didn't he understand that he was charged with murder? How was she supposed to investigate and respect his privacy at the same time? "You listen to me, Pete Fontana, you are in a heap of trouble. Either you start leveling with me or I am going to forget I ever knew you. Now, you tell me about TotalCom.''

"It was an excellent investment opportunity. Computer software for communication systems. I got in with my clients when it first went public.''

"Do you know anything about the other people who invested?''

His eyes shifted, just a fraction, before he said, "No.''

"Then, how'd you hear about it?''

"I pick up things here and there. Can't recall exactly who it was that told me about TotalCom.''

"You're lying to me, Pete.''

Behind her, she heard the prison guard make a snorting noise in the back of his throat as if to say that lying was to be expected from a prisoner in his jail. Maybe Pete wasn't talking because of the guard.

"I don't know what you want to hear, Maggie. It was a good investment, and I put every one of my clients into the pool.''

"How did you know when it was going to pay off?''

"I got a letter, about two weeks ahead of time, informing me about the most lucrative timing.''

"And that's when you contacted Kyle?''

"Right.''

He gave this information without hesitation, and Maggie had the feeling that he was telling her the truth. He'd received a letter, then contacted Kyle and, presumably, all his other clients.

If the timing on this letter had been manipulated—by Ezra Dean—the defense attorney and his team and his associates, many of whom were the scum of the earth, would know exactly when Kyle Johnson could be found in New Orleans.

"This is very important, Pete. Who sent you the letter?"

"I guess it was from TotalCom."

"Was there a signature?"

"I'm sure there was, but I can't remember."

Was he lying? Maggie hated to think that Pete might have been a party to a scheme luring Kyle to his death, but there was a possibility.

"Maggie, I didn't kill him."

But he might have helped set it up. That sort of premeditation was almost more despicable. "I'm trying to believe you, Pete. Is there anything else you want to tell me?"

His eyelids lowered. "I'm sorry, Maggie. I got nothing to say."

As she watched him shuffle from the room, Maggie's anger erupted inside her like a volcano spewing hot lava. Someone had beaten her friend. It wasn't right. Now he was scared to talk to her, scared of his own shadow.

And Maggie knew how that felt. She remembered from when she was a kid. Afraid to speak. Afraid of being seen.

She couldn't allow this to happen.

Storming away from Parish Prison, she charged along Broad Street, past the splendid courthouse and down a block to the Orleans Parish Police Station.

She was still steaming when she walked inside the crowded, filthy building where cops, perps and lawyers bumped around desks and processing areas. Maggie wasn't in the mood to waste time with regular procedures. She went straight to the top, demanding directions until she approached the secretary who guarded the door to the office of Royce Monk, police chief.

"I'm here to see Chief Monk," Maggie said. "I'm Maggie Deere."

When the secretary buzzed the inner office, the response

was immediate. Royce Monk bobbed out of his office, staring at her with the kind of apprehension that most people reserved for encounters with deadly reptiles. "Get in here," he said.

She stepped inside and primly sat. "Nice to see you again, Chief."

"What the hell are you doing here? I've had enough trouble with all of you protected witnesses on the DeCarlo case. One of them is a homicide. And there was that Gleason woman who blew the whistle on this whole police corruption scandal. I can't take much more of this."

Maggie didn't feel the least bit sorry for the man.

He glared at her. "What are you planning to do? Tell me there's an explosive planted in the morgue?"

"I'm not the Unabomber, sugar. I just need your assistance on two matters. First off, I need to get my vehicle out of your impound lot."

"You give me the plate number and I'll send somebody over to pick it up and bring it right out front." Hopefully, he added, "Then will you leave?"

"And I would like to register a complaint about the treatment of Pete Fontana, who is being held in the Parish Prison for the murder of—"

"I know who Fontana is," he snapped impatiently. "What's this about?"

"I'm a friend of Pete's," she said. "I just paid him a visit and discovered that he had been beaten."

"Not my problem," Monk said. "Talk to the prison warden."

"I'm filing a complaint with you. I believe the charge would be assault and battery."

"I won't accept your complaint."

"I think you will, Chief, because I'm going to wait right here until you see fit to do the right thing." She widened her eyes, assuming innocence. "I sure hope nothing happens to me, being a protected witness and all."

"If you're hinting that my cops are dangerous, you're wrong." He cleared his throat. "But there are more than cops wandering around here. This is a police station. We have people being arrested and charged and picked up for questioning. Bad people, Ms. Deere. I can't let you hang around."

"Thank you, sugar. So, I guess we'll be doing things my way. I really do appreciate—"

His secretary tapped on the office door and poked her head inside to interrupt. "There's a telephone call for Ms. Deere on line three."

A phone call? Who knew she was here?

She accepted the receiver from Monk. "Hello?"

"I warned you once." The voice was whispery. Masculine, but not identifiable.

"Excuse me, I can't hear you. Who is this?"

"You know damned well who it is. This is the last time I'm going to tell you nicely, Maggie Deere. Leave town and don't come back. If you take the witness stand, you're a dead woman."

"Who is this?" She stalled, waving to Monk, trying to signal him to trace the call. "I have a few projects I need to finish. Maybe we could get together and discuss—"

"My next warning won't be so polite. I know where you are, Maggie. Every minute of every day. I'm watching you."

The telephone went dead in her hand.

Chapter Eight

"I'm not blaming Roy for this latest trouble," Travis said in a low, dangerous voice. His fingers gripped the steering wheel of his BMW so tightly that his knuckles were white. "This wasn't Roy's fault. You sweet-talked him with some story about your damned car. You said nothing about visiting Pete Fontana, and you sure as hell didn't tell him that you intended to flutter around the courthouse like a sitting duck and then go to the police station."

Maggie might have pointed out that sitting ducks don't flutter, but she didn't dare tease. She had never seen Travis this angry, though he'd been plenty mad before. There was the seething rage when he confronted Ezra Dean. And he'd been annoyed with her several times, very annoyed. But this was different, almost out of control. His jaw clenched. His face was red. A vein in his forehead throbbed. His anger was like a pit bull, snapping and snarling, held back by a slender leash.

"Where are we going?" she asked, hoping he'd cool down with a change of subject.

"I'm taking you home, where I fully intend to lock you in the upstairs bedroom like my crazy Aunt Ida."

"And what if I don't want to be locked up?"

"Doesn't matter," he said. "You can't be trusted."

That stung. Maggie felt a little prickle of her own irritation. After all, she'd been the one who was threatened. "It's no big deal, Travis. Nothing happened."

"Nothing?" The leash went taut. She could see the struggle as he barely hung on to his self-control. "Repeat what that guy told you on the phone."

"Some stupid threats." She was trying to dismiss his words, trying to pretend like it was nothing. Still, when she remembered the sound of his whisper, her insides quivered like a leaf in a storm. "He said something about how he was going to get me if I didn't leave town. He would kill me if I testified."

"And he was watching you," Travis reminded. "Let's not forget that this psycho is stalking you."

"Don't you think he made that part up?" Her question was hopeful. "I mean, you haven't noticed anybody following us in your car, have you?"

"How would I notice? I'm an attorney, not a trained bodyguard." The tires of the BMW screeched as he braked for a stoplight. "Believe me, Maggie, I would like nothing better than to turn you over to the Marshals and let them take care of you."

"But you can't."

"Especially not now. Everywhere I look, the law enforcement is tainted. You got that call in the police station, in Police Chief Monk's office. And the call came from a pay phone right outside. That pretty much says it all. The cops aren't safe." Travis exhaled in a curt sigh. "Dammit, Maggie, I wish you had the good sense to be frightened by these threats."

"Don't worry too much about that, sugar. I'm scared, all right."

"Not enough," he said. "Hell, you won't even stay put when I tell you to."

"I can't let fear run my life, Travis. I made that decision when I was eight years old and my mother died. I was so scared that I wanted to curl up in the grave beside her. But I didn't. I couldn't."

If only he could understand what was going on inside her head! She didn't want him to think she was so foolish that she didn't acknowledge danger. But explaining was hard. It meant exposing the ghosts of her childhood.

She sucked in a deep breath, prepared to speak from her soul, from the secret core of her being. "I know about fear, Travis."

He must have sensed her struggle because his voice softened. "From when you were a kid?"

"That's right. I'm not saying that most of the foster homes where I got placed weren't wonderful and kind and good. But there were others, too. I was bounced around a lot before I turned fifteen and took off for good."

"Tell me about it, Maggie."

She glanced at his profile while he was driving. Did she dare to tell the shameful terrors of her past? Confronting the evil was like reaching into her own chest, ripping out her own heart and holding it in her hand for him to examine. Could she trust this man? "I don't like to dwell on it."

"I want to know. Tell me about your fear."

She stared straight through the windshield at the rear bumper of the car in front of them. Her peripheral vision danced with dark horrors that she would not confront head-on.

"I was just a little girl, like every other little girl. I had dreams and hopes. I wanted to be pretty. And to be loved."

But it never happened for Maggie.

"I was scared. Fear." She whispered the word. It was

too powerful to say out loud. "Fear is a belt strap and a beating."

She could still hear the snap as the leather strip tore at her flesh.

"Fear comes when you wake up every morning and a woman who claims to be your foster ma tells you that you're nothing but a worthless pig and a liar. I never told lies. Never!"

But she'd been accused and condemned because there was no one to defend her.

"Fear is knowing you're going to be hit because you got your socks dirty. Fear is being handcuffed in your bed at night because you ran away. Oh, yes, I can tell you all about being scared. Fear is when the man who is supposed to be your foster pa shoves you up against the kitchen cabinets and breathes in your face with his whiskey breath, then tells you that he'll come to you at night, after it's dark and the house is silent. And nobody can save you. Nobody."

Travis had pulled the car over to the curb. She felt his hand on her shoulder and she shrugged it off. "Keep driving, Travis. That's all I've got to say."

"I'm sorry, Maggie."

"Don't be. It's over and I learned from it." She could have buckled under the duress of her early life, could have turned to drugs, could have snagged a husband or a sugar daddy, could have committed suicide. Instead, she got strong. "I'm a survivor, Travis. I'm going to make it."

"Let me help."

When she turned her head and faced him, the anger was gone from his eyes. There was an aching gentleness that she wanted to accept. "Let's go home, Travis."

He started the low, purring engine and drove for a way in silence. She could feel her fears begin to settle, like dust after a tornado. It should have felt good to finally tell someone about the secret terrors that sometimes grew so fierce that they shook her awake in the night, but right now she only felt drained.

Travis cleared his throat. "Did you find out anything this afternoon when you talked to Pete?"

"Nothing much." She laced her fingers together on her lap. It was time to return to the present.

"Why did you want to see him today?"

"I was thinking about him."

She didn't want to tell him about the possible link between Pete and Ezra Dean. Travis was, after all, an officer of the court. Whatever she told him, he was obliged to report. And she had a very bad feeling about TotalCom and the investors.

Instead, she focused on the assault. "Somebody beat him up, Travis. He wouldn't tell me who, claimed he fell down. But we're looking at police brutality."

"Why do you think a cop beat him?"

"Either they did it, or they stood by watching while it happened. This was a thorough job—he had bruises all over. It took some time."

"Is Pete willing to press charges?" Travis asked. "Because I would love to have a good reason to get right in Chief Monk's face and force him to clean up his department."

"Pete's not tough enough to make a stir. They told him to keep quiet, and that's exactly what he's going to do."

"It's a good thing he has someone like you to fight his battles for him."

Maggie had always taken that role. In the foster homes, even when she wasn't the oldest, she somehow became designated protector of the other kids. "I don't mind taking care of other people," she said. "That's why I want to become a lawyer."

"To protect the rights of others," he said. "That's noble of you, Maggie. I wish, with all my heart, that lawyers could pin their aspirations to that lofty star, to run every case as if it were a search for justice."

"But it doesn't work that way?"

"You've seen me in action for the past couple of days. I'm wallowing in the mud, not reaching for the stars."

Travis opened the gates to his home with the remote control. It was the first time they had approached his house before dark, and Maggie marveled at the sultry charm of this place. What would it be like to live here? To sit on the porch swing at dusk and share a cup of espresso would be so genteel. So very elegant.

She left the car and stepped up on the veranda, where she waited for Travis to unlock the front door. "Are you still planning to stash me away in the attic like crazy Aunt Ida?"

"Not unless it's okay with you." He unfastened the lock and held the door for her. "Don't get settled down because we're going to have to leave in a couple of hours. I'm meeting with Sharon and Dave to talk over the strategy for their meeting with Sandor Rossi. This could be a long night. I'm going to change into comfortable clothes."

"Me, too."

When he started up the stairs to his bedroom, she was right behind him. As they went through these mundane actions, there was an unspoken intimacy. *Clandestine intimacy*, she thought, because it was secret. Neither of them could admit to feeling close, even though they were, in effect, living together.

In her bedroom, Maggie hummed to herself as she strolled across the soft carpet. Her gaze flicked to the bed.

There was something out of place, something wrong. At first, her mind didn't register what her eyes had seen. A photograph lay on the pillow where she had rested her head.

In one instant, all her fears came true. He was after her. He was watching her. He knew where she was.

Her eyes glazed over as she stared at the snapshot she'd last seen in Pete Fontana's apartment. It was Maggie herself with her platinum hair. She was laughing in the picture, mocking the panic that now surged through her veins.

In the center of the photograph, right where her heart would be, there was a dagger.

She needed to call Travis, but the muscles in her throat had constricted. She could hardly breathe. As if the dagger were plunged into her own heart instead of scarring the surface of the snapshot, she felt an overwhelming wrenching in her chest. This must be what a voodoo curse was like.

She stumbled backward, catching herself on the edge of a rosewood table. It overturned, crashed to the floor.

Suddenly, Travis was in the room. She hadn't seen the door open, hadn't heard him approach. But he was here.

He reached for the dagger, and she cried out. "No! There might be fingerprints."

When he looked at her, it seemed that their eyes met for the first time. There was no distance between them. They shared the panic. She recognized the naked concern that she had discovered in Travis and in no other man. He was holding her arms, easing her into one of the velvet chairs.

Though she wanted to be strong, she was trembling, gasping, sweating. Oh, why couldn't she be serenely distressed, like a damsel in a novel? Maggie knew her jaw was shaking in a most unbecoming manner.

"He's been watching us, Travis. This photo came from Pete's apartment. He must have followed us there."

"And he followed us here," he said darkly. "You've got to pull yourself together, Maggie. We have to get out of this house. Now."

"Where will we go? What will we do?"

"Pack up. I need you to get moving, pronto."

She tried to obey, but her knees felt weak. Her hands were shaking so badly that when she held them before her eyes, her fingers were a blur. "I can't."

"You're tough, Maggie. You're the strongest woman I know. Don't fall apart on me now."

She knew he was right. The alternative to escaping from his house was to sit here and wait to be attacked. Gritting her teeth, Maggie plunged into motion. Clumsily, she threw her clothes back into their suitcase in a jumble and forced the zipper to close.

Travis returned to her side quickly. He had a suit bag of his own.

"How'd you pack so fast?"

"Scooped up a handful of hangers and zipped them in here." He had something else in his hand. It was a shoulder holster of black leather. He slipped into it.

"My God, Travis, are you packing a gun?"

"Afraid so. The guy who attacked you shot off the door lock in the stairwell. If we've got somebody with a gun coming after us, it makes sense for me to be armed and dangerous."

He picked up a black automatic pistol from the dresser where he'd laid it, snapped in a fresh clip of ammunition and fitted the gun into his holster.

"I should warn you that I'm a lousy marksman," he said. "I got this gun about six years ago when I was prosecuting somebody who swore revenge. The only time I've fired it is at the police range. About once a year, I go in and try to hit their targets.''

''I don't like guns,'' she said.

''Me, neither.'' He slipped into his suit jacket, covering the holster. The bulge near his left arm was barely noticeable.

At the front doorway, Travis cautioned her. ''He might be out there right now, waiting.''

''And watching.''

They scanned the bushes and the thick oak tree overhung with Spanish moss.

''Maybe we should wait until it's dark,'' she said.

''I'd rather take my chances now. If this guy has a rifle, it probably has a night scope. This way, I might be able to see him, to return his fire.''

This seemed so unreal. She looked up at him. ''Travis?''

''Yes?''

''If you're going to return fire, sugar, you might want to take the gun out of the holster.''

''Right.'' He blessed her with his magnificent smile. ''You're going to be okay, Maggie. We're going to be okay.''

With Maggie hauling their luggage and Travis leaping around with his gun as if he knew what he was doing, they made their way to his car. He fired up the motor, and they sped away from the house.

Maggie didn't see the slightest signal of an attack, which was, in some ways, more frightening than if they had been met with a barrage of bullets. This hit man, this psycho, was toying with them, letting them know that he could find them anywhere, anytime. He could track her down in the police station and reach her by telephone in the offices of the police chief himself. He'd known she used the stairwell to sneak out of Travis's offices. He'd been in Pete's apartment. He'd been in Travis's house, his pristine home.

The stalker was always there, unseen but watching.

In the car, Travis was following the most bizarre route she could ever imagine, winding down one street, then another, then cruising onto a stretch of main thoroughfare, then back through an alley. Finally, she asked, "Where are we going?"

"I'm shaking anyone who might be trying to follow us," he said, glancing in the rearview mirror. "Unless they're using half a dozen different cars, I think we're safe."

"What do we do now?"

"The best place to lose ourselves is in the crowd, with the tourists down in the French Quarter."

"We'll never get a room down there, Travis. Not during Carnival. The city is booked."

"I already have a place for us to stay. My family leases a small room in the Quarter so we always have a front row seat for the big parade on Fat Tuesday."

He switched lanes, veering dangerously across traffic. Travis wanted to leave his car as soon as possible. It was too easy to trace. There might even be some kind of tracking device hidden in the car.

"I don't understand," she said. "Your family rents a hotel room all year so you can watch the Fat Tuesday parade?"

"It's in use other times, too. But not right now. Nobody's there."

His mother and father had used the hotel room as their own private escape, especially during the hectic Mardi Gras season. When his father had died, three years ago, his mother gave the key to Travis, saying that she couldn't face the memories. The only times Travis had used the room were when there were workmen in his house and when he needed total privacy to work on a case. He had never been there with a woman. Not until tonight.

After more twisting and turning, he parked his BMW outside a shabby little house off St. Charles on Constance Street. "Welcome to my roots, Maggie. This is the Garden District, otherwise known as the Irish Channel. Everybody thinks of New Orleans as being mostly French, but hundreds of Irish immigrants settled here in the 1800s. They were dirt poor, lower than slaves."

"But the Shanahan family prospered."

"Yes, we did." Grabbing Maggie's hand, he pulled her to the door of the simple house where his great-great-grandfather once lived. Some years ago, Travis had arranged to sell this place to the elderly black woman who had rented here for years. She answered the door when he rang. As soon as she recognized him, she threw open the screen and wrapped Travis in a huge embrace.

"Hi, Marie." She was a large woman who worked in a bakery. He could barely enclose her in his arms. "How're you doing?"

"Just fine. It's so good to see you." She shook a finger in his face. "You haven't been to visit Marie in a long time."

"And now I come to ask a favor."

"You're in a rush. Always running, Travis. Aren't you going to introduce me to your lady?"

As they stepped into the house and Travis introduced the two women, he remembered Marie's penchant for voodoo. Wildly painted masks and drums hung from the walls. There were strange little charms scattered all over. The smell of incense mixed with the ever-present aroma of cooking.

"I have king cake," Marie said. "You sit down and have some with me. And chicory coffee."

"I was looking for voodoo," Maggie said excitedly. "I need some powerful good luck, Marie."

Knowingly, Marie nodded. She waddled to a bookshelf and removed the top from a carved wooden box. Reverently, she took out a long piece of green yarn with knots tied at irregular intervals. To Maggie, she said, "Hold out your hand. Palm up."

Marie looped the yarn over Maggie's wrist and tied a loose bow knot. All her actions had a mystery to them, and Travis remembered when he had been a boy and totally fascinated with this woman and her charms. She grabbed his hand and draped the string over his wrist. "There's your luck, Maggie. You stick with him. He'll keep you safe."

As she removed the yarn from Travis, she leaned close to him. "She be the one, young man."

Deftly, she plaited the yarn into a bracelet for Maggie and stepped back to regard her handiwork.

"Thank you," Maggie said. "I want to pay you. It's bad luck not to pay for voodoo."

When she dug into her huge purse, half the contents spilled onto the floor. "Now, look what I've done."

When Travis bent down to help her gather her belongings, he noticed a round, shiny object about the size of a button. From his work with the U.S. Marshals on wiretaps and surveillance, he knew enough to recognize a tracking device. This little button sent out a signal that allowed a follower to always know where they were. He must have planted the device when he attacked her in the stairwell. That was how the stalker had been able to keep watch on Maggie. She carried that damned purse with her everywhere.

He explained the device to Maggie and Marie. "Looks to me like our luck has changed already."

Maggie handed Marie a twenty dollar bill. "Thank you."

The big woman turned to him. "Now, what can I do for you, Travis? I see you crazy to get moving."

He held out his car keys. "Can you take care of my car for a few days?"

"Can I drive it?" Her eyes sparkled.

"Yes, ma'am. It's all insured."

"Ooh-la-la," said Marie. "This be a favor I like."

After accepting a king cake wreath, wrapped in foil, Travis and Maggie set out on foot, carrying their luggage. On St. Charles Street, he dropped the tracking device into a drainage ditch.

"Now where?" Maggie asked.

"We catch the trolley."

"The streetcar named Desire?"

"You might say that."

Maggie glanced down at the green yarn Marie had given her. "I like her, Travis."

"She's a good person." He wrapped his arm around her shoulder. "And so are you."

On the trolley, they rode into the French Quarter. Dusk had settled into evening, and the romantic glow of street lamps shone on the narrow cobblestone streets. Only Bourbon Street was flashing neon, and Travis took care to avoid the heavy crowds. There were enough revelers on the less popular walkways to make them inconspicuous, and he was able to keep a vigilant eye, scanning for suspicious characters. Without the tracking device, he figured they had some time before the stalker resorted to old-fashioned methods of finding them.

He felt safe when he directed her into a small hotel on

Royal. The second-floor room was gracious and airy with French doors that led onto an iron grillwork balcony.

"I love this," Maggie said. She went to the French doors and pushed them open a crack. From down the street, Maggie could hear sweet jazz. A saxophone and trumpet, accompanied by an easy backbeat, echoed the rhythm of her heart.

The lamp between the two double beds shone with a soft, golden light, softening Travis's features as she looked up at him. "I guess you need to leave," she said. "You have that meeting with Sharon Gold and Dave Dermott."

"The hell with the meeting. There's only one job I have tonight and that's keeping my star witness safe."

"Is that all I am to you? A witness? Oh, Travis, I could be so much more." Her hand flew to cover her mouth. She hadn't meant to say that—such comments could only lead to humiliation.

"Forget that," she said, "I don't know what came over me. It must be the atmosphere in this room, the soft light, the jazz music."

"The French Quarter weaves a romantic spell," he said. "I've lived in New Orleans all my life, and I'm still not immune. This is the real magic in this city. Not voodoo."

"But I like Marie's good luck. She tied me to you."

"I won't leave you, Maggie. I might not be the most skillful bodyguard in the world, but I am definitely the most trustworthy, considering the leaks with the police and the Marshals."

"I'm sure you're the best protector in the whole world."

"Why's that?"

"Because I've never felt so safe."

He peered deeply into her eyes. "You asked if you were nothing more than a witness to me."

As he paused, anticipation shot through her, wakening

her senses, sharpening her hearing and her sight. Travis was going to tell her how he felt about her. Finally. Finally, she would know if she had a chance with him.

"I don't have the right words," he said.

"It's all right." She bobbed her head, hiding her disappointment. He was going to tell her that he respected her and was very fond of her and all those other words that were meant to let her down easy. What had she expected? "You don't have to say anything. I understand."

"I don't think you do." Gently, he pulled her closer. Their bodies were almost touching. She could feel the heat of him, flowing toward her, mingling with her own warmth. And when she looked up at him, the glow in his eyes told her of a deep caring she dared not believe. Was it possible? Long buried doubts assailed her. Was it possible that this man would be different than all the others, that he could care for her?

In a fierce burst of energy, he crushed her against him. Maggie was so surprised that she didn't have time to object. His lips slanted across hers in a deep, passionate, primitive kiss.

Instinctively, she kissed him back. All the suppressed longing in her soul gave way. She leaned toward him, aching with need. Her ears rang with a throbbing desire that rose on the jazz riffs, the beat of the city.

When the kiss ended, she was breathless in his arms.

"That's how I think of you," he said gently.

"You break my heart, Travis."

"That's not my plan. I want to take care of you, to heal you. I want to be a part of you."

She glanced over at the two double beds. Would tonight be the occasion when she lost her virginity? She hadn't ever believed her maidenhood—practically spinsterhood at her age—was a sacred trust or anything like that, but this should be a special moment. With Travis, she knew this might be the best night of her life. A fulfillment.

Walking slowly, imagining her feet buoyed by white, fleecy clouds, she went to the nearest bed. Since she had spent most of her life avoiding sexual relationships with men, she wasn't sure of how to flirt in this way. Oh, sure, she was good with a wink and pose. But when it came to making love, she was...a virgin.

Perched on the edge of the bed, she removed her shoes. What was she supposed to do next? Her body felt tense. Her movements seemed jerky and disjointed.

Then Travis was beside her. Without the least bit of arrogant male condescension, he leaned her back against the pillows and stroked the hair from her eyes.

Her breathing accelerated. Was she going to be good at this? Would she please him? "Travis, I don't know—"

"Hush, darling. Let me take care of you."

With infinite gentleness, he massaged her feet, stroking the high arch and stretching her toes. "That feels so wonderful." She groaned. "Foot massage is heaven to a waitress."

"But you're not a waitress anymore."

Not today, anyway. Maybe tomorrow or next week she'd be back at work, serving tables and going to school on the side. But tonight, she felt like a princess.

Travis kissed her again, tasting her lips and exploring the soft, slick interior of her mouth with his tongue. Sheer delight spread through her in delicious waves. As he caressed her, her body rose to meet his hand.

He unbuttoned her blouse and spread the material aside. His light kisses rained over her naked skin, refreshing as dewdrops at dawn. When he unfastened her bra and his mouth nuzzled her breasts, she felt a fire light within her.

Soft moans of pleasure escaped her lips. She wanted him so desperately.

His teeth caught her nipple, and she yipped at the sudden pleasure and pain.

"I won't hurt you," he said. "I won't ever hurt you."

How many times had a man spoken those words to a woman? How many times had he lied? Maggie's past rose up within her, and the hard lessons she learned when she was young warned her to stop him. Stop him now!

"Don't make promises," she said.

"I'm not lying to you. Trust me."

"But you don't know me. You can't understand what might cause me pain." Frantically, she pushed him away. "I haven't gone my whole life without falling in love to give in right now."

Her gaze met his, expecting to see rage and frustration. Instead, he looked down upon her with sadness.

"It's okay," he said. "I'm here for you, Maggie. Whenever you're ready."

And when would that be? A lump of regret caught in her throat. Why had she stopped him?

Maggie climbed from the bed and stumbled to the bathroom to prepare for sleep. When she confronted her reflection in the mirror, she looked normal. A little flushed. Her blouse hung open and she clutched the material together. Had she been irreparably damaged by her past?

Tears spilled down her cheeks as she silently wept. She could face psychos and thugs more easily than she could face one man who cared for her. All the bruises and years of abuse would hurt far less than the unending pain of a broken heart.

Chapter Nine

Travis slept with his eyes half open, exercising vigilance as he watched the reflection of lights through the sheer curtains on the French windows and listened to the sound of Carnival, an unending party in the streets. They were safe here. No one but his mother and sisters knew of this hotel hideaway.

He drifted in and out of sleep, unsure if he were awake or dreaming, knowing that he had almost made love to Maggie Deere, a witness for the most important case he had ever tried.

Such an act wasn't grounds for disbarment, but it surely was questionable ethics. If Ezra Dean got her on the stand and asked about their relationship, her testimony would be compromised if she told the jury that she was literally in bed with the prosecuting attorney. What had he been thinking of? Since when were his brains in his trousers?

In the soft light of dawn, he studied the features of the woman in the bed next to his. In repose, her face was lovely, somehow more innocent than when she was awake and animated.

He had never known anyone who could get into hot water so deep and so fast. Maggie Deere was a name that was rapidly becoming synonymous with trouble in his mind, but he was endlessly glad that he knew her. Yesterday, she had trusted him with the darkest secrets of her past. Last night…

Their kiss told him a lot about her. Her sexuality was not far below the surface. She was yearning to make love. He could feel her passionate craving in the way she responded to his touch. And yet, when she kissed him, there was a tender clumsiness and exploration, as if she were making love for the first time. Was it possible that she really *was* a virgin?

Travis wanted to believe that she'd told him the truth when that admission slipped from her. He wanted to believe that she and Pete Fontana were not lovers but friends. Was it possible?

The evidence seemed heavily weighted to the contrary. When he'd met Maggie, she'd looked like a tough waitress, flaunting her remarkable bosom in snug sweaters and wearing enough makeup to make any man think she was advertising the fullness of her lips and inviting them to come close.

In the D.A.'s office, Travis saw a lot of women who had a history like Maggie's. They were the wives who had been beaten, the daughters who had been abused, the abandoned mothers who had too many children. They were the victims of the system, battered and bruised by the endless tragedies of their lives.

Maggie was like them but different. She wouldn't allow herself to be a victim. Over and over, she told him that she was going to make something of her life, and Travis believed her. He understood why she was afraid to be too close.

He should learn from her cautious fear. His desire for her was foolhardy and imprudent. Still, he wanted to be the man who introduced her to passion, gently teaching her the sweet pleasure of making love.

As he watched, her eyelids fluttered on the verge of wakening. The dawn of another day for Maggie meant another battle. He admired her strength and her fearless willingness to fight. But he was captivated by her vulnerability.

"'Morning, Travis," she murmured.

God, she was beautiful. "Did you sleep well?"

"Just fine, but I must be hungry because I was dreaming about food, a huge banquet, and I was starving. Can we order room service?"

"No room service in this hotel. We could eat Marie's king cake."

She pulled a face. "Too sweet."

"Or we could get into gear, head out and have a real breakfast. There's a lot to do today."

Lazily, she rolled onto her side and gazed across the carpeted chasm that separated their beds. "Like what?"

"First, we've got to hustle over to the courthouse so I can check in with Dave and Sharon before their meeting with Rossi. Then we've got to buy you a party dress."

"Why?"

"Because tonight is my mother's annual Carnival party, which is always on the first weekend after Twelfth Night. And I am required to attend. Which means that you're going with me."

"I am truly sorry, Travis, but fancy Carnival dresses are not in my present budget."

"I'm paying. You have to have a long skirt, you know. It's bad luck to wear a short dress."

"Is this a Crewe Ball?"

He shook his head. "It's at Mother's house, not at the Municipal Auditorium. Just a casual get-together for two or three hundred of Mother's nearest and dearest friends, insuring that she will be invited to the best parties and balls throughout the rest of the season. There's lots of food, enough to feed a couple of Third World countries if they could be convinced to exist on pâté and canapés. Women in jewels. Men in tuxedos. A dance band.''

"Why, it sounds purely fabulous," Maggie said.

"We'll see." He swung his legs out of bed, aware that he was only wearing his shorts, and headed for the bathroom. Behind him, Maggie giggled, and he turned. "What's so funny?"

"You are elegant to the core, Travis. Even your underwear is silk with a monogram."

"I like to have soft material next to my skin."

Maggie heard herself purring as she studied the handsome man who stood before her. His body was perfectly proportioned, wide at the shoulders and tapering down a strong, lean torso to narrow hips. He was endlessly handsome and well-groomed—even the hair on his chest seemed combed. When he went into the bathroom and closed the door, she had a glimpse of his backside, which was nearly as sexy as the front view.

Maggie fell back on the pillows. Why had she said no to Travis last night? Making love with this wonderful man who had dedicated himself to protecting her would be a moment she could cherish forever.

But it wouldn't last, she reminded herself. There couldn't possibly be a relationship between them. Not while he was a wealthy prosecuting attorney and she was a witness who was destined to go back into the protection program and disappear forever.

It was safer to keep her distance, to close off her heart and run a fence of barbed wire all around it. If she got too involved with Travis, she'd start expecting things, and that could only lead to disappointment.

Trying not to bump into each other, they dressed and were out on the street in a matter of moments. The French Quarter in early morning seemed tawdry and exhausted, like the aftermath of a wild party when you need to open the windows and air out the stench of cigarettes and pick up the dirty glasses.

There weren't many commuters who lived in this part of town, so the streets were mostly deserted. Travis suggested that they head over toward Canal Street where there were big hotels and lots of cabs.

Maggie fell into step beside him. "If somebody's following us, I sure can't see them."

"I'm pretty certain that the stalker's surveillance was limited to that tracking device in your purse. By now, he must have figured out that he needs to follow us in person."

With a shudder, Maggie shoved that thought right out of her head. Instead, she resolved to enjoy the morning. She always liked this time of day when everything was fresh and new. It was a time for hoping, and she was pleased that today's weather was temperate, almost warm.

After catching a cab, they arrived at the D.A.'s offices at eight o'clock. As soon as they got off the elevator at the third floor, Sharon Gold poked her head out of her office. "Travis, I need some backup. Dave has this wrong, all wrong."

With a barely audible groan, he went into her office with Maggie at his heels.

"Sorry that I didn't make our meeting last night," Travis said. "Something came up."

Sharon couldn't have cared less. "Dave has the wrong idea about how the questioning should proceed. He wants to concentrate on the logistics of the alleged frame on Ben DeCarlo. I told him that what we want is names.''

"You want both," Travis said. He glanced over at Maggie. "You shouldn't be listening to this."

"I'll close my ears."

Sharon continued, "We already have this improbable scenario about several people setting Ben up for the murder of his parents. That's in his blanked-out testimony. We need to know who did it. Then we can call them as witnesses." She added, "And Dave thinks that at least one of us should wear a wire so we have a record of this poor excuse for a deposition."

"No wire," Travis said firmly. "That was one of Ezra Dean's conditions. No recording equipment of any kind."

Apparently pleased with herself, Sharon grinned. "That's what I told him."

"Don't be too hard on Dave. He's still learning."

"It's not my job to teach baby lawyers. It's my job to convict."

Maggie didn't like Sharon's attitude. "Maybe I'm being naive here, but I thought it was your job to discover the truth."

"Very naive," Sharon said. "By the way, Maggie, I heard you went back over to the prison yesterday to talk with your buddy, Pete Fontana. Is there new evidence you need to share with me?"

"No," Maggie lied. She wouldn't betray Pete to this lady piranha. "But I was most disturbed to find that he'd been beaten. I'd call it police brutality."

"Damn." Sharon scowled fiercely. "Travis, you've got to do something about Royce Monk and his gang of Keystone Kops. Pete Fontana is an open-and-shut case, a sure win for me. If they mess it up by interfering—"

"Hold it!" Maggie said. "You're missing the point. An unarmed, helpless prisoner has been violated."

"Right. And juries are sympathetic to things like that. I could lose the case."

Maggie gritted her back teeth. This wasn't about winning and losing. Justice wasn't a game. Sharon's attitude didn't set well with her, but before she could object, Travis was leading her out the door. "What time is the meeting with Rossi?"

"Four o'clock at some cheesy little restaurant." Sharon sneered at Maggie. "You probably know the place."

Steaming, Maggie followed Travis to his office. Dave Dermott was waiting inside. The strain of doing jury selection and of working with Sharon Gold was beginning to show on the redheaded laywer. There were dark circles under his eyes. This morning, he looked less like Huck Finn and more like someone had slipped him a Mickey Finn.

"I can't work with her," Dave said.

"Amen to that." Maggie took the chair next to him.

"Both of you stop it," Travis said. "Sharon might be abrasive, but she's a good attorney."

"She wants to push Rossi to get names," Dave said. "I can tell you right now that he's not going to give us squat. Travis, do you think we could wear a wire?"

"No." Travis was curt but not unkind. "I've dumped a lot on your plate, Dave. Do you need more help? Is there anything Janine can do?"

"When I found out about the interview with Rossi today, I pretty much dumped the rest of the jury selection stuff on her. Should I get her in here?"

"Please do. And Dave, I think you and Sharon will work well together. Let her be the aggressor, then you come in behind with encouragement. Rossi might open up to you."

"Fat chance. Even if he starts to, Ezra Dean is going to be with him to put a cap on anything useful he might say."

Maggie was banished to the lunchroom when Dave brought Janine into the office to study the profiles of potential jurors and come up with a final panel they could live with.

Instead of sneaking around and listening, Maggie used the time to ponder. A good attorney, like Sharon Gold, didn't seem too concerned about finding out the whole truth. And that was bothersome.

At the same time, Maggie's own attitude about Pete Fontana was much the same way. She'd discovered a connection between Pete and Ezra Dean in the TotalCom investment, but she hadn't told Travis. She was protecting Pete. From the whole truth?

When Travis came into the lunchroom, she quietly said, "Let's go into your office. I've got something to tell you about Pete."

In his office, she dug the computer runoff from her purse and placed the pages on the desk in front of him. "This is a listing of investors in TotalCom, which was a very lucrative project for Pete. And for Kyle. The payout from this investment is why Kyle returned to New Orleans."

"And?"

"Glance down that list, Travis. You'll find a familiar name. Ezra Dean Slaughter. He appears to be the majority stockholder in TotalCom."

Travis grasped the implication immediately. "The timing of the payoff might have been engineered by Ezra Dean so he would know exactly when Kyle would be in town."

It pained Maggie to confirm that Pete might have had a

part in setting up the murder of his friend, but she nodded. "Ezra Dean could have dropped a word to the right people, friends of DeCarlo."

Travis was scanning the list. "I'll be damned. Look who else is on here. Charles Weston."

Maggie didn't recognize the name. "Who?"

"It's the witness protection name for Gord Hoskins." He looked up at her. "Remember how Bascombe said there was something worrisome about Hoskins?"

"I can't believe it. He was a regular customer at Augustine's. I thought it was real brave of him to come forward because it meant giving up his career as an accountant."

"An accountant who invested in TotalCom."

"Might be just a coincidence," she said. But Maggie had the feeling that the TotalCom list had peeled back the lid on a can of worms, and something ugly was about to crawl out.

TRAVIS HOPED THERE WOULD be nothing ugly about that evening.

The rest of Friday had gone well. First and foremost, there had been no further threats to Maggie, who was, for a change, being cooperative and seemingly content to sit in an office on the third floor reading her novel. In Judge Howell's courtroom, the jury selection was complete, and the trial was scheduled to begin after the weekend. Sharon and Dave had not dismembered each other before they set out for their meeting with Rossi.

As soon as Travis concluded a confidence-boosting conference with Janine, he leaned back in the chair behind his desk to contemplate the strategy for the DeCarlo trial. But a vision of Maggie popped into his mind. The real Maggie was next door, chatting with Roy. His fantasy Maggie was a memory of smooth, tanned skin and silken hair. Damn, she was pretty. Thinking about last night aroused him. And tonight? Would they sleep in separate beds? Travis didn't know where he was going to find the willpower to resist his natural urges.

He shoved away from the desk and went to fetch her.

Maggie was waiting. She'd arranged to retrieve Junior from the impounding lot and her little car was right outside.

"Why?" he asked.

"Because we're shopping, Travis. I need a car."

"We should take cabs. What if we're followed?"

Her lips slid into a grin. "You've never seen me drive, sugar. Junior might only be a Toyota, but he's fast."

As if to prove her point, she raced to a boutique. Travis settled down to wait, but Maggie was decisive. True to her nature, she picked out the floor-length dress with the most sparkle and left wearing it, yanking off the tags as they went out the door. "Now shoes," she said.

Selecting a pair of high-heeled pumps only took a moment.

Back in his car, they debated about whether they dared to return to Travis's home so he could pick up his tuxedo, then decided against it. His mother would have to be satisfied with a plain, dark suit. He did, however, visit the dry cleaner and grab a clean shirt.

It was just past seven o'clock when he directed her to the circular drive outside his mother's palatial residence. Maggie stared through the windshield. Tall white columns graced the front of this elegant, antebellum mansion. "I'd say the Irish Shanahans have done real well for themselves. Looks like Scarlett O'Hara should be living here."

"That's Mother's secret identity. She's originally from Atlanta and still holds a grudge against General Sherman."

After convincing her that it was all right to turn her car keys over to the uniformed valet, Travis took Maggie's arm and escorted her into his mother's home.

The glittery decorations, he thought, were excessive. There was too much dazzle in the chandelier and too much gleam from the dozens of mirrors that marked the path to the ballroom at the rear of the house. The shimmer seemed false to him—as if by glistening and gleaming his mother could hide the lack of real happiness in this house.

His father had died three years ago, only a month before this annual party, and he had resented Mother's decision to go ahead with the event, pretending that life went on and they would all flourish, despite sorrow and grief. Without his father, the Shanahan Carnival party had lost much of its meaning. In his day people had referred to this event as the Power Ball, where important men and women met in fancy dress to wheel and deal.

His father, a prominent attorney, had always taken this occasion to encourage Travis toward a career in politics. *Maybe someday, son, you'll be governor of Louisiana.* But Travis didn't want to be governor, didn't even want to be District Attorney. Travis was happy in the courtroom.

"It's beautiful," Maggie said.

"I can't believe it. Mother set up a fountain in the middle of the ballroom."

Cascades of crystalline water shot from the mouths of dolphins and splashed into a huge, marblelike basin. The trickle of water underlined the soft jazz played by a tuxedo-clad pianist at a white-and-gold baby grand.

Travis gestured toward long tables draped in white linen, where the catered buffet had been spread. "Let's hit the snack bar."

"Seems a shame that people aren't using this floor for dancing," she said.

"That comes later." Right now, there were only fifty or so people milling around the ballroom. "Later on, there will be hundreds of people and a dance band. They start at precisely eight-thirty."

With any luck, he thought, he would have fulfilled his social obligation and could be gone by then.

"Brace yourself," Travis said. "Here comes Mother."

Jenny Lynn Shanahan was a delicate, petite woman in her late sixties. Her white hair was arranged in a towering mountain of curls atop her head. For the past three years, she'd worn the same brilliant green silk dress to this party because it complemented the emerald-and-diamond necklace her husband had planned to give her on the Christmas morning two weeks after he passed away.

The timing was ironic, Travis thought. His father had died from a heart attack within a few days of the date when Ben DeCarlo had murdered his parents. Possibly, Travis's hatred for Ben DeCarlo came, in part, from his own grieving.

"Mother," Travis said, "I'd like for you to meet—"

"I know this girl. It's Maggie Deere. She was a witness at the DeCarlo trial." Jenny Lynn extended her gloved hand. "I love your new style. Black hair is pretty. And you're so slim!"

"Thank you, ma'am. And I must tell you that this is the most elegant home I've ever been inside as a guest."

"And how else would you be inside, if not as a guest?"

"I used to work for a caterer in Birmingham," Maggie said. "And I went to a lot of grand events. I loved those at-home weddings with the striped tents set up on the lawn."

"I adore a good wedding." Jenny Lynn cast a baleful eye on her son. "Someday I'm hoping Travis will participate in such an event as the groom. I have two other children, both girls, and they're married.''

"One of them has been married twice," Travis interjected. "Or is it three times?"

"Now, Travis, you know I don't gossip about family."

"You don't?" As far as he knew, scandal was his mother's primary hobby. Sometimes, she knew things about him *before* they happened.

"Which reminds me," Jenny Lynn said brightly, "I happened to hear that you've undertaken a special sort of protection for this witness. Is that right, Maggie?"

"I'm not sure what you mean."

"What she's asking," Travis explained, "is if we're sleeping together. The answer is no, Mother. And where did you hear this rumor?"

"Well, that nice girl from your office—Sharon Gold— is already here. Right over there, by the bar."

"Thanks, Mother." Travis bent and kissed her forehead. "I hope the party goes well."

For an instant, her socializing smile fell away. She met his gaze. "Every year, it gets more difficult, Travis."

Her candor surprised him, as did the hurt he saw behind her brilliant smile. "Mama, are you okay?"

"I miss your Daddy so much. People tell me it's supposed to get easier, but there's an ache inside that will not go away."

"Next week," he promised, "no matter what else is going on, you and I are going out for dinner."

"Next week," she informed him, "I intend to be at the trial every single day, making sure you do a good job. Your father would want me to be there, cheering you on."

"It's not a high school football game, Mother." He fondly patted her cheek. "But I appreciate your support."

As Jenny Lynn swept across the ballroom floor to greet

her arriving guests, Travis guided Maggie to the long, mirrored bar where Sharon Gold stood with a highball glass clenched in her fist. Though she was wore a togalike gown of soft pink, Travis thought she looked hard enough to chew nails. Still, he said, "You look very lovely this evening, Sharon."

"How gentlemanly of you to notice."

Travis cut directly to the matter that was at the forefront of both their minds. "How did the interview with Rossi go?"

"With Ezra Dean instructing, Rossi gave us practically nothing. He claimed to be terrified of revealing names of the people who supposedly engineered this frame, and he referred to them by nickname. The main instigator was called—ridiculously enough—The Nose."

"It's something," Travis said. "The Nose? Maybe Chief Monk has some idea who that applies to."

"He also mentioned a bunch of other silly epithets. It sounded like a conspiracy of the Seven Dwarfs." She tossed back her drink. "Sorry, Travis. I don't have a single person to call as a prosecution witness. Except for Dominick DeCarlo, Ben's uncle who took over the family business after his brother was murdered, and you already had planned to get him on the stand."

"Dominick is guilty of something," Travis said. "Did Rossi say anything about him?"

"Dominick, according to Rossi, who isn't exactly a paragon of truthfulness, was devastated by his brother's death, even though Antonio had been trying to clean up his act so his son could get elected to the Senate. And the cleanup was cutting profits."

"So Dominick—despite being distraught—had a motive for wanting his brother dead."

"Big deal, Travis. There's no lack of people with motives for killing Antonio DeCarlo."

"But why would they kill his wife?" Maggie asked. "She seemed like such a sweet woman, and it wasn't like they had to kill her because she was a witness to the crime."

Travis turned to stare at her. "You're not supposed to be listening to this."

"Cocktail chitchat?" She rolled her eyes. "Sugar, you haven't said anything I didn't already know. Except that there's somebody called The Nose who wanted to kill Mr. and Mrs. DeCarlo, and that's pure hogwash."

"I don't agree" said a voice from behind them.

Both Travis and Maggie turned at the same time, coming face-to-face with Farris Quinn, the reporter for the *Times-Picayune*.

"Hi, sugar," Maggie said with smile.

"I didn't expect to see you here," Travis said coolly.

"Nor did I." Sharon Gold backed him with a cold front of her own.

Ferris ignored their obvious enmity and spoke to Maggie. "In my opinion, there was somebody else behind these murders. We're ultimately going to learn that Ben DeCarlo is innocent."

"Oh, please! I saw him do it with my own two eyes." Maggie wasn't quite sure how to take Quinn's prediction. She respected him and thought he was a savvy reporter, but his idea that Ben DeCarlo was innocent was bunk. "Ben is guilty."

"Maybe not."

"When you have proof," Travis said, "I trust that you will see fit to inform my office before taking off on a wild-goose chase, like the one with Brentley Gleason and the rogue cops."

Quinn turned back to Maggie. "I understand that you're friends with Pete Fontana. Maybe we could schedule an interview about his case."

"Not a chance," Travis interrupted. "Not until after the trial."

"I wasn't aware that you could enforce a gag order on witnesses. Isn't that the job of the judge?"

Maggie sensed the conversation heating up, and she wished to defuse it. "Isn't this the most amazing thing? I see someone else I know. Won't you excuse me?"

She beat a retreat in the general direction of Janine Carlson, who looked very pretty and very nervous at the edges of her smile.

"How are you doing, Maggie?" Janine asked.

"Can't complain." She amended, "Well, maybe I can, but it would be unworthy. And yourself?"

"I'm overwhelmed. I probably shouldn't have come here, but everybody says it's important to be seen and to mingle if you want your career to take off."

"Good luck," Maggie said.

She'd spotted another familiar face among the people who had begun to fill the ballroom. It was Francine Bentley, of all people, and she was leaning against the bar as if she'd had too much of her fancy Château Louis Noir to drink.

Maggie sidled up beside her. "How nice to see you again, Francine."

It took Francine's eyes a moment to focus, then another few seconds before she recognized Maggie. "You're Emmet's friend."

"Yes. It must be hard for you, coming to these parties. I know your fiancé, Kyle, would have loved this evening."

"He would have adored it. He was so handsome in his

tuxedo. All the other ladies envied me." She raised the glass to her lips. "It's a lovely night. Romance in the air."

"Kyle was a romantic man, wasn't he?" Maggie was a bit ashamed of herself for prodding when the lady was inebriated. On the other hand, Francine might slip with some important information. "Tell me about your courtship."

"I particularly remember one night, a soft summer night, with the warm breeze swirling around us. Emmet and I were drinking my favorite wine—"

"Château Louis Noir."

She sighed. "Perhaps were both a teensy-weensy bit drunk. Not falling down drunk, but tipsy. And we made love until dawn."

Like her other story, this had the ring of fantasy, but Maggie chose to ignore it. "You mentioned all the other ladies. Did the two of you spend much time with friends?"

"Oh, no. He preferred being alone with me."

A deep voice resounded in Maggie's ear. "Ms. Deere. We meet again."

She didn't even have to turn around to know that the speaker was Ezra Dean Slaughter. Maggie introduced him to Francine.

"I already know Ezra Dean." Francine giggled and gushed in a manner totally unsuitable for a lady of her years.

Attempting to escape from the defense attorney, Maggie pretended to see someone else across the room. "Excuse me."

"And me," said Ezra Dean as he took her arm.

"I don't want to be rude," Maggie said, gazing up at him. "But if you touch me again, I will scream like a banshee."

"Oh, but Ms. Deere, you are no stranger to the admiring caresses of men."

"What are you saying?"

"Your reputation, Maggie, is about to catch up with you."

If he was trying to get a rise out of her, he had succeeded. "Sir, I take offense at your suggestion."

"Be offended all you want. Nobody is going to believe you."

"I wasn't aware that I was on trial."

"But you are." He displayed his even white teeth in an expression that was far too vicious to be described as a smile. "In the last trial, I made the mistake of not challenging the credibility of the witnesses. There were too many of you, and a couple were unassailable. But you, Maggie, are eminently vulnerable to a character assault."

Maggie's blood pounded in her veins. What was he talking about?

"You might think that you're safe, now that you don't look like a cheap slut. But I will use that to my advantage, showing how you are hiding your real self. The liar. The cheat. The girl who constantly ran away from home."

"It doesn't matter what you say about me," she shot back. "I know what I saw."

"What matters is how the jury perceives you after I call a few character witnesses."

"Who?"

"You'll see." His laughter was pure evil. "When I'm done with you on the witness stand, nobody will believe a single word you say."

Chapter Ten

As she had done before, so many times in the past, Maggie lifted her chin, stiffened her spine and walked away. She left Ezra Dean Slaughter standing there, mired in his own cruel accusations. His lying words stung like nettles, but they wouldn't kill her. She'd been called much worse and still survived.

The dance band had just set up when she found Travis, who was chatting with a group of fine Southern gentlemen. Though most of them looked real spiffy in their tuxedos, none could compare with Travis. When he caught her eye and flashed one of those patented killer grins, her anger about Ezra Dean faded as quick as a jackrabbit hightailing it into the woods.

She wouldn't let Ezra Dean ruin this party for her. There hadn't been many beautiful occasions in her life, and she intended to enjoy herself.

On the small stage, the leader of the dance band combo stepped up to the microphone. "Ladies and gentlemen, I have been asked to welcome you on behalf of the Shanahan family, most especially, Mrs. Jenny Lynn Shanahan."

He gestured in her direction, and heads turned. There was a polite round of applause, and Maggie wondered how many of these fine folks actually knew Travis's mother.

How many were here because this was the smartest place to be seen on the first weekend after Twelfth Night?

The bandleader continued, "Our first song for the evening is a slow one, but we take requests, ranging from tangos to rock 'n' roll. And now, maybe we can ask Mr. and Mrs. Shanahan to start off our evening of dancing with 'Embraceable You.'"

There was a moment of confusion because, of course, Jenny Lynn was a widow and unpartnered. Maggie saw an expression of distress on the lady's face as she waved to the crowd. "Everyone, please—"

Travis stood before her. He bowed from the waist. "Mother, may I have this dance?"

When that delicate silver-haired lady stepped into the arms of her handsome son, Maggie swelled with pride. Travis was the boy that every mother hoped to have. He was gallant, sensitive and affectionate. His behavior reflected his good upbringing, and Maggie noticed that he wasn't a half-bad dancer, either.

When the song ended, he kissed his mother's hand and led her to another gentleman. Then he came toward Maggie.

"Care to dance?" he asked.

"I'd like that a lot."

The band was playing "Young at Heart," and when he clasped her lightly in his embrace, Maggie felt like fairy tales sometimes did come true. His touch was gentle but firm, and he directed her movements with a subtle strength.

His hand tightened at her waist. "Let's try a dip."

She followed his lead and arched back, feeling graceful as a swan. They moved as if they were made to be together. But when the band swung into a medley from the sixties, Travis guided her away from the floor. "I never learned to twist," he admitted.

"Me, neither." When she looked up at him, she felt like the room was shimmering with magical light. The water from the fountain splashed in refreshing sparkles. And the lovely long dresses of the ladies swirled in a brilliant montage.

"I saw you talking with Ezra Dean."

Crash! Her aura of pleasure splintered and exploded around her. No matter how much she wanted to pretend, Maggie wasn't Cinderella at the ball. This glamour was make-believe. She needed to watch out or she'd turn into a pathetic fantasizer like Francine.

"What's the matter?" Travis asked.

"Ezra Dean gave me a little preview of his trial strategy. It seems that his focus is going to be attacking the character of the witnesses, and he promised to find people who would testify that I'm a liar and a cheat."

"Bastard," Travis muttered. "I'm sorry, Maggie. If this is too painful for you, I won't force you to take the stand."

"I don't turn tail and run. Not from a bully like Ezra Dean. He got my dander up, Travis. There's nothing that would keep me from testifying at that trial."

"Don't underestimate him," Travis warned.

"How could I under-evaluate the belly of a snake?"

He leaned down and dropped a light kiss on her forehead. "You've got real courage."

"Don't make me into Joan of Arc," she warned. "You might be disappointed."

"In you? Never."

For the next several hours, they danced and ate and enjoyed themselves. Though Maggie never lost track of the fact that this elegant life-style was not her birthright, she was much too happy to feel embarrassed or out of place.

Not even when Travis's much-married sister hinted that Maggie might be interested in Travis for his money.

Not even when Police Chief Royce Monk snubbed her until she pinched his arm and whispered in his ear, "Would you call this civilian brutality to a police officer?"

Laughing, he'd acknowledged her, and Maggie decided he wasn't such a bad guy, after all. If she ever visited the police station again, she'd remember to bring him doughnuts.

She hadn't even felt bad when Sharon Gold brought her over to a group of men and women who were all attorneys, politicians, doctors and engineers. Apparently, they were having a discussion on the merits of raising the minimum wage.

Sharon prodded her into the fray by saying, "Maggie might have an especially pertinent opinion."

One of the women asked, "And what do you do, Maggie?"

She could have opted out and said she was a student, but she wasn't ashamed. "I'm a waitress. And believe me, sugar, the minimum wage needs to be higher."

Within a few minutes, she was expressing her opinion, using almost all her vocabulary words. And, amazingly, people were polite enough to listen.

What a night this had been! She felt beautiful and smart. If only this could go on forever.

Police Chief Royce Monk stepped up in front of her and asked for a dance.

"I'd be purely delighted."

Being clasped against the potbelly of the police chief was nothing like dancing with Travis, but at least he didn't step on her toes. "I need to talk to your partner in crime, Maggie."

"You mean Travis?"

"Help me get him alone for a minute, would you?"

She glanced over toward the buffet table where Travis

stood beside his mother, chatting to a couple of men she recognized as senators, then she looked back at Royce Monk. "Why, Chief Monk, I thought you asked me to dance because you were taken with my ladylike charms. And all you wanted was to get Travis."

"Well, I am, you know, taken by your charms and all, but—"

"Let's go, sugar."

Maggie waited for her opportunity, then pulled Travis away from the group. As they strolled side by side, she noticed the beginning of fatigue in his smile. The finely etched lines around his eyes had deepened. But when she told him that Royce Monk wanted to meet him on the veranda, Travis was alert. "Why?"

She shrugged. "Don't know."

"I'll find him. You wait in here, Maggie."

Like heck she would. This time, it was easy to find a place for eavesdropping in the shrubberies beside the gracious flagstone veranda that looked out on a wide expanse of perfect green lawn and a gazebo.

Royce Monk was smoking a cigar when Travis stepped up beside him.

"We've got a little problem, Travis."

Maggie could see both of their faces if she craned her neck, and the two men made quite a contrast. Travis was an aristocrat, through and through. The police chief looked like a bulldog who'd just lost his favorite bone.

"Is this about the DeCarlo case?" Travis asked.

"Hell's fire, Travis. That's all anybody can talk about. Is it true you've already got a jury and will start on Monday?"

"Looks that way," Travis said.

"Judge Howell is running this thing like the Indy 500."

"That's just fine with me. I can't wait to see Ben

DeCarlo locked up for good." Travis pressed onward with business. "So, what's the problem? Anything wrong with your forensics?"

Royce took a drag on his pungent cigar before speaking. "I told you before and I'll tell you again, I can't promise the evidence wasn't tampered with. We had rogue cops and they had access."

"But how could they do it? The blood on DeCarlo's cashmere overcoat was a match with the victims'. It was distributed in a spatter consistent with the position that our witnesses said Ben had taken."

"Right. Plus there was powder residue from the gun."

"How could that be faked?"

"It couldn't be," Royce said disgustedly. "But, as you recall at the first trial, Ben DeCarlo claimed that it wasn't his coat."

"What about the blood in his car?"

"That could have been a setup," Royce admitted. "We had blood samples from the victims, and one of the bad cops could have planted all the other blood evidence we found."

Travis shrugged. "I guess it doesn't matter. I'm not basing my case on forensics, anyway. There's no need as long as I still have my witnesses."

"Just so you understand. I'm trying to be forthcoming."

"I appreciate that." Travis stared out across the lawns. "By the way, have you ever heard of anybody called The Nose?"

"Sure. Jimmy Durante. Or was he called the Schnoz? I'm dating myself here."

"I was thinking of someone a little closer to home," Travis said, and Maggie detected a hint of impatience in his voice. "Rossi said the alleged frame on DeCarlo was engineered by somebody he called The Nose. Got any ideas who that might be?''

"Not off the top of my head, but I'll ask around.''

"Okay, Royce. Now, what was the problem you wanted to talk to me about?''

"It's about Maggie.''

"Why am I not surprised?''

"I'm not sure that one of my boys wasn't responsible for that phone call and for the attack in your offices.'' He exhaled heavily, deflating. "Dammit, Travis, I wish I could swear to you that my department is clean, but I don't know. I've worked with some of these guys for years. I don't want to believe they're dirty. Like Kit Wells. I would have trusted that officer with my life, and he turned out to be a miserable, back-stabbing crud.''

"What makes you think a cop attacked Maggie?''

"Whoever jumped her in your office building was licensed to carry a concealed weapon. How else would they get past the metal detectors?''

"That could have been a cop, a bailiff, the FBI or the Marshals. Any of the federal law enforcement people.''

From where she was hiding, Maggie saw Travis unbutton his suit jacket to show the police his own shoulder holster.

"And me,'' Travis said. "There are a lot of people who don't go through the metal detectors. Familiar faces. The attorneys and the investigators who work for them.''

"That's true,'' Royce said.

"So, why would you think the attacker was a cop?''

"After Maggie came to my office, asking about Pete Fontana, I remembered something. A letter.''

Maggie almost betrayed her hiding place with a gasp of surprise. She'd written to Pete in jail and told him when she expected to arrive in New Orleans. She'd promised that her first order of business would be to bash down the door of the D.A.'s office and prove him innocent. But how would Royce Monk know about that?

"What letter?" Travis demanded.

"I seemed to recall that Maggie wrote to Pete and told him the date she was going to be in town. As you know, we routinely check mail to prisoners, especially if it might pertain to an ongoing murder investigation."

How dare they! Maggie was incensed. That was invasion of privacy, tampering with the U.S. Mail. But Travis seemed unperturbed. "Why would you recall this letter in particular?"

"She signed it Maggie Deere and I knew she was one of your protected witnesses. Anyway, I made a copy of the letter and stuck it in Pete Fontana's file before it was delivered to him."

"Well, damn," Travis said. "She announced the date of arrival. And you filed it. How secure are the files?"

"People are supposed to check the information in and out. But sometimes they don't. Plus, we've got a mob of nonpolice personnel, including your attorneys and the defendant's attorneys, poking around the station all the time."

"You're hedging, Royce. There's something you're not telling me," Travis concluded. "Did you check the file? Was the letter in there?"

Royce sucked on the butt of his cigar. "That's the problem, Travis. After Maggie left, I asked my secretary to fetch the Pete Fontana file."

"And?"

"It's missing. The whole file is gone."

"I was afraid you'd say something like that."

Another evidence of a leak, he thought. When would it

end? Where would it lead? He clapped Royce Monk on the shoulder. "Thanks, Chief. I appreciate your honesty."

"It wasn't easy. I hate that some of my cops are dirty. Hate it." Royce Monk turned and lumbered back toward the party. "Anything I can do to help with the trial, you let me know."

Stay the hell away from it, Travis wanted to say. "I'll let you know."

Whether by inefficiency or deliberate design, Travis could feel the loose ends of his carefully knitted case against Ben DeCarlo coming unraveled. The DeCarlo retrial was the only reason that someone would bother to steal the Pete Fontana case file from the police department.

Maggie slipped up beside him. "Hey, good-looking."

"Were you listening? Again?"

Shamelessly, she nodded. "That's right."

"Maggie, I can't begin to tell you how wrong that is. You are a witness. Everything you hear or see can become testimony."

"But this didn't have anything to do with DeCarlo," she said. "It was about my friend, Pete Fontana."

"Of course, this is about the retrial. Why else would anybody steal Pete's file from the police station?"

"The person who murdered Kyle Johnson might have reason to steal Pete's file," she said.

"Why? Pete's already in jail. The police aren't looking for any other suspects in Kyle's murder."

"They ought to be."

Ignoring her righteous indignation, he continued, "The DeCarlo retrial is why Pete's file was stolen. There must be a clue in the file that would tie Kyle's murder to DeCarlo."

"How about TotalCom? That's a link."

"And it's something I mean to deal with."

Travis had already decided that if Pete was aiding and abetting the scheme to bring Kyle Johnson to town, the D.A.'s office would work a deal. If Pete would testify against Ezra Dean, his charges would be lessened. Hell, Travis would drop charges and offer lifetime immunity for a chance to nail Ezra Dean Slaughter.

"This must be hard for you," she said. "You can't help thinking about the leak, wondering about the person who stole the file. It could have been an attorney. One of your own staff might have sold out. You've got the same problem as Chief Monk."

"Except—at the risk of sounding snobbish—it's even harder to pick out the bad apples in a barrel full of lawyers. They're smarter than cops. Usually."

"At least, they think they are."

"It feels like I can't trust anybody."

"Trust me."

Travis looked down at the woman who stood beside him. She was pretty as a picture. His developing relationship with her was the one good thing that had come from this whole sorry mess. "I can't believe I'm standing out here in the moonlight with you, talking about trials and murder."

"I don't mind," she said. "To tell the truth, I was getting a little bored with all the glitter. There are only so many canapés and flutes of champagne that one gal can handle."

"Then you don't mind if we leave now?"

"Not a bit."

As they strolled back inside, the Carnival party was fully under way with dancing, merriment and drinking. Though Travis tried to look upon this gala scene as a place of celebration and amusement, his view was colored with suspicion.

Someone had leaked information. Someone had stolen the Pete Fontana file. While Royce Monk feared it was a cop, Travis had to consider that it might be one of his staff. Someone on their team—an attorney, a paralegal, an investigator—might have contacted the man who attacked Maggie and informed him that she was there, in New Orleans, and vulnerable as a newborn colt.

He spotted Sharon Gold, dancing in the arms of Wiley Henderson. She wouldn't even have to steal the file. She had her own information on Pete Fontana. Could Sharon be the informant? She seemed utterly dedicated to her career advancement, but was she happy in the D.A.'s office? Was she planning to move on to greener, better-paying pastures?

Travis spotted Dave's flaming red hair in the crowd. And what about Dave Dermott? What could he have to gain by passing information to the bad guys? He was chatting with Janine, who seemed so sweet that she was above suspicion.

Nearby, he saw Ezra Dean. And Royce Monk.

Still at the bar, Francine Bentley gestured wildly with another drink. She was talking with Judge Leland Howell.

"Just like Mardi Gras," Travis said quietly.

"What do you mean?" Maggie asked.

"Everyone is wearing a mask. It's nearly impossible to guess what's really inside."

After they bid his mother good-night and picked up Maggie's Toyota from the parking valet, Travis shifted his mind to his most immediate problem—keeping Maggie safe for another night.

"I don't want to park your car near the hotel where we're staying," he said. "If they find your car, they'll know that we're nearby."

"Oh, Travis, do we have to play hide-and-seek?"

"Afraid so."

"Okay, I won't argue."

After such a lovely evening, it seemed impossible that there could be danger. Still, she followed his directions, driving to the hotel where they'd caught a cab that morning. When she'd parked in the lot, she pleaded, "Please, don't let's walk to the Quarter. Can we take another cab?"

"You bet." Travis stepped to the curb in front of the hotel and signaled to the next taxi in line waiting for fares.

Maggie caught a glimpse of movement from the corner of her eye and turned her head in the opposite direction, away from the taxis. A dark sedan with tinted windows barreled down the street and swerved. The car was headed directly toward them.

"Travis, look out!"

He glanced in the direction she was pointing, then dove toward her, hurtling through the air, knocking her off her feet and throwing her almost against the side of the hotel.

The black sedan crashed along the sidewalk, missing them by inches.

Before she had time to react, they were on their feet and running. Maggie regretted her high-heeled shoes that made swiftness impossible. "Are they coming? Travis, are they coming after us?"

He pushed her into a recessed doorway. When she pivoted she saw Travis, standing in a crouch. His handgun was out and ready. He squeezed off one shot, then another and another.

Maggie covered her ears. Panic shot through her. Fear for Travis. If they shot him, it would be her fault, and she couldn't bear it. This had to stop. There had to be a way to end it.

Slowly, Travis lowered his gun. He tucked it back inside his holster.

"They're gone, Maggie. Let's get out of here." He linked his arm with hers and they walked briskly, rounded a corner, crossed the street and went down an alley.

Her breath came in gulps. The perfect shimmering world she'd found at the Carnival party was as ragged and frayed as an old sweatshirt. Only the fear remained.

Still walking, putting distance between themselves and the hotel, Travis cleared his throat. "I don't think we'll inform the police about this."

"We can't keep hiding," she said. "They were shooting at you."

"Actually, they weren't. I seemed to be the only one with a gun. As soon as I fired, they ran." He shrugged. "I kind of enjoyed it. Attorneys don't usually get to—"

"Are you crazy? This is serious, Travis. I don't want you to be hurt."

"Unfortunately, I don't think they were after me."

They were after her. Those men in the sedan were trying to kill her. She would have liked to pretend that car wrecks and bullets didn't scare her, but there was only so far that her imagination would stretch without springing back to reality.

She needed some good luck, some magic, something to protect her from fear. Pulling away from Travis, she entered a crowded café. They had reached the French Quarter in full Carnival celebration on a Friday night. The streets were hopping with tourists and resounding with jazz. But she didn't pay any attention to any of it. She stood inside the door to the café, digging in her huge purse, frantically searching.

"What are you doing, Maggie?"

"I need my good luck charm. I told you about it, remember? The charm that I got from the voodoo woman."

"Why?"

"I need some more magic, and I need it now." She fished deeper among her belongings. "Oh, Lord, I hope I haven't lost it."

"Maggie, we need to keep moving. These guys might be following us."

"Got it!"

She held up the plain, round rock. It was a half globe with a jagged edge and strange red-and-black scribbles on one side. Maggie wrapped her fingers around the *mojo*. She wasn't praying, but wishing. Wishing with all her might for protection and safety.

Travis took her hand and opened her fingers. His gaze filled with astonishment.

He reached into the inner pocket of his jacket, right above his shoulder holster and withdrew a rock. A plain, round rock with one serrated edge. When he fit the stone against hers, the edges matched precisely and the markings became a star and a waning moon.

FOR YEARS, THEY HAD EACH carried half of the charm. When it fit together, it was as if a destiny had finally been fulfilled. At least, that was what Maggie told herself when she and Travis collapsed together in the small hotel room with louvered French windows and two wicker frame beds.

She didn't worry about what was happening between them. Her only concern was the burst of excitement that he aroused in her so easily. His clever, skillful hands caressed every part of her body. His kisses drove her to the edge of ecstasy.

The awkwardness of last night was gone as Maggie allowed her natural instincts to direct her movements. Making love was like dancing in his arms, with Travis leading her to dip and twirl and arch.

When he poised above her, about to enter her most private, inner place, she clung to him. She was ready, more ready than she had ever been. He thrust into her, hard and swift, and she trembled uncontrollably around him. A cry escaped her lips, half pleasure and half pain.

Slowly, he moved, and she couldn't believe the unbearable tension that curled and tightened within her. The moment accelerated, and she felt like she was ascending in a magnificent spiral, rising higher and higher into the stratosphere where the air was thin and she could hardly breathe. Then she melted. Her very bones turned to mush. She was limp. Helpless. Unable to move.

Travis gently cradled her naked body beside him and held her until she felt like she had returned to mundane earth.

Her tongue licked her lips, moistening them. She must have been sweating because she could feel the perspiration drying on her skin. In a lazy, sultry voice, she said, "I don't know why I waited so long."

"You were waiting for me, Maggie Deere."

Maggie knew he was right. As she cuddled against him, she knew that Travis was her destiny. He was her other half.

THE NEXT MORNING was Saturday, and Maggie indulged herself by sleeping late. It was ten o'clock when she drifted awake and snuggled against the handsome man who lay beside her.

Her hand reached up to stroke the crisp hair on his chest. Instead, she encountered buttons. "Hey, you're dressed."

"But I brought coffee."

She inhaled the fragrance, took the foam cup in her hands and tasted. "Mmm. You're forgiven."

She gazed up at him, knowing that he was going to kiss

her and adoring the intimacy of that knowledge. When their lips met, it felt too good to be true. Soft and sexy.

"Now I'm a fulfilled woman. Shouldn't I be feeling more serene and wise? Like a goddess?"

"How do you feel, Maggie?"

"A little sore."

He laughed, and the sound crept into her ears and spread through her entire body, like a perfect song that strikes a chord in your soul. "I love to see your smile," she said.

"I feel the same about you, Maggie." He traced her lips. "Your mouth is so pretty."

"I'd better watch out," she said, "if I keep thinking like this, I'm going to turn into a romantic fool, like Ms. Francine Bentley."

"Did you talk to her at the party?"

"I did like you said, Travis. Tried to get her talking about her relationship with Kyle. And it was all walking in the moonlight and making love, always with her bottle of fancy wine."

"Purchased from DeCarlo's shop."

"Right." Reluctantly, she returned to the case. "Did I ever tell you about that list? Roy and I managed to pull up a copy of the Crescent Wine Cellar's mailing list, and there was Francine Bentley's name—big as day."

"Was Dave Dermott on the list?"

"Nope."

"Thank goodness."

She sipped her coffee, allowing the warm liquid to soothe her. It seemed like a lazy day, a time for pleasure. "Can we take the day off? Or is there no rest for the prosecution?"

"I need to go to the office," he said. "I want to prepare for the trial today because tomorrow morning, Gord Hoskins is being brought into town by the federal Marshals."

"Right." She just didn't seem to have any energy. "What about tonight?"

"We come back here, and I make mad, passionate love to you all night."

He took the cup from her hand and set it on the bedside table. Lightly, he kissed the tip of her nose, then her chin. He pushed down the sheets and the comforter to nuzzle her throat. Maggie felt her engine start running, like a finely tuned automobile. Then, Travis went lower. His tongue circled and teased at her taut nipple, kicking her motor into high gear.

Playfully, he stepped away from the bed. "Later."

"You don't think I can wait, do you?"

"I hope it's hard, real hard."

She drawled, "So do I."

As she dressed, Maggie figured that she had managed to restrain her carnal urges for years and years. One day should be a piece of cake. But it wasn't.

She couldn't think, couldn't concentrate. Her mind wandered into daydreams while she followed Travis to the office and sat around, content to be lazy and sultry. Her lips kept smiling for no reason. Every so often, she heard herself exhaling a purely satisfied sigh. She didn't even mind being excluded from the attorney's strategy sessions.

When Travis charged into the office, she was in the middle of the ten thousandth mental replay of the night before.

"Lunch," he announced. "Hungry?"

"Starved." But she wasn't talking about food.

There were three restaurants near the courthouse that were usually patronized by the legal staff—a fast-food joint, a fancy dining establishment and the Green Door.

Sharon, Dave, Janine, Travis and Maggie circled around a wooden table at the dimly lit Green Door where the menu was a single page and the cocktail list was as long as a novella.

"After reviewing your reports of the interview with Rossi," Travis said, glancing at Sharon and Dave, "it's safe to assume that we gained nothing."

"Here's something," Dave said, scowling below his red eyebrows. "Rossi presented himself pretty well. The guy seemed sincere and scared as hell about revealing too much."

"He's a good con man," Sharon concurred.

As they bounced perceptions back and forth, Maggie was drawn into their talk. And she found it perplexing. "If he's lying, what difference does it make if he looks like a saint?"

"In a jury trial," Sharon explained, "first impressions are almost more important than truth. If Rossi comes across as a penitent hoodlum who is fighting his demons and trying to go straight, a jury might believe him."

"That's why I want Janine to question him on the witness stand," Travis said. "Nobody does fawn-eyed sincerity better than our quiet little Janine."

"Why, thank you," she said, widening her huge brown eyes and quivering her little chin. She looked as innocent as a lamb when she said, "On the witness stand, I'll rip out Rossi's black heart."

Maggie chuckled. "Y'all are Academy Award-winning actors, aren't you."

She glanced around the table. If she'd been casting a movie about trial law, she couldn't have selected better players. Janine projected a sweetness that would touch the heart of the most hardened juror. Redheaded Dave was wholesome and believable as the kid next door. Maggie knew that Sharon, though caustic, could be a fierce prosecutor, capable of demolishing a witness on the stand. And what was Travis? He was too young to be a father figure, and too old to be boyish. From the first trial, she knew that he had a trial face that was serious, dogged, determined and, sometimes, passionate.

She sighed. *Passionate*.

"Drama," said Sharon, "can be the essence of trial law. We've all seen cases where the defendant was guilty but not convicted because the lawyer convinced the jury that the law-breaker was, as he claimed, innocent."

She glanced up at the waitress who was waiting to take their orders. "I'll have the chicken and almond salad. And to drink, I'd like a glass of wine. Château Louis Noir, if you have it."

Chapter Eleven

That wine, again! Travis exchanged a glance with Maggie. That damned Château Louis Noir. And Sharon had specifically asked for it. After the other orders had been taken, he turned to Sharon. "Is that a good wine?"

"Excellent. Full-bodied with a fine bouquet. We had it in the office the other day. Remember?"

He nodded. "You brought that bottle?"

"I thought we needed to upgrade our tastes."

"How generous!" Dave said sarcastically. "Gosh, Sharon, thanks for trying to educate our yokel palates."

"It would take more than one bottle."

"I had no idea that you were a connoisseur," Travis said.

"I'm not really. But I ran across this wine when I was investigating the first DeCarlo trial and I had to snoop around at the Crescent Wine Cellar. I am hooked on that place."

Dave snarled, "I can't believe that you would patronize a business belonging to Ben DeCarlo."

"Just because he's a murderer, it doesn't mean he's not an excellent judge of fine wine."

Travis experienced a real sense of relief. The coincidence of the Château Louis Noir preferred by Francine

Bentley and by a member of his staff was nothing more than that—a coincidence.

For the rest of the meal, they talked about inconsequential matters. Construction on the highway. The annoying influx of tourists for the Carnival season. The football playoffs and the upcoming Super Bowl.

When they returned to the office, Travis banned Maggie from a brief strategy meeting wherein they planned the first day of the DeCarlo trial. The plan was simple. Travis would present an opening statement, playing up the eyewitnesses to the crime. No matter what surprises Ezra Dean might pull from his legal bag of tricks, he could not get around the witnesses.

"What order for the witnesses?" Dave asked. "Who goes first?"

"We'll start with Maggie. Let's get her testimony under way on the first day so the jury leaves the courtroom with a clear picture of Ben DeCarlo killing his parents."

Dave nodded. "We'll time her so that we don't complete her testimony and Ezra Dean has no opportunity to cross-examine."

"I have a suggestion," Janine piped up. "I think Dave should handle Maggie on the stand."

Though the same thought had occurred to Travis, he was displeased that someone else mentioned it first. "Why?"

"Well, you and Maggie seem to have gotten kind of close, and there might be hints—right or wrong—of impropriety."

"Don't be ridiculous," Dave said. "Maggie's in the witness protection program. After this trial, she gets zipped away, and he'll never see her again. Travis isn't so dumb that he'd get involved when he knew—"

"Excuse me," Travis said. "I would prefer that we

don't discuss the level of my intelligence or lack thereof while I am sitting here listening."

"I apologize," Janine said. "I'm sure it's nothing. I know you wouldn't lead Maggie on just to dump her after the trial."

"I assure you, Janine, hurting Maggie is the furthest thought from my mind."

Yet, he knew that pain and regret might be the outcome of their time together. The witness protection program would stand between them like a bulwark. It wasn't safe for her in New Orleans. But this was his home.

He didn't want to think about what would happen when Maggie completed her testimony.

That night, when they were safe and alone in their secret room in the French Quarter, she brought it up. "I was wondering, Travis, how flexible is the witness protection program? Can I pick where they send me?"

"If you could, where would you go?"

"I'd like to stay close to New Orleans."

She stretched out on the bed, fully clothed. Her shining black hair spread carelessly across the white pillowcases. The tan of her complexion emphasized the sea blue of her eyes.

His gaze wandered lower, allowing himself the pleasure of undressing her in his mind, layer after layer, until she was magnificently naked before him.

He traced the firm line of her chin down her throat. Her response was a slight, sexy movement that encouraged him to unfasten the buttons of her blouse.

"Travis, I want to stay close to you."

He wanted that, too. Oh, God, how he wanted it!

"What if I decided not to testify?" she asked. "Could Ben DeCarlo be convicted if there were only two eyewitnesses?"

"I don't know. And we shouldn't be talking about this."

As he bent down to kiss her, she pushed at his chest. "When do I have to make the final decision about whether or not I'll testify?"

"Two days. Dave is going to direct your testimony, probably starting on Monday."

"Hold on." Pushing him away, she struggled to a sitting position. "How come Dave is questioning me instead of you?"

"I don't want to take a chance that our, um, relationship would come to light."

"We haven't done anything wrong, Travis. You haven't tried to influence my testimony in any way."

"Oh, yeah." His tone was sardonic. "I'm sure that a jury would believe that we were sleeping together and I didn't influence you."

"But it's the truth." Remorse flickered in her expression. "Oh, Travis, have I gotten you into trouble?"

"Nothing I can't handle."

"I shouldn't have seduced you."

"You didn't force me, darling."

When he leaned forward and lightly kissed the tip of her nose, she surprised him by grabbing hold of his ears and hanging on. "I sure as heck did seduce you," she said. "I've been waiting all my life to be a seductress."

"And you're a damn good one," he replied, grinning. "But, if I remember rightly, I was initiating all the first moves."

"Well, then…" She ran the tip of her tongue around her lips. "We'll have to reverse that process tonight, won't we?"

"You call the shots, Maggie."

Playful and sexy, she revealed a talent for seduction that

he wouldn't have believed if he hadn't experienced it himself.

THE NEXT MORNING, in the safe house arranged by the U.S. Marshals, Travis and Maggie sat down across a kitchen table from Gord Hoskins, who had just been picked up by the Marshals at the airport and escorted to this place.

Maggie was familiar with this type of housing from the first time she was a witness. A quiet place, surrounded by a chain-link fence with a heavy lock on the door. The neighborhood was nondescript. The furnishings were without character.

She knew that the safe house was wired to the hilt, and surveillance cameras kept a constant watch on the front and rear approach. All the drapes were drawn. No matter what they called it, she'd felt like she was in prison when she'd been in the care of the Marshals.

"So, Gord," she said, "how've you been, sugar?"

"Keeping busy. You look mighty fine, Maggie, but I liked your hair better the other way."

Gord was quick to notice hair on other people because he had very little of his own. He must have been in his mid-fifties because he was always talking about retirement, but he looked younger. His eyes had a twinkle, and his face was ruddy. Maggie remembered him being a heavy drinker who used to spend his whole afternoon at Augustine's, sampling the beer and talking up a storm with Pete Fontana.

"Did you hear about Kyle?" she asked.

"Yes, ma'am, and I don't like it one bit." He swiveled his head toward Travis. "You people are crazy if you think Pete Fontana is a murderer. That was a gangland execution if I've ever heard of one."

"You see!" Maggie chimed in. "Gord thinks like I do. Pete would never, ever do anything wrong, would he?"

"Not a chance. Pete's a good boy."

Encouraged by this confirmation of her own opinion, Maggie plunged forward. "Gord, you've got to tell us about TotalCom."

"Whoa, Maggie." Travis halted her. "Let's back up a few paces."

"No need," Gord said calmly. "I invested in TotalCom. In fact, I brokered a couple of other people and advised others to get into it. The investment paid off real well."

"Was Ezra Dean Slaughter one of the people you brokered?

"Without my records, it's hard to say. I know Ezra Dean. I might have suggested investments to him."

"You'd sure as shootin' remember this," Maggie said. "He invested over a million dollars."

She didn't like the way Gord seemed to be avoiding her gaze. "I'd remember that," he said.

"Here's my big concern," Travis said. "From what I understand, Ezra Dean intends to base much of his defense case on discrediting the eyewitnesses to the crime. That's Monique, Maggie and you."

Gord shifted his weight, crossed his arms. Maggie wasn't an expert on body language, but she could tell he was edgy.

Travis continued, "Is there anything we should know about you, Gord? Anything that Ezra Dean can dredge up and use to make you look bad?"

Gord Hoskins swallowed hard. "I think I might be needing to have my attorney present, if you don't mind."

"I CAN'T BELIEVE THIS." Travis paced in the tiny bedroom of the safe house. "My whole case is falling apart. I don't know what the hell Gord Hoskins is involved in, but it doesn't sound good."

Nor did the name of the law firm who represented him, Maggie thought. He was a client of Dermott, Pike and Rosewell, the firm where Dave's father was senior partner. Once again, it seemed Dave had a connection with the bad guys.

"I can't lose Gord Hoskins," Travis said.

"If I back out," she said, "it's another big, fat hole in your case, isn't it?"

He paused in his endless route and stopped in front of her. Maggie was leaning with her back against the primrose-patterned wall of the bedroom, and when Travis fixed his penetrating gaze upon her, she felt like he was staring clear through to the other side, counting the little yellow flowers on the wallpaper.

"I don't want to leave you," she said. Yet their relationship might compromise her testimony.

But if she didn't testify, he could lose the case. Ezra Dean would make the most of the disappearing witnesses. He'd use their refusal to appear as proof of his own lying allegations that the witnesses were part of an elaborate frame.

How could she let that happen?

"Before this," she said, "I didn't have anything to lose. When I agreed to start over in the witness protection program, it was an adventure. But now, I don't know."

She waited for him to jump in and tell her that he wanted her to stay, that he would find a way to handle the case without her testimony, that she was more to him than a witness.

But Travis said nothing.

Hesitantly, she said, "Maybe I've got this all wrong. Do

you want me to go? To disappear into the witness protection program?''

"No." The single syllable felt as if it had been wrenched from his throat.

"It's okay if you do. I could live with it."

He pulled her into his arms and held her tightly against his chest. His lips nuzzled her hair. "I want you to stay, Maggie. I want to take care of you."

Relief poured through her like a soothing balm, aloe to all her aching doubts and questions. He cared about her. That much was clear. Though she wished he might have said the more traditional words, like "I love you, Maggie" or "Let's get hitched, Maggie," she'd be content with protection. It was a start.

"Mr. Shanahan, sir?"

The voice came over the intercom on the wall. Travis and Maggie broke apart as quickly as a couple of teenagers caught necking on the front porch.

"Yes." Travis pushed down the intercom button to speak. "What is it?"

"The attorney for Mr. Hoskins is here."

"Thank you, we'll be right out."

"What's with all the mechanical stuff?" Maggie asked as she pushed her hair back into place.

"It's like a baby monitor," Travis said. "The marshals in the front room can hear if there's any disturbance in here while the witness is sleeping."

"Oh, my God!" Her eyes opened wide. "Were they listening to us? Just now?"

"Let's hope not."

They returned to the kitchen table where Gord Hoskins's attorney, a silver-haired man who looked like he'd come directly from the golf course, introduced himself. "I'm

Hank Woodrow, and this had better be all-fired important to drag me over here on a Sunday afternoon.''

Travis nodded and introduced him to Maggie, then he turned back to her. "I'm sorry, Maggie. This conversation is going to be confidential. Would you mind waiting in the bedroom?''

"Not at all.'' On her way out of the room, she redirected her route, fetching a glass of water and arranging to bump against the kitchen intercom to turn it to on. With any luck, she could listen in without anyone being the wiser.

In the bedroom with the door closed, she tested the intercom. The voices of the men in the kitchen came through, loud and clear.

Travis ran through a brief explanation of the trial and the importance of Gord's testimony, pointing out that it was Gord's legal obligation to testify because he'd signed a promise with the federal Marshals.

Mr. Woodrow had a Southern accent so thick that the intercom practically oozed. "I appreciate your candor, Travis. But I don't rightly see your problem.''

"Much of the defense case will rest upon discrediting our witnesses. When I asked Mr. Hoskins if he had any past history we should know about, he wanted you present. So, you tell me,'' Travis concluded. "What's wrong?''

"Would you mind if I conferred with my client for a moment?''

"Go right ahead.''

Unfortunately for Maggie, the attorney and Hoskins had apparently moved away from the intercom. She couldn't hear anything but the shuffling noises of Travis and the marshal who was in the kitchen with him. Poor Travis! His entire case was falling to pieces.

She was really hoping that Gord Hoskins had exaggerated about his lawbreaking. Maybe it was some nothing little thing that only seemed important to him. He was an accountant, after all. Maybe he'd cheated on his income tax or something.

Mild-mannered Gord didn't look like a criminal. But, then, neither did Ben DeCarlo.

In a few minutes, she heard the voice of Hoskins's attorney. "Travis," he said with a solemnity that was previously absent. "We might be needing Wiley to sit in on this discussion."

"Why would I need the District Attorney?"

"I can't very well have my client incriminating himself from here to Baton Rouge without a promise of immunity."

"Tell you what, Woodrow." She heard the rage in Travis's voice. "Your client can unburden himself here and now to me. Or he will find himself in a cell at Parish Prison."

"Are you threatening me?"

"Stating facts," Travis said. "What's it going to be, Gord?"

"I'll tell you, Travis, because I know how much you want to win this case. And you need me to do it." He gave a nervous, breathy chuckle. "You don't have any choice but to grant me immunity in exchange for my testimony."

"Go ahead."

"Without going into details, I have been involved—in a very minor way—in an operation that might be considered money laundering. And fraud."

"That's enough," Woodrow cautioned. "We're going to need guarantees of some kind."

Money laundering and fraud? Maggie couldn't believe this! How could Travis let Gord get away with this?

"If I can convince Wiley to arrange for immunity,"

Travis said, "Gord will have to testify in a separate trial on these scams."

"Absolutely not," Gord said. "I won't name names."

"Why not? You've already got the DeCarlo family after you. Your life couldn't get more threatened. Unless..." When Travis paused, Maggie could almost feel the rising tension in the kitchen. "Unless Sandor Rossi is telling the truth, and you were set up as an eyewitness to frame Ben DeCarlo."

"No way," Gord vehemently denied. "I was there in the restaurant. I saw what happened."

"But maybe you turned it to your advantage. You're a smart guy, aren't you? Witnessing this murder might have been a big opportunity for you. You could work a deal with DeCarlo's enemies, then turn around and be Ezra Dean's man on the inside."

"My client," said Woodrow, "will not be saying one more word unless we have a deal."

"Not a chance," Travis said. "If your client is a liar and a fraud, he's worthless to me as a witness."

She heard the sound of chairs scraping back. Travis spoke to the marshal who was in the room with them. "Arrest this man. Gord Hoskins, I charge you with—"

"Hold on, Travis," Gord said. "Haven't you forgotten something? Haven't you forgotten TotalCom?"

"Tell me about it, Gord."

"The company is a legitimate concern, but the trading for this particular stock was based on insider information that I shared, for a piece of the action, with Pete Fontana."

Maggie groaned inwardly. How could Pete be such a doggoned fool! What had he hoped to gain?

"It was a fast payoff," Hoskins said. "The profit was all in the timing. There were other people involved in this. I could give you names. The majority investor in

TotalCom was somebody you want. You want him bad, Travis.''

"You'd be willing to betray Slaughter?''

His attorney spoke up. ''That's enough. You don't get any more information until we have immunity. What's fair is fair.''

"Fair?'' Travis sounded like he was about to explode. ''Coming from you, that word is profane. Woodrow, you're the kind of slimeball that gives attorneys a bad name.''

"How dare you—''

"Don't push me.'' Tersely, Travis continued, ''I will contact Wiley and we'll discuss arrangements.''

"What kind of arrangements?'' Gord wailed. ''I don't—''

"Hey,'' Travis said, cutting him off. ''I'm gone. I can't stand to be in the same room with you two.''

Maggie turned the intercom to silence. Though she had always known, in the back of her mind, that these kinds of bargains went on, she never fully comprehended the utter mendacity. *Mendacity.* Lying. Cheating.

How could Travis be involved in such filth? He was a decent man. How could he stand to take testimony from scum like Hoskins?

When he returned to the bedroom, an aura of outrage clung to him. The tension around his eyes suggested that he was in pain, physical pain. He couldn't even force a smile. ''Let's go, Maggie. I want to get out of here.''

"Can I help? Isn't there something I can do?''

"Just try to stay out of trouble, Maggie.''

After he talked briefly with the marshals and made a few phone calls, they were back in her car. Before she could fire up the ignition, he reached past the gearshift and took her hand. When his fingers closed around hers, she looked into his eyes.

"I'm sorry, Maggie."

"For what?"

"For everything. I had promised not to hurt you."

"What are you saying, Travis?"

"More than anything, I want to take you back to our hideaway in the French Quarter and make love to you."

Her heart beat faster, just hearing those words. They might only have a few days left. In a matter of hours, she might be forced to leave him. Forever.

"But the trial is bearing down on us like a runaway train. We're going back to my house."

"No," she said. "I'll go back to the French Quarter and wait for you."

"I have a lot of work to do. This could take all night. I can't leave you in the Quarter, alone and unprotected."

"I'll be okay. I promise."

"I've already arranged for two federal marshals to meet us at my house. Janine and Dave, too. We need to prepare additional pretrial motions, and I have to talk with Wiley."

The darkness in his expression frightened her. It was as if he were already saying goodbye. Though she had always known that their time together would have to end when she went back into the witness protection program, she had dared to hope for more. Maybe not a lifetime with Travis. But a week. A month.

"Then, it's over," she said. "You have a trial to run. There's no more time for me."

He squeezed her hand. "I didn't want it to be like this. You've got to believe me, Maggie."

"It's all right," she said, hiding the pain, the frustration, the regret. Finally, she'd found the man of her fantasies, and hard reality wouldn't allow her to dream.

She pulled her hand away from his grasp and started up Junior's engine. "I knew what I was getting into."

"I'll make this up to you, Maggie."

"And how are you going to do that? After I get done with my testimony, I'm going to disappear. It'll be against the law for you to contact me."

"Sometimes, the laws can bend."

Like in that kitchen, she thought, where he was fixing to offer immunity to a man who had confessed to fraudulent dealings. The legal system bent over backward for criminals. Average people, like herself, got swept under the carpet.

When they arrived at his home, Clayton Bascombe's men were already there, securing the premises and complaining about all the windows and shrubbery. Within minutes, the other two attorneys joined them.

Maggie was relegated to her bedroom, where she tried to relax by taking a long, hot bath. She tried to read her novel. Tried to think about something else. But it was impossible. Maggie wasn't accustomed to sitting around and twiddling her thumbs when there was work to be done.

But there was no way she could be useful. Except...maybe she could talk with Pete Fontana. Pete was central to understanding what went on with Gord Hoskins and with Kyle's murder. He might open up to Maggie. He might confide in her.

But what if he told her something incriminating? How could she betray him?

How could she not?

Before she could wade deeper into ethical waters, Maggie decided to act. She yanked open the bedroom door. Outside, in the hallway, a federal marshal had been posted to guard her. He was a young man, probably only in his early twenties.

"Excuse me," Maggie said, "but I need to go downstairs."

"My instructions, ma'am, are to keep you on this floor."

"You can escort me. You can announce me so that the lawyers can pick up all their documents. You can wrap a blindfold around my eyes." She braced both fists on her hips. "But I am going downstairs."

He spoke into a walkie-talkie. "She's on the move. I repeat, Sugar Lips is coming downstairs.

"What did you call me? Sugar Lips?"

The marshal shrugged. "It's a code name, ma'am."

Her eyes narrowed. This code name had better not be any sort of reference to her relationship with Travis. "And what does it mean?"

"I guess it's because you call everybody sugar. And, according to Marshal Bascombe, you talk too much."

Maggie patted his cheek. "Escort me downstairs, sugar."

In Travis's elegant dining room, the three attorneys had made a mess. There were three laptop computers, all in various stages of creating documents. And there were law books, spread like autumn leaves across the long dining room table. Dave and Janine looked as tired as their boss, but Maggie hardly noticed them. Her gaze flew to Travis. Even now, ravaged by exhaustion, she saw a reflection of her own longing in his eyes. He cared about her. She could see it, clear as day. How could he let this happen? Why would he let her go?

"I was thinking," Maggie said, "that Pete Fontana seems to be messed up in this case in all kinds of ways. If I talked to him, I might be able to get some answers that he'd be afraid to tell anyone else."

"I thought he was your friend," said Dave Dermott.

"He is. And I am still certain that Pete didn't kill Kyle. But there are other things, like TotalCom, that he might have answers to."

Janine smiled encouragingly. "It couldn't hurt."

"You're a witness," Dave said. "It's not right for you to be investigating."

"Here's a news flash for you, Mr. Dermott. There's only one reason that I'm a witness. I want to see Ben DeCarlo convicted. Now, maybe I'm just a waitress, but it seems to me that your case is based entirely on five eyewitnesses. One's dead. Another is excused from testifying. Gord Hoskins is a mess. All that's left is me and the ex-model, Monique. Are we enough? Seems to me like you need more evidence."

"Tomorrow after court," Travis said, "I'll take you to see Pete. But I will have to be present when you two are talking."

"Well, that kind of defeats the whole purpose. He might not open up to me if you're there."

"Unless he talks to me, it doesn't do any good."

He softened his words with a slight smile that touched her soul. She wanted nothing more than to soothe away the shadows beneath his eyes, to caress his stubbled cheek. She wanted to kiss away all his worries. But all she could say was, "Okay, Travis."

And so, she was dismissed. She returned to her bedroom and stretched out on the bed, which seemed so empty without him. It was strange, she thought, that she'd slept alone for most of her life, only sharing with another kid when she was growing up. Now she didn't think she could rest without feeling Travis's warm, masculine body beside her.

Her bedside clock showed that it was after two when she heard noises outside her room. The key turned in the door lock.

"Travis," she whispered, instantly alert.

Straight as an arrow, she ran through the darkness toward the door as it opened wide.

Maggie halted. The rest of the house was dark and extremely quiet. In the dim reflection of moonlight from a window, she saw the outline of a man who stepped into her doorway.

Something was wrong. Silently, she eased back into the shadows.

Where was the young marshal who was supposed to be here standing guard?

Maybe Travis had convinced him to take a break. But why would he come through the dark? Why would he—

"I warned you."

She knew the voice from the stairwell. Maggie dove for the floor as she heard the muffled crack of a pistol with a silencer.

If she yelled, he would know where she was. There was nowhere to hide.

The pistol sounded again and again.

On her hands and knees, she scrambled into the bathroom, locked the door, turned on the light, threw back her head and screamed bloody murder.

He was at the door. She could hear him.

Maggie jumped into the bathtub, hoping the porcelain walls would be a shield. And she kept on yelling for help. Where was everybody?

The wood door to the bathroom was no protection against three bullets, fired in rapid succession.

After all this, he was coming to get her. He was going to kill her. Oh, Lord, this was not funny, but she was praying that she wouldn't die here, in a bathtub. It would make a hell of a coffin.

There was noise outside the bathroom, and Maggie stopped her screams.

She heard Travis's voice. "Maggie, are you all right?"

"What do you think?" She leapt from the tub and ran to the bathroom door. Throwing it open, she pointed to the bullet holes. "Do you see these holes? Do you?"

Travis nodded.

"How can you be asking me if I'm all right? A psycho maniac almost killed me!"

Behind Travis, she saw the young marshal. He had been wounded. Crimson blood marked his hairline. "I'm sorry, ma'am. I must have closed my eyes. I didn't see him coming."

She wished that she could reassure him, but she was too furious. She had spent most of her day in forced inactivity so that she would supposedly be safe. For what? So she could be attacked while she slept?

The other marshal, the one who had been stationed downstairs, was at the bathroom door. He reported, "I don't know how he got in here. I didn't hear a thing. He must have had a key. This isn't a safe house."

"Hold your excuses for Bascombe," Travis said.

"He has been called, sir. And an ambulance."

"Not an ambulance for me," Maggie snapped. "I will not be going to the hospital."

"You need to be in a safe house," said the older marshal.

"I am not going anywhere," she raged, "until Clayton Bascombe himself agrees to guard me. Do you understand me, gentlemen? I'm tired of being shoved around in this system. I'm tired of being told what to do, when to speak and when not to listen."

She stormed past Travis into the bedroom. With the overhead light shining brightly, she saw the bullet hole in the lacy white comforter. If she had been sleeping, she would be dead right now.

Maggie did a sharp about-face and returned to the bathroom. "If you gentlemen will please excuse me."

She closed and locked the door. With her eyes closed tightly, she fought for control. Everything was crazy, upside down. Her chest heaved. Though she hadn't been hurt, her entire body was wracked with pain. Maggie fell to her knees on the cold tile floor. She vomited into the toilet.

Chapter Twelve

The next morning, Maggie was driven to the courthouse by Clayton Bascombe himself, who had not been pleased about being wakened in the middle of the night and called to protect her. Neither of them spoke one word to the other until they were in sight of the marble columns of the Criminal District Court.

Marshal Bascombe cleared his throat. "I'm sorry, Maggie. The attack last night never should have happened. The marshal guarding your door was too green. I should have known better."

"Yes, sir. You should have." She wasn't about to let him off the hook. "I shudder to think of my fate if I had delivered myself to your custody from the beginning of my stay in New Orleans."

"Your unauthorized stay," he reminded her.

She looked down at her hand where she held the voodoo charm. Marie's green plaited bracelet decorated her wrist. Right now, she needed all the luck she could muster.

"Life is short, Clayton. When that madman tried to kill me, I was reminded. If you want anything done, you've got to do it for yourself." She reached over and touched his arm. "Help me today, Clayton."

He made grumpy noises in the back of his throat, but he said, "That depends, Maggie. What do you need?"

"Don't make me stay in the basement of the courthouse, twiddling my thumbs and waiting to be called as a witness. I need to go to the D.A.'s offices."

He shook his head. "No way."

"Please," she said. "It's not like I'm asking for a trip to the mall so I can buy a new hat. I'm investigating. I want to see Ben DeCarlo convicted. Otherwise, everything I've gone through is for nothing."

"If anything happens to you, it's my head on the chopping block."

"If anything happens," she said, "I'll be dead."

He pulled the car up to the curb in front of the District Criminal Court and parked. When he looked at her, his expression was sympathetic. Marshal Clayton Bascombe truly was a kind, gentle man. "Please," she repeated. "Do the right thing."

"All right," he conceded. "But I'm sticking with you like glue. If they need you, you're ready for court, aren't you?"

"You bet." Since there was a possibility she would testify this afternoon, she'd dressed in a plain, black, sleeveless sundress, which she wore like a jumper with a simple white blouse underneath. "First stop, Travis's office."

"Lord help us all." Marshal Bascombe sighed as he started up the car and drove to the parking lot beside the building where the D.A. kept his offices.

Maggie's heart was fluttering when she stepped into Travis's office. He rewarded her with a dazzling smile that made her forget the many things she wanted to tell him. She had hoped to tell him that she understood about yesterday. She didn't blame him for putting her aside. From the start, she'd known that they couldn't be together.

But when she faced him, all she wanted was to love this man, to be with him, night and day, forever and ever.

Briskly, he stepped out from behind his desk. "Thank you, Clayton. I'd like to talk with Maggie alone."

"I'll be right outside," he said as he closed the door.

He took her into his arms. Hungrily, his lips claimed hers, igniting a flame of passion that she had never known with another man. She was breathing hard when he ended their kiss and clasped her firmly against his chest. "I've missed you."

"I was hardly gone."

He grinned at her. "When I told you to dress conservatively, Maggie, I didn't expect a Pilgrim outfit."

"You don't like this?" She snuggled against him, feeling her hope take flight. "I could probably make Clayton take me back and change clothes. That poor man is suffering from such guilt that I could ask him to jump through a hoop and he would gladly comply."

"He should feel guilty," Travis said. "Last night was too close."

Though she knew Travis had only a few hours of sleep, he looked vigorous and strong. "You appear to have gotten more rest, sugar. You got the color back in your face."

"Adrenaline," he said. "I have to psyche myself up before a big trial like this. If I drag into that courtroom like a whipped puppy, I might really get whupped."

"I like to see you this way, Travis. Full of fight."

She went up on her tiptoes and kissed him lightly but thoroughly, gliding close to him, savoring the friction of her bare forearms against the rough woolen fabric of his suit jacket. These kisses were a piece of heaven. Greedily, she took as many as she dared, storing up for when they were apart.

When he gazed down at her, concern flickered in the

shadows of his eyes. "We probably won't call you today, Maggie. I think Judge Howell is going to be busy with all our pretrial motions."

"I'll be ready," she said. "Don't forget. Later today, we're going to visit Pete Fontana over at the prison."

This was a crazy conversation, she thought, for two lovers who might never see each other again. Why were they talking about prisons and trials when they should have been pledging their devotion? "Good luck in court, Travis."

"I'm going to need it."

He opened the door. Clayton Bascombe was standing just outside.

"Oh, Travis," Maggie said, "would you please inform Marshal Bascombe that it's all right for me to stay over here before I testify? And that I have the run of these offices."

"Anything she wants," he said to Clayton. "Keep her safe."

With Clayton sitting in the chair opposite, Maggie settled down behind the desk in Travis's office. Amid the clutter, she found a fresh legal pad and began making notes.

Her first assumption was that Kyle had been lured back to New Orleans and killed to keep him from testifying. His murder had the bonus effect of scaring the other witnesses. But there were still so many questions she needed answers to.

Did Ezra Dean manipulate TotalCom to pay off at this particular time so he knew when Kyle would be here?

Did Pete know about the payoff scheme?

What about the other money Kyle said he was expecting to get? And the plane tickets to Paris?

Who stole Pete Fontana's file from the police station? Why?

The second problem was Maggie, herself. She had been attacked and threatened within hours after her arrival in New Orleans. Who would know she was in town?

She wrote the word *leak* on the yellow legal pad. If she found who was leaking information to the bad guys, she would have the answers.

She dropped her pen on the pad and peeked over at Clayton Bascombe, who was reading a novel. "What are you reading?"

"Elmore Leonard. I love the way he makes the U.S. Marshals sound so cool." He dog-eared his page. "What do you need, Maggie?"

"I need to go down the hall and check out the Pete Fontana file in Sharon Gold's office."

"Fine. Travis said anything you want. If you're trespassing, it's his problem."

Sharon was out. It probably wasn't correct procedure for Maggie to be riffling through her files, but she needed answers and she remembered the file drawer where Sharon had stashed Pete Fontana's file.

After a quick search, Maggie selected the correct tab on a fat manila folder, wound twice with rubber bands. "Getting at this is too easy," she said to Clayton. "Shouldn't there be more security?"

"It's been my experience that if somebody wants information, they can find it. Whether it's on a computer or stuck in a file drawer. Just a matter of knowing which buttons to punch."

DeSharko, Maggie thought, remembering how she and Roy had invaded the files at the U.S. Marshals' offices. It was probably best not to mention that breach to Clayton.

She settled down at Sharon's tidy desk and flipped open

the file. A copy of her letter to Pete was there. How foolish she'd been! She'd given the date of arrival, bold as you please. She also found pages of forensic information. Copies of police interviews with witnesses. A copy of the unused plane ticket. Receipts from the rental car company.

Maggie felt the edges of glossy photographs and swallowed hard. She didn't want to study the actual pictures of the crime scene, but this was part of the investigation, part of the process, the dark side of law. What had Travis said to her? *Always remember the victim.*

She gritted her teeth, but she couldn't force herself to confront those pictures. Death was too close, already. She flipped past the photographs.

At the end of the file, she realized that something was missing. An important document.

Sharon Gold came through the door. "What are you doing?"

"Taking a gander at Pete Fontana's file."

"What the hell?" She glared at Clayton, then at Maggie. Her features were rigid. "You don't have authorization, Maggie."

"I'm just a waitress, Sharon. You wouldn't expect me to understand that."

"Get out."

Maggie stepped around her and paused in the doorway. "By the way, sugar, something is missing from in there."

"When I need your help, I'll ask for it."

Maggie returned to Travis's office with Clayton at her heels. He chuckled and said, "You sure yanked her chain."

"Doesn't seem to bother you."

"I can't stand that woman. When she was working on the first DeCarlo trial, she was always over at our offices, digging up information on the Dixie Mafia, demanding special favors. Pain in the rear. That's what I call her.''

''Is that her code name?''

''No, Sugar Lips. But it would make a good one.''

Maggie picked up the phone in Travis's office and put through a call to Chief Royce Monk. As soon as she recognized his voice, she said, ''I never thanked you for the dance, Chief.''

''Maggie Deere?'' Monk's voice was apprehensive. ''What do you want?''

''You know, sugar, I'm doing a little work for Travis, and he was wondering if you had located the Pete Fontana file yet.''

''Matter of fact, I have.'' He sounded relieved. She imagined a smile on that bulldog face. ''It was just misplaced.''

''Could you check that file for me, Chief? I was wondering if you had a copy of that anonymous tip that directed you toward Pete Fontana. I think it was hand-delivered, to your attention.''

''I know what you're talking about. You want a copy or the original?''

''Either is fine. You can contact me in Travis's office.''

At noon, Clayton brought her a sandwich and a Pepsi from the machines in the lunchroom. She'd only taken a bite when Travis came storming into the room. He slammed the door. ''Judge Leland Howell is either being paid off or he is the dumbest son-of-a-gun I have ever encountered in the entire judicial system.''

''Tell me.'' She leaned forward avidly. His dynamic presence, after an entire morning of paperwork, was a magic elixir. Her brain had been working all morning, but now she felt like her blood was moving again. When she was near him, she was alive. Away from him, she was only marking time.

"I don't need to go through the whole courtroom ordeal," he said. "In every single instance, Judge Howell ruled for the defense."

"When does the trial with the jury present begin?"

"Tomorrow. Aw, hell, Maggie. I wish we had more time."

"So do I," she whispered. But her reasons for wishing were far from the courtroom and justice. She wanted more time with Travis. Any time, any way.

Clayton rose from his chair and stretched. "What's next, Travis?"

"I need to take Maggie over to Parish Prison so she can talk to Pete Fontana. If we find anything new, we'll have the rest of the day to deal with it."

"If you're going to be running around," Clayton said, "I'm calling for backup. I need a break."

Under escort of the federal marshals, they went to the prison and directly into the small room reserved for interviews with prisoners. Pete was shown into the room almost as soon as they arrived.

When the guards and marshals left the room, Maggie hopped out of her chair and hugged him. She studied his face for new bruises and found none. "No more accidents?"

"None. They've been treating me real nice."

"Sugar, I've got some hard questions for you, and I brought Travis along with me in case you decide you might want to work out some kind of deal for leniency."

"A deal?" He rolled his eyes. "I've got nothing to deal with. I don't know anything."

"Tell me about Gord Hoskins." She sat down opposite

him. "He's the one who advised you to invest in TotalCom, isn't he?"

"Sure is. Gord has always been helpful to me in learning about investments and accounting."

So trusting, Maggie thought. How did Pete stay so naive? "Did you ever think he might be pulling something illegal?"

"Like operating on an insider tip?" Pete nodded. "It occurred to me, especially when TotalCom paid off just the way Gord said it would. But Gord never shared that information with me. Far as I knew, I was acting in good faith, taking some friendly advice."

"But you were in contact with him," she pointed out, "after he was in the witness protection program."

"Him and Kyle, too. I knew what city they were in, but that was all. I sent their letters to a post office box. Never knew their addresses." He squinted at her. "Something's different about you, Maggie."

"Like what?"

"I don't know. You're more serious or something."

"Well, somebody tried to kill me last night. That kind of thing tends to take the giggles right out of a person."

She told him about the attack, then eased the topic back to TotalCom and Ezra Dean and Gord. But Pete had nothing new to tell them.

She glanced down at the legal pad where she'd scribbled her notes. What about Francine Bentley? "What was Kyle like when he was in town? Anything unusual?"

"I've been thinking a lot about Kyle, trying to figure out if he had some hidden reason for staying at my place. But I can't think of a thing. I was so proud of him, Maggie."

"How come?"

"He still wasn't drinking. Kyle stuck to his Alcoholics

Anonymous vows. Even when he went out partying, he only had soda pop as far as I could tell.''

An echo resounded in Maggie's head. "Not drinking at all. Never even got tipsy?''

"Not a bit. He'd been sober for five years before he died.''

But Francine Bentley claimed that they had shared many bottles of her favorite wine. She'd told Maggie that they were half loaded when they made love. That was her lie. Not a fib, but a full-blown lie. The deceit wasn't her brand of wine, it was her claim that they were drinking. Didn't she know that Kyle was a dry alcoholic? Did she know him at all?

"I've got an idea, Pete.'' She reached across the table and clasped his hand. "I might get you out of here yet.''

After he'd been escorted from the room, she explained her reasoning to Travis. "I don't think Kyle was any kind of boyfriend to Francine at all. She invented the whole courtship.''

"Why?''

"To get him here. To get him back to New Orleans. Renting a car for him. Setting him up with a place to stay. Doesn't it sound suspicious to you, Travis?''

"Let's bring her in.''

In the prison offices, Travis grabbed a phone and called the police station. Though he doubted that Francine Bentley was any sort of criminal mastermind, she might be able to provide a critical piece to the puzzle. After dealing with the likes of Gord Hoskins and Ezra Dean, Francine would be a welcome relief.

Travis had Royce Monk on the phone. "Pick Francine Bentley up for questioning, and don't be any too nice about it.''

"What do you mean?''

"If she resists, tell your boys to use handcuffs."

"Travis? Are you going to get me in more trouble with the rich people in this town?"

"All I'm trying to do is hang a killer."

TRAVIS FIGURED there was no reason Maggie couldn't sit in on the questioning of Francine Bentley. In the first place, Francine was really part of the Kyle Johnson murder instead of the DeCarlo case. In the second place, Travis doubted that Ezra Dean would open this particular line of questioning. He'd been adamant in their pretrial motions and discussion in chambers about excluding reference to the murder of Kyle Johnson.

Suspicious, Travis thought. Many of the events since Ben DeCarlo's first conviction had suspicious overtones. It was almost as if a master puppeteer was pulling the strings, making the witnesses dance against a background of crazy evidence that shifted and changed like shadows in the bayou.

He lightly touched Maggie's shoulder. It was difficult to keep himself from caressing her. When they were near, he had to avoid looking at her or else he would be overwhelmed.

"Maggie?"

When she looked at him, her blue eyes were bright and intelligent. Her lips took on that eternal smile. He'd only seen it vanish once, last night, when she was angry and scared.

An amazing woman. He wanted to tell her that. Instead, he asked, "Would you like to help me question Francine?"

Her cheeks dimpled with a full-fledged grin. "Can we play good cop, bad cop?"

"I think we can just ask our questions," he said. "With

the mood I'm in, there's no chance that I might be too gentle."

When he and Maggie entered the small interviewing room, Francine bristled with indignation. Her voice was high and whiny as she said, "There seems to be some sort of horrible misunderstanding, Mr. Shanahan. I wish to go."

"Fine with me. I just have a few questions."

"I've answered more questions than I want. This is an outrage!"

"Would you like to have your attorney present?"

Her disdainful expression slipped a bit. Her eyes blinked. She was frightened. Good, Travis thought. Scared people didn't use the best judgment.

She said, "Do I need to have my attorney here?"

"Up to you, Ms. Bentley."

"Oh, go ahead. I know your mother. You wouldn't dare ask me anything too awful."

He glanced over at Maggie, encouraging her to start. Enthusiastically, she leapt right in. "You have an unusual and expensive taste in wines, Ms. Bentley. Do you always buy your Château Louis Noir from the Crescent Wine Cellar?"

"I order all my wines from the Crescent Wine Cellar. I have for years and years."

"Are you acquainted with the owner, Ben DeCarlo?"

"Of course."

She shifted in the hardwood chair and carefully centered her black leather purse on her lap. Her knees were pinched together, and Travis could guess by looking at her that this woman was not typically a passionate temptress. She wasn't Kyle Johnson's type at all. How could he have accepted her assertion that she was his girlfriend?

Maggie continued, "We talked before about your friend,

Kyle Johnson, and how you and he used to share a bottle of Château Louis Noir."

"Yes, we did."

"I think you told me," Maggie said, "that you and Kyle got kind of tipsy on the special date when you became intimate. Is that right?"

She glanced at Travis. "It's a little embarrassing to talk about this, but we were both in high spirits."

"Both sipping at the wine."

"Yes."

"Except for one problem," Maggie pointed out. "Kyle was a recovering alcoholic. He didn't drink."

Her lower lip began to tremble. "But he was a bartender."

Maggie nodded.

"He recommended drinks to me. I'm sure he did."

"How well did you know Kyle, Ms. Bentley?"

She scooted her purse up close to her stomach. "I think, perhaps, I should contact my attorney."

Travis stepped in. "Very well, Ms. Bentley. We surely want you to have adequate representation. What law offices will you be contacting?"

"My attorney in Atlanta, of course. He handled all of my late husband's affairs and now he takes care of me."

"We'll bring you a telephone," Travis promised. "And you be sure to tell your Atlanta attorney that you'll be waiting for him right here. Until he arrives."

She gasped. "Perhaps I'm not understanding correctly. Are you saying that I am to stay here, in the police station, until my attorney arrives?"

"Yes, ma'am."

"But he has to come from Atlanta. He might not be here until tomorrow." Panic raised her voice several octaves. "I can't stay in a jail overnight."

"I'm sure you understand," Travis said smoothly. "It seems that you didn't tell us the whole truth when you gave statements to the police. And this is a murder investigation."

Maggie slid in behind Travis. "Maybe we can clear up this confusion with just a few more inquiries."

"I'll answer any questions." Her eyes darted, as if she were seeing spiders in the corners of the plain green-painted room. "I can't stay here. It is simply too mortifying."

Maggie pressed on. "So, you and Kyle weren't really all that close, were you?"

"He was a friend. An acquaintance. Maybe he'd teased me a little bit with occasional hugs and a kiss on the cheek. And maybe I'd done the same with him."

"But you weren't lovers," Maggie clarified.

"No."

"I'm just not understanding. Maybe I'm dense or something, but I don't see why you would pay for his rental car and have him check into a hotel room at the Lafayette."

"It was a business arrangement," she said.

"What kind of business?"

"Well, Emmet—or Kyle, rather—proposed it. He was a little short on cash, and I said I'd help him get to New Orleans since I was coming here myself and could use the rental car and room after I arrived."

"It was all Kyle's idea?" Maggie frowned as if she didn't believe that. "You let him take advantage of you like that?"

"I didn't see it that way."

"Francine, sugar, I thought you were way smarter than that. A wealthy, classy lady like you? Getting played by a wise guy like Kyle? Letting him walk around with your credit card? Sounds mighty foolish to me."

Francine said nothing. Her mouth pursed in a tiny bow.

"You knew better than that," Maggie said. "Never let a con man control your pocketbook."

"I was the one in control," Francine said venomously. "I was always calling the shots and making the decisions. I knew exactly where he was and what he was doing. I knew every second of the time."

"Even when he was staying at Pete Fontana's?"

"Of course. I knew—" Her hand flew up to cover her mouth, but the confession was already there.

Travis leaned back in his chair. Francine had engineered Kyle's return to New Orleans, to the city where he met his death.

Stiffly, she said, "I will speak to a local attorney."

"Any preference?" Travis asked. "Or should I call the public defender's office?"

"I wish to speak with Ezra Dean Slaughter."

Travis couldn't have asked for this interrogation to fall more neatly into place. He and Maggie left Francine Bentley to stew in the roiling pot of trouble she'd created for herself.

Outside in the nondescript halls of the police station, he wished he could take Maggie into his arms and twirl her in celebration. Finally, things were coming clear. There had been a conspiracy to lure Kyle to his death. Francine, Gord Hoskins and Pete had been a part of it. But the puppeteer was one man: Ezra Dean.

"Good job, Maggie. You're going to make a fine attorney."

He wished with all his heart that they could be alone, away from the marshals who guarded her. He longed to turn back the clock to two days ago when they would have been returning to their hideaway in the French Quarter. But tonight, Maggie would be sleeping under guard in a safe house. And he would be sleeping alone.

On their way out, Royce Monk caught up with them. Without preface, he said, "Dammit, Travis. I'm sorry."

"For what?" What had this fool done wrong this time?

"I should explain." Maggie stepped up beside him. "I called Royce from your office, asking for information on Pete Fontana's file, which the chief said he'd found. I'd gone through the stuff in Sharon Gold's office, and I couldn't find that note that was the anonymous tip."

"Neither could I," said Royce. He stuck a cigar into the corner of his mouth and fired it up, despite the No Smoking signs posted all over the building. "I went through that doggoned file half a dozen times, and I checked with the guys who keep evidence. Nothing. It's gone."

Travis wasn't sure what was going on, but Maggie's obvious disappointment told him that the anonymous tip was important.

"Damn," Royce said. "Every time I think I've got everything under control, it slips away from me. I do have something else, though."

"What's that?" Travis asked.

"I have the forensics report on the note. You know, we checked the type of paper and the ink and such."

"And fingerprints?" Maggie asked.

"Yeah, but that was a dead end. The only prints were from the officer who opened the envelope, and from Sharon Gold."

Sharon Gold? Why would her prints be on that note? Travis couldn't think of any reason she might have handled it before forensics did their work. Though the NOPD was developing a bad reputation for mishandling evidence, Sharon herself would have known better.

It was just possible that he had found his leak. Sharon Gold might even have sent the note.

Beside him, he could feel Maggie's excitement. She was bursting to talk. "Not now," he said.

"When, Travis? We haven't got much time."

He nodded to Royce Monk. "Thanks for your efforts, Chief."

"Anytime." He chugged away from them, puffing smoke from his cigar like a steam engine.

"Sharon Gold," Maggie whispered to him. "She touched that note. Maybe she even sent it."

"That's a leap of logic." He turned to the marshals. "We're going to step into this office for a moment."

Travis closed the door to the office that was more like a cubicle with clear glass windows, giving them a view of the duty room of the police station and allowing the marshals to keep an eye on them. He turned to Maggie. "Sharon was the prosecutor assigned to the Kyle Johnson murder. It's logical that she would handle the evidence."

"Before they tested it? Come on, Travis, I admire your loyalty to your staff, but Sharon Gold is your leak. There's the Château Louis Noir, and the fact that she patronizes the Crescent Wine Cellar." She snapped her fingers. "Ezra Dean arranged for her to be at the deposition with Rossi."

"But Ezra Dean asked for Dave Dermott."

"He knew you wouldn't send Dave by himself. Who else would you have sent besides Sharon Gold?"

It sounded true. Ezra Dean had manipulated him to get exactly what he wanted. He wanted Sharon Gold.

Unfortunately, Travis also understood her motivation. Sharon was ambitious. What better way to advance her career than doing a few favors for Ezra Dean, one of the most prominent attorneys in New Orleans?

She could easily be the leak. She knew everything. She had access to everything. But she wasn't a murderer. Travis was sure of that.

"Maggie, you've got to keep quiet about this."

"Why? Why can't you arrest her?"

"Due process. Reasonable evidence. We're still working on suspicions."

"How about this? Arrest Ezra Dean. At the very least, you have hard evidence that he was involved with insider trading."

"I can't."

She dragged her hands through her curling black hair. "Why not, Travis? Is this another deal, another bargain?"

"You don't understand, Maggie. If I pull the plug on Ezra Dean, DeCarlo is sure to get yet another retrial. He'll have a valid claim for incompetent representation by his chief attorney." This issue had been bothering Travis from the moment he saw Ezra Dean's name on the TotalCom list. "Sometimes, in the search for a higher truth, the letter of the law must be flexible."

"But *I'm* supposed to obey it," she said. "I'm supposed to testify even if it means giving up my life, moving away from New Orleans."

"I know it seems that way, but—"

"No, Travis. It seems that the law is something you can use to suit your own purposes."

"This has nothing to do with me personally."

"I don't believe you, Travis. I've been watching you work one deal after another, bending the law, sliding around the hard edges. Now it's time for the truth."

"What are you talking about?"

"Us. You and me. You had an affair with me, but you

didn't want more. How convenient for you, Mr. Prosecutor, that the law will force me to leave you.''

''Maybe that's what it looks like—''

''I know what I see. I'm a witness, Travis. That's all I've ever really been to you.''

She yanked open the door of the fishbowl cubicle. ''Goodbye, Travis.''

Chapter Thirteen

"The prosecution calls Maggie Deere to the stand."

At half past three o'clock in the afternoon, two federal marshals escorted her from the basement holding area. The bailiff held the door, and Maggie entered the spacious courtroom of Judge Leland Howell.

Though the DeCarlo trial might be a travesty of justice, the courtroom was awe-inspiring, with its rows of wooden pews, dark wood wainscoting and the massive elevated desk where the judge sat waiting to render life-and-death decisions. It *looked* like justice, she thought. Heavy. Stern. Majestic.

Maggie approached the witness stand down the center aisle, between the many onlookers, just like a bride without the wedding march. She was dressed for court in her linen suit. Her makeup was properly subdued. Though her gold jewelry was Woolworth's finest, nobody but a jewelry snob could tell from a distance.

Nor could they guess that last night, in the anonymous safe house, she'd been through agonies of soul-searching. Had she been a fool to care for Travis? Or had she been blessed with a once-in-a-lifetime love affair?

Obviously, Travis didn't feel blessed. With all his wheeling and dealing, he could have worked out some kind of witness protection deal for her so she could stay close to him. If he had wanted a solution, he could have found one. But he hadn't offered her any alternative to witness protection.

Ergo, Maggie could only conclude that Travis didn't want her around anymore. She shouldn't be surprised. Wasn't that just like every other man she'd ever known?

Maggie stood in the witness box and raised her right hand.

"Do you swear to tell the truth, the whole truth and nothing but the truth?"

"I do."

She glanced toward the prosecution table and saw him. So handsome, so elegant. With the lift of his eyebrow, he started her heart to pumping. She wanted to hate him, but she couldn't. He had given her the sweetest moments in her life. He had released her from the self-imposed sentence of restraint and taught her how, just for a moment, to trust another person.

But it was over now. She was a witness. He was the prosecuting attorney. That was the only relationship that mattered to him.

She expected Dave Dermott to come forward to direct her testimony, but it was Travis who approached the stand.

As he came nearer, her breathing accelerated. She was trembling. Maggie clenched her hands together in her lap. She couldn't let anybody know how she felt when he was near.

"Miss Deere," he said. "On December 15, 1993, what was your occupation?"

"I was a waitress at Augustine's restaurant, and it was the very best job I ever had. Nice people, great food and the tips were outstanding."

"Did you have any regular customers?"

"Sure did. There were lots of people who came in several times a week and always sat at my tables." She glanced over at the jury. "I prided myself on being able to remember what they liked to order and what they preferred to drink. One of the house specialties was the hurricane cocktail, which is rum and passion-fruit punch—"

Travis subtly cleared his throat, and she knew she was embellishing too much. When she looked at him, there was such a deep fondness in his gaze that her gush of words stopped short.

"Miss Deere, do you remember Antonio and Bethany DeCarlo?"

"Yes, I do." There, she thought, that was a brief answer. He ought to like that.

"Can you tell us about them? In your own words?"

"They were an older couple, nice-looking people. It seemed to me that they were comfortable with each other and still very much in love."

"Objection," shouted Ezra Dean Slaughter. "The witness is neither a psychiatrist nor a close personal friend of the family. This is conjecture."

She glared at him and at the other two attorneys in their expensive suits who sat at the defense table. Other members of his defense team were present. A couple of aides and investigators. The devil's assistants, she thought. Also at the table was Ben DeCarlo himself.

Travis continued, "Were Antonio and Bethany DeCarlo in Augustine's on December 15, 1993?"

"You bet they were."

"Did they sit at one of your tables?"

"Yes."

"Did you speak with them?"

"Of course I did. I had to take their order, didn't I?" Though her words remained casual, it was killing her to look at him, to remember all that had happened between them, to imagine what could have been.

"Miss Deere, tell the court about your conversation with the DeCarlos."

"Antonio DeCarlo placed the order for both of them. He always did. He'd say what Bethany DeCarlo wanted, then he'd look at her and raise his eyebrows, checking to see that he'd got it right. And she winked at him and patted his arm."

Since Travis did not stop her, Maggie continued with her description of a long-married couple who loved and respected each other as well as being kind to Maggie and everyone else. As she talked, she looked over at the jury and sensed that they understood her plainspoken words and the underlying message that Antonio and Bethany DeCarlo were good people.

Members of the jury smiled at her when she explained about her vocabulary words and *clandestine tryst*. Though Ezra Dean interrupted a few more times with his objections and Judge Leland Howell sustained them, she noticed that even the judge seemed kindly disposed toward her.

Maggie felt like she was doing the right thing by testifying, and when she looked at Travis she knew it. The truth was bigger than both of them.

Skillfully, Travis led her through a description of her chat with Kyle Johnson at the bar, including her thoughts at the time when she said she was saving up her tips for Christmas presents.

"Who were you planning to buy Christmas presents for?"

"Objection!" Ezra Dean was on his feet, fuming. "Her Christmas list is hardly relevant to a murder trial."

Travis said, "Your Honor, I am establishing the character of this witness, trying to show just what kind of woman she is."

"Objection overruled," said Judge Howell. "Continue, Miss Deere."

"I have no real family," Maggie explained, "but I was fixin' to buy presents for my friends." She listed several names, concluding with Pete Fontana. "Also, I was saving up for a computer on account of I was taking some correspondence courses and I thought it would help with my studies."

"While you were waitressing," Travis said, "you were also going to school?"

"I've always planned to make something of myself, someday. I blush to tell you that I never did finish high school, but I went back and got my equivalency degree. Right now, I'm enrolled in a college."

"And did you purchase your computer?"

"No, sir. When I decided to become a witness at the first DeCarlo trial, I had to spend all my savings just to live."

"Objection! Incidents that occurred after December 15, 1993, are not relevant to the testimony of this witness."

"Your Honor," Travis said, "I am trying to show the sacrifices this woman made in the interests of serving justice."

"Objection overruled."

Travis led Maggie through the final moments when she recognized Ben DeCarlo walking through the door of Augustine's.

"Is the person you saw in Augustine's on December 15, 1993, present in the courtroom today?"

"You bet he is."

"Would you point him out?"

Maggie raised her arm and aimed her index finger toward Ben DeCarlo. "That's him. Ben DeCarlo."

Maggie knew this was always a dramatic event, the actual naming of the accused, but as she stared toward the defense table, the moment took on double significance for her.

Seated directly behind Ben DeCarlo, among several other members of Ezra Dean's staff, was a hard-looking man wearing a black suit coat, white shirt and a vest. His longish hair hung around his face in limp strands. On his left cheek, his face was marked with red welts, as if he'd been scratched.

When he tucked his hair behind his ear, she saw a gold hoop earring. Was he the man who had attacked her? The man who'd tried to kill her?

Her gaze was riveted to his face while Travis returned to the prosecutor's table and shuffled papers.

"Your Honor," she heard Travis say, "I will have several more questions for this witness. Perhaps this would be a good time to recess for the day, and I can start up again tomorrow."

Judge Howell checked his wristwatch and nodded. "Though the court does not appreciate being told when to quit, I agree."

He gave instructions to the jury and to Maggie, then rapped his gavel. "Adjourned until tomorrow morning at nine o'clock."

As the people in the courtroom dispersed, Maggie kept watching the man in black. Was it him? Was she imagining things? Her two federal marshals were waiting to take her back into protective custody, but she ran to the prosecutor's table instead.

She knew it wasn't appropriate for the prosecutors to congratulate her on her testimony or even to speak to her while the jury was still in the room because it looked too much like collusion, but she grasped Travis's arm. "I saw him. The man who attacked me."

"Is he here?"

She turned her head toward Ezra Dean's table, but the man in black was gone. "He was sitting right over there. Behind Ben DeCarlo."

Travis glanced over her head to the waiting U.S. marshals. "Take Maggie downstairs and wait for us."

"Only for a moment, sir. We have orders to take Miss Deere to the safe house immediately following her testimony."

TRAVIS ENTERED THE holding room on the basement level of the courthouse where the marshals were holding Maggie. With him was Dave Dermott, Janine Carlson and Sharon Gold. Though he had reasons for suspecting Sharon, there was no hard evidence that she had tampered with evidence or leaked information to Ezra Dean.

As soon as he saw Maggie, all other thoughts flew from his mind. Today, in court, he had been so proud of her. She was smart. She was utterly believable. She talked to the jury as if they were old friends.

But she was so much more than that. Only a witness? Not in his heart.

When he looked into her beautiful blue eyes, he wanted to take her into his arms and kiss her. When this was over, he would not let her go. Without her, his life was bleak and ugly. She was a beacon of decency in the murky confusion of this trial.

Travis didn't trust himself to speak, so he nodded to Dave Dermott, who said, "Maggie, you said that you saw the man who attacked you. How did you recognize him?"

She explained in a rush, her words tripping over one

another. "Scratch on his cheek. Earring. I'm not one hundred percent sure it was him. Aw, heck, how could it be? How could he have the nerve to show up here and sit right behind Ben DeCarlo?"

"I know who she means," said Sharon Gold. "He works as an investigator for Ezra Dean. His name is Lester Parsons."

"An investigator," Dave Dermott crowed. "Of course!"

"Why do you say that?" Maggie asked.

"A lot of the investigators are licensed to carry concealed weapons. They're like private detectives. And they're in and out of the courthouse, our offices, the police station, even the prison. This character would have access to all kinds of information, and nobody would think twice about the fact that he was armed." Dave looked to Travis. "We should pick him up for questioning."

"Does this mean I'm safe?" Maggie asked. Her gaze rested on Travis. "That I don't have to go back to the safe house?"

"I'm sorry Maggie." Travis had never wanted her so much. His need to comfort her was a painful ache in his chest. "You have to go with the marshals."

The disappointment in her eyes struck him like a physical blow. "Okay," she said. "I understand."

"Don't worry," Sharon Gold said. "Tomorrow, this will all be over and done with."

THE NEXT MORNING, the trial resumed.

At the end of the narrow aisle between the oak benches, Maggie saw Travis, the man she'd thought she loved, the man who had seemed to be her destiny.

Her testimony today might be the last time she spoke to him. When she left the witness stand, she would be whisked into the witness protection program and given yet another identity. She would never see Travis again, never kiss him, never touch him. Never again would they lie together with their hearts beating as one.

As she proceeded slowly down the center aisle, forcing herself to move toward the emptiness of her future, she heard a hissing noise to her left. Someone in the courtroom audience called her name.

Maggie turned her head. The woman was older now, but Maggie instantly recognized the thick lips that were permanently fixed in a sneer.

How could *she* be here? Maggie wished that she was imagining, but she wasn't. The woman was here, in the courtroom. Her hands rested in her lap, waiting to attack like sharp talons that had, many years ago, closed around Maggie's arm and pulled her hair while the cruel mouth accused her of seducing her husband, Maggie's foster father when she was fourteen. *I've seen you stick out your little breasts at him.*

"No," Maggie said under her breath, "it's not true. I hate him. He smells bad."

She shivered. Had she actually spoken aloud?

Her foster father sat beside his wife in the courtroom. His dirty brown hair had turned to dirty gray. The lines in his face cut deeper. His eyes were as flat as a rattlesnake's. When he looked at her, his tongue flicked out.

She recoiled, remembering every word he had spoken. *Can't have little Maggie talking like that. Can't have her saying that I smell bad.*

Slowly, he had unfastened the buckle on his belt. The sinuous leather came away from his belly.

And the talon fingers held her tight.

She backed away from them. From behind, she heard another low voice, "Hello, Miss Maggie."

This one was obese and awful to look at. Maggie couldn't even see her eyes inside her red, puffed-up cheeks. She flapped her sausage fingers, waving. And she smiled with her tiny mouth. A mouth that had accused her and lied to the police, telling them that it was Maggie who had drugs in her possession rather than her own darling daughter.

Maggie forced herself to walk forward. The judge's bench and the witness stand seemed miles away.

In the very front row was the foster father who was called Preacher, though that wasn't his name. When she ran away from home, she was caught and brought back to him because everybody believed he was such a good man. Every night, when she went to bed, he handcuffed one wrist to the bed frame. If she ran away again, she'd go to jail. *And we don't want that, do we, Maggie? You must learn obedience. For the Lord.*

She hated him most of all. Every night, when he locked her up, he promised it would be the last time. Every day, he found another reason that she needed to be punished. *Your hair is a mess, Maggie. A shameful sight. You know what that means.*

She shook her head. This couldn't be happening.

Desperately, she wanted to run from them. All her adult life, she'd been running from them, her tormentors.

She stumbled through the wooden gate that divided the court. All these creatures from her past stood ready to accuse her. This was the surprise Ezra Dean had threatened her with at the Carnival party. He'd promised that when he was done with her, nobody would believe her. And she feared he was right.

These horrible people. He had found them, and they would shame her with their lies.

The distance to the witness box seemed impossibly far.

Her steps were leaden. Her shoulders slumped as she dragged herself forward. If there actually were a merciful Lord, he would let her be struck down by lightning right now.

When Travis touched her arm to help her into the witness box, she jumped away from him. The concern in his eyes threatened to shred the last remnant of her self-control. His touch, which had so recently wakened the most tender passion, felt harsh and cold.

"Miss Deere?" Judge Leland Howell peered down from his lofty bench. "Are you ill?"

She wanted to say that she was very sick and couldn't be here. Maggie would do anything to escape from this courtroom. Even lie? No! She hadn't come this far to be intimidated. There had been enough deception. She needed to speak. Her testimony would put a killer in prison. "I'm all right."

"I remind you, Margaret Elizabeth Deere, that you are still under oath."

She nodded.

Travis came close to her and leaned over the wooden banister. "Maggie, what is it? What's wrong?"

How could she tell him? It barely seemed possible to speak while they were all watching her. How long would it be before one of them leapt to his feet and pointed the accusing finger at her and shrieked, "Liar! Blasphemer! Whore!"

If they did, would she fall back in time and become that pathetic little girl whose life was in the control of others?

"Maggie?" Travis whispered. "What is it? I'm going to ask for a recess."

"Let's get this over with."

"Your Honor," Travis said as he approached the bench. "My witness is not well. Could we take a short recess?"

Judge Howell beheld her with hostile eyes. "Miss Deere, are you physically capable of giving your testimony?"

"I think so."

"Go ahead, Mr. Shanahan. I've had enough of your stalling. Stop wasting the court's time."

"Miss Deere," Travis said, "yesterday you told the court that you were a waitress at..."

She concentrated only on Travis, training her gaze away from the courtroom. His deep voice soothed her as he recapped her prior statements. He seemed so logical, so normal.

Nothing could happen to her here. No one could attack her. She was in a court of law, and Travis was near. He wouldn't let them hurt her. She was safe.

"Is that the gist of what you told us yesterday, Miss Deere?"

She concentrated on Travis. "Yes."

"Would you again point out the man you saw walk through the door of Augustine's, raise his handgun and pull the trigger."

Keeping her gaze turned toward the jury, so she wouldn't accidentally see one of her former foster parents, Maggie aimed her finger in the general direction of the defendant. "It was him. Ben DeCarlo."

The judge leaned down. "I need for you to look directly at the defendant, Miss Deere. For purposes of identification."

Sucking breath from the depth of her lungs, as if preparing to scream, she looked at the man who had killed his parents. "Him. Benjamin Wilson DeCarlo."

Beside him was Ezra Dean Slaughter, cool and well-dressed. Behind him was Preacher. He was truly there. She hadn't imagined that stern and vicious man from her past.

"Miss Deere," Travis called to her. "Would you tell us, in your own words, what happened after Ben DeCarlo fired the gun?"

She was terrified. Every single utterance she forced through her lips was an effort.

"I dropped the tray I was holding." She tried to recall precisely, but too many other memories were getting in the way. "The glasses broke on the flagstone floor."

And then, she would be punished, she thought, remembering her childhood. She'd broken the glasses. She was a bad girl.

Maggie forced herself back to the present. "I was running to stop him, but he'd already fired. So I stepped into his path to keep him from getting away."

That moment flashed clearly in her mind. "I could not believe what I'd seen. I had met Ben DeCarlo once or twice before, and he seemed to be a perfect gentleman. How could he do such a terrible thing?"

"Objection." That came from Ezra Dean.

"Sustained. Miss Deere, please report only what you saw."

"I looked directly into his face." Those eyes, she remembered. They were the soulless eyes of a cold-blooded killer. "We were no more than a few inches apart. He kind of pushed around me and ran out the door."

Travis had returned to his chair at the prosecution table. "Your witness, Mr. Slaughter."

She didn't watch as Ezra Dean approached, but she knew that he was near the witness stand. She could smell his expensive cologne. His evil aura surrounded her.

"Would you call yourself an honest woman, Miss Deere?"

"Objection." That was Travis.

"Your Honor," said Ezra Dean. "We covered this issue

in pretrial discussion. Mr. Shanahan knows that I intend to explore the character of his witnesses. Character has everything to do with truth, if the witnesses were paid off.''

Judge Howell ruled quickly. "I will allow this line of questioning. Proceed, Mr. Slaughter.''

"Well, Miss Deere? Are you an honest woman?''

"Yes.''

"Have you ever been arrested?''

"Never as an adult.''

"But as a juvenile, you had quite an extensive court record." He consulted a sheet of paper attached to a clipboard. "Let me see here. You were picked up twice as a runaway. On another occasion, you were charged with possession of drug paraphernalia.''

"All before I was fifteen, sir.''

He turned away from her and spoke to the judge. "Your Honor, this witness has a history of embellishing her testimony. Would you caution her to only answer my questions?''

"You are so cautioned, Miss Deere. No speechifying or you will be charged with contempt.''

"Yes, Your Honor." Her spirit shrank. She felt herself becoming small and vulnerable. The judge had taken away her ability to defend herself.

Ezra Dean continued, "In school, your grades were poor. Several of your teachers marked on their report cards that you were incorrigible. You were caught fighting in school more than seven times. You dropped out of high school. Is that correct?''

"Yes." She wanted to tell the jury that she had also tested high in IQ and achievement tests. There were teachers who liked her, too. They said she was smart. They encouraged her.

"At home," Ezra Dean continued, "you were placed in

nine different foster homes between the time when you were eight until your fourteenth birthday. Correct?''

"I don't remember," Maggie said. "That sounds about right."

"Perhaps you remember some of your foster parents," he said. "Look around the courtroom. Do you know any of these people?"

Their eyes accused her. Their faces despised her. She knew the venom that would pour from their mouths. She knew the pain of those talon claws, slapping her face. She remembered the belt, whistling and snapping across her backside.

"Miss Deere? Do you recognize any of these people?"

"Yes."

Her voice quaked, but she wouldn't cry. With all her strength, she fought the tears that she had always held inside. She couldn't allow them to win, not after all these years.

Ezra Dean had flashed an old photograph of Maggie on the large screen that faced the jury. Her platinum blond hair fell in disarray to her shoulders. Her heavy makeup was smeared. Her low-cut blouse revealed too much cleavage. Even in Maggie's eyes, she looked cheap.

"Is this a snapshot of you, Miss Deere?"

"Yes."

"You've changed your appearance considerably," Ezra Dean said. "Was this picture taken during the time you worked at Augustine's?"

"I don't know. Might have been."

"Regarding your relationships with men, Miss Deere. Have there been many?"

"No."

"Isn't it true that you are currently sleeping with—"

"Objection!" Travis stormed. "Your Honor, Maggie

Deere isn't on trial here. Mr. Slaughter is using lewd and unfair tactics to discredit the testimony of a woman who rose above her abusive past and became a contributing member of society. She has always worked to support—"

"Objection overruled," the judge interrupted. "And I caution you, Mr. Shanahan, against further outbursts."

Ezra Dean approached her again. "Miss Deere, have you, during the past week, slept with a man?"

Her heart shattered within her breast. For the first time in her life, she felt truly hopeless. The magnificent dream of love she had shared with Travis seemed tainted, tawdry, ugly.

"Answer my question, Maggie Deere."

"Yes."

When she looked up, the courtroom seemed to be spinning around her, as if she were caught in the eye of a cyclone, unable to escape, while the debris of past despair circled around her, coming closer and closer. Out of control.

"Is that man present in this courtroom today?"

"Yes."

Travis was objecting again. He requested a recess. Demanded that this line of questioning cease.

Ezra Dean leaned toward her. In his booming orator's voice, he demanded, "Maggie Deere, are you sleeping with the chief prosecuting attorney, Travis Shanahan?"

The courtroom erupted. Vaguely, Maggie was aware of reporters racing toward the door. Was Travis's mother here today? How could Maggie face that kind, elegant lady? Maggie covered her eyes, hiding her shame.

From far away, she heard the banging of the gavel, calling for order. Each resounding crack penetrated her consciousness, more painful than the blows she'd received as a child, more devastating than any humiliation she'd felt before. She wanted to give up. She couldn't take any more pain.

"In my chambers!" Judge Howell shouted. "Mr. Shanahan. Mr. Slaughter. In my chambers, immediately."

Travis was holding her hand. She saw his lips moving, then she heard the words that he spoke softly, for her ears only. "I love you, Maggie. Remember that. No matter what happens. I love you. And that is the highest truth that has been spoken in this—or any other—court of law."

She saw the love in his eyes, and that glow gave her hope. His love was one slender guy rope thrust into her grasp at the moment when she thought she could no longer withstand the whirlwind disaster.

"Be brave, Maggie. I won't let them hurt you. Never again."

"Recess," the judge shouted.

Travis stepped away from the witness box. He was strong and solid in the midst of dizzying chaos. "Trust me, darling. I love you."

Then he was gone. Into chambers.

Staring at the floor, she clung to her precious hopes, her only chance for survival, and allowed herself to be led, jostled by people she dared not look at, cursed by voices from her past. Outside the courtroom, the confusion intensified. It was a mob.

Someone shoved her and she went along. They were leaving the noise. That was all that she wanted. Silence.

Where were they going? A man's hand closed on her wrist and she allowed herself to be led. Downstairs. He closed a door, blocking the noise and confusion and hurried her along a corridor into another room.

"Thank you," she whispered.

Maggie raised her eyes and looked into the face of Gord Hoskins.

"You were screwing Travis?" He chuckled. "Oh, Maggie, if you needed loving that bad, I would have been happy to oblige."

She wrenched away from him. She must have been insane to come with him! That wasn't far from the truth. Temporarily, she had been shocked into craziness. "Where are we? What do you want from me?"

"We're in a quiet little corner of this great big courthouse. Did you know that this is one of the largest, oldest courthouses in the country? It's going to take your U.S. Marshal watchdogs a little while to find us."

"I'm getting out of here."

When she started toward the door, he grabbed her arm and held on tight. "You aren't going anywhere. This is my last favor for Ezra Dean. With the money he pays me, I'll disappear where even the U.S. Marshals won't find me."

"Ezra Dean was behind all this?"

"That man does not like to lose."

"Then he arranged for Kyle to be murdered."

"That's right. He used TotalCom as a lure, and Francine Bentley provided the means for Kyle to come to New Orleans on account of she owed Ezra Dean for some legalwork. I was sorry about Pete, though. I always liked that boy."

Maggie's mind cleared. In an instant, she regained the old familiar sharpness that had allowed her to survive years of abuse. Surveying her surroundings, she saw a plain room with bars on three basement windows. There was a wood table and a couple of chairs. She went to one of them and sat.

Since she wasn't physically strong enough to overpower Gord, she would have to talk her way out of this. "When I look at you, Gord, I don't see a killer. You might have done some bad things, but I don't think you intend to murder me."

"Me? Hell, no. I could never do that, Maggie. In fact, if I could go back in time, I would never do any of the things I've done. I'm not a bad person."

"I understand, sugar. Let's go upstairs and find Travis. He can work out a deal for you."

"It's too late for that. Best thing I can do is take my money and run."

"They'll track you down, Gord. You can't live like that."

"It's better than the damned witness protection program."

"But you started your insider trading with TotalCom before you even left New Orleans."

"That was nothing, Maggie. Just a tip. Everybody slides around the edge of the law. It wasn't until Sharon Gold contacted me that I figured out how to make a really big payoff."

"Sharon Gold was the leak," Maggie said.

"She was a whole lot more than that. The initial impetus and the financing might have come from Ezra Dean, but the details of Kyle's murder and the attacks on you were pure Gold. Strictly designed to eliminate the witnesses and let Ben DeCarlo get away with murder." He gave his nervous chuckle and looked toward the door to the small room. "Miss Gold is going to make a fine attorney. She'll be working for Ezra Dean within the year."

"So, they paid you off. What about Kyle?"

"Hell, yes. They paid for his tickets to Paris. Only problem was that Kyle suspected something and stayed with Pete instead of the hotel where he was supposed to be."

"But he told Francine about that."

"Right. And she told the people who needed to know."

He was eyeballing the door again as if he was waiting for somebody.

"Gord, if you come forward with this information, the D.A. is going to take care of you. Let's go back upstairs and—"

The door to the room opened quickly. A man in a policeman's uniform stepped inside. "Sorry I'm late, Gord-o. That scene upstairs got a little crazier than we thought it would."

"No problem, Lester. Have you got my money?"

Lester Parsons took the sidearm from his holster. "I'm going to enjoy killing you, Maggie. You caused a lot of trouble when you identified me yesterday. Made me go into hiding." He rubbed the badge on his uniform. "Lucky for me, I've got friends in the department."

"My money," Gord said. "Pay me and I'm gone."

"You're gone, all right." He sneered. "Gord-o, my man, didn't you learn anything from when I killed Kyle? It's a hell of a lot cheaper and tidier to kill a witness than to pay him off."

Lester raised his gun and fired into Gord Hoskins's chest. He blasted three bullets before Gord fell to the floor. Then he turned the pistol on Maggie. "I warned you."

"No!" She dove behind the table, flipping it over like a shield.

She heard the door crash open. A voice yelled, "Hold it right there!"

My God, what was happening? Was that Travis? She heard the sharp report of a pistol. More gunfire echoed. A barrage.

Maggie should have stayed hidden, but her love for Travis overwhelmed her common sense. She leapt out from behind the table. Without thinking, she raced toward the tall man with the gun in his hand. "Travis. Are you all right?"

His eyes reflected horror and pain. "I think I killed him."

Trembling, she stood only a few feet from him. "He deserved killing."

"That's not for me to say." The gun fell from his hand. "I'm not the executioner. Not the judge. I've spent my whole life protecting the law, the due process."

"You did what you had to do! Would you have let him kill me? Would that be justice?"

"No, Maggie." His shoulders straightened. No smile touched his lips. She had never seen him so serious. "I need you. I need your instincts to show me what's right."

"You believe me? Instead of all those other people, those witnesses?"

"You are my shining truth." He held out his arms. "I'll never let them take you away from me again."

She stumbled toward him. When she felt his arms encircle her, Maggie felt like she'd finally found her home.

Chapter Fourteen

Travis raised a glass of fine champagne from the Crescent Wine Cellar and toasted the six other people who sat around his dining room table. "Here's to Clayton Bascombe, who kept us safe in spite of ourselves."

"Hear, hear," they shouted and took a sip.

"And here's to Dave Dermott and Janine Carlson, who are running the DeCarlo retrial just fine without my help."

Janine rose to her feet, a little wobbly. "Thank you, Travis. We couldn't have done it if Sandor Rossi hadn't developed amnesia on the stand. I think we'll be starting the New Year right. With the conviction of Ben DeCarlo."

"Yes, indeed," said Travis. "Now, let's raise our glasses to Pete Fontana, who served time for a murder he did not commit."

"Here's to Pete."

Dave Dermott added, "We're sorry, man."

Pleasantly, Pete said, "Let me handle your investment portfolio and all will be forgiven."

"Most of all," Travis said, "here's to Maggie Deere."

He gazed, with pleasure, at the woman who stood at the other end of his table. This was her place, he thought. She looked just right with her glass raised and a wholehearted smile curving her beautiful lips.

"Hooray for Maggie."

Janine Carlson piped up, "I kind of feel like we should toast Sharon Gold and Ezra, too, for making it so easy to pull this case together. But that seems nasty, doesn't it? I mean, they're both in so much trouble."

Vigorously, Dave said, "May they rot in jail!"

"Don't be naive," Janine said. "With all their maneuvering, they'll probably only serve a couple of years. But at least neither one of them will be able to practice law again."

"Travis," Maggie said, "you haven't offered a toast to your mother yet."

"I was saving the best for last." He put his arm around his mother's slender shoulders but kept his gaze fixed on Maggie. "Here's to the patience of my mother, Jenny Lynn Shanahan. She has waited these many years for me to make this declaration."

For a moment, he communicated silently with Maggie. She understood him better than anyone. Her courage and honesty fulfilled him.

"Heavens, Travis," his mother said, "what is it?"

"Here's to you, Mother. I'm getting married."

He gave her a squeeze and went around the table to stand beside Maggie Deere, his bride-to-be. "I have proposed to this lady, and she has accepted. I wish to take this occasion to announce my engagement to darling Maggie, the bravest and most stubborn woman I have ever known."

When he kissed her, Travis knew he had made the wisest deal of his entire life. "Now you can give Farris Quinn that interview he's been pestering you about."

She turned to the others at the table. "Of course, I will not be taking that marriage vow about obeying."

Travis said, "I know better than to ask you to obey."

"You're right about that, sugar. And I guarantee you that I will not be—"

He cut her off with a kiss. It was his favorite way of keeping Maggie quiet.

Ring in the New Year with babies, families and romance!

FREE VALENTINE'S BROOCH!
$9.95 U.S. retail value

This Valentine's Day Harlequin brings you
all the essentials—romance, chocolate
and jewelry—in:

VALENTINE *Delights*

Matchmaking chocolate-shop owner Papa Valentine
dispenses sinful desserts, mouth-watering
chocolates…and advice to the lovelorn, in this
collection of three delightfully romantic stories
by Meryl Sawyer, Kate Hoffmann and Gina Wilkins.

As our special Valentine's Day gift to you, each copy
of *Valentine Delights* will have a beautiful, filigreed,
heart-shaped brooch attached to the cover.

Make this your most delicious Valentine's Day
ever with *Valentine Delights!*

Available in February wherever
Harlequin books are sold.

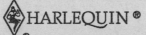

HARLEQUIN ®

Harlequin and Silhouette celebrate
Black History Month with seven terrific titles,
featuring the all-new *Fever Rising*
by Maggie Ferguson
(Harlequin Intrigue #408) and
A Family Wedding by Angela Benson
(Silhouette Special Edition #1085)!

Also available are:
Looks Are Deceiving by Maggie Ferguson
Crime of Passion by Maggie Ferguson
Adam and Eva by Sandra Kitt
Unforgivable by Joyce McGill
Blood Sympathy by Reginald Hill

On sale in January at your favorite
Harlequin and Silhouette retail outlet.